KT-525-592

MORE THAN MEETS THE EYE

Recent Titles by J. M. Gregson from Severn House

Lambert and Hook Mysteries

AN ACADEMIC DEATH
CLOSE CALL
DARKNESS VISIBLE
DEATH ON THE ELEVENTH HOLE
DIE HAPPY
GIRL GONE MISSING
A GOOD WALK SPOILED
IN VINO VERITAS
JUST DESSERTS
MORE THAN MEETS THE EYE
MORTAL TASTE
SOMETHING IS ROTTEN
TOO MUCH OF WATER
AN UNSUITABLE DEATH

Detective Inspector Peach Mysteries

DUSTY DEATH
TO KILL A WIFE
THE LANCASHIRE LEOPARD
A LITTLE LEARNING
LEAST OF EVILS
MERELY PLAYERS
MISSING, PRESUMED DEAD
MURDER AT THE LODGE
ONLY A GAME
PASTURES NEW
REMAINS TO BE SEEN
A TURBULENT PRIEST
THE WAGES OF SIN
WHO SAW HIM DIE?
WITCH'S SABBATH
WILD JUSTICE

MORE THAN MEETS THE EYE

A Lambert & Hook Mystery

J.M. Gregson

This first world edition published 2012
in Great Britain and in the USA by
SEVERN HOUSE PUBLISHERS LTD of
9–15 High Street, Sutton, Surrey, England, SM1 1DF.
Trade paperback edition first published
in Great Britain and the USA 2013 by
SEVERN HOUSE PUBLISHERS LTD.

Copyright © 2012 by J. M. Gregson.

All rights reserved.
The moral right of the author has been asserted.

British Library Cataloguing in Publication Data

Gregson, J. M.
More than meets the eye.
1. Lambert, John (Fictitious character)–Fiction. 2. Hook,
Bert (Fictitious character)–Fiction. 3. Police–
England–Gloucestershire–Fiction. 4. Detective and
mystery stories.
I. Title
823.9′14-dc23

ISBN-13: 978-0-7278-8198-4 (cased)
ISBN-13: 978-1-84751-449-3 (trade paper)

Except where actual historical events and characters are being
described for the storyline of this novel, all situations in this
publication are fictitious and any resemblance to living persons
is purely coincidental.

All Severn House titles are printed on acid-free paper.

Severn House Publishers support The Forest Stewardship Council [FSC],
the leading international forest certification organisation. All our titles that
are printed on Greenpeace-approved FSC-certified paper carry the FSC logo.

Typeset by Palimpsest Book Production Ltd.,
Falkirk, Stirlingshire, Scotland.
Printed and bound in Great Britain by
MPG Books Ltd., Bodmin, Cornwall.

To Patricia Cooper, who has enjoyed many of the great gardens of England and contributed much to them, and who in another life was a splendid college registrar.

Our England is a garden that is full of stately views,
Of borders, beds and shrubberies and lawns and avenues,
With statues on the terraces and peacocks strutting by;
But the glory of the garden lies in more than meets the eye.

Rudyard Kipling

AUTHOR'S NOTE

Garden enthusiasts and National Trust members will easily recognize the great English garden in which this story is set. I have chosen to call it Westbourne Park. For obvious reasons, I wish to emphasize that though the setting is real enough, the characters and events are wholly fictional.

ONE

'I bet you could have killed her on the spot!'

Dennis Cooper started guiltily. It was so near to what he had actually thought at the time that he stared hard at his wife. Probably she hadn't meant the suggestion seriously. But these days he could never be sure what Alison was thinking.

He took a sip of his wine, watching her surreptitiously as she ate. She picked her way expertly through runner beans, broccoli and new potatoes, then left her pork chop as clean as if it had been attacked by a scavenger. Her knife and fork sped round the plate as swiftly and deftly as a surgeon's scalpels. She seemed to have become quicker over the years, as if developing this small, deadly skill had been her primary aim in life.

He said, 'I certainly wasn't pleased with her. But Lorna's very knowledgeable. You have to allow her a certain latitude.'

Alison frowned, setting her knife and fork down on the empty plate as precisely as if she had been setting a clock to midnight. 'I don't see why. You seem to me to put up with far too much from the guides. And from Lorna Green in particular. You're the man in charge – or you should be.' A tiny flicker of contempt creased her thin lips for a moment.

Dennis sighed softly, preparing for an explanation he had offered to her many times before. 'There are a lot of privileges with this job. One of the drawbacks—'

'I haven't noticed many privileges myself. But then I'm just a normal person, forced to live with you in this abnormal environment.'

Dennis wondered if she had prepared this little paradox in advance; it seemed to give her some pleasure as she delivered it. He said patiently, 'There aren't many full-time resident National Trust curators in the country. The Trust can't afford many and takes care that the ones it does employ are placed in important centres like this. We are fortunate to live here. I am reminded of that every morning when I wake up and look out over our wonderful gardens. It makes you glad to be alive.'

'Correction: it makes *you* glad to be alive. It makes *me* think how odd and frustrating it is to be stuck here miles from the normal advantages of civilization.'

'You don't consider Westbourne Park to be civilized?' He couldn't prevent a small sneer as he delivered what he considered a crushing riposte.

It was a mistake. Derision only increased his wife's aggression. 'Indeed I don't! If your idea of civilization is to be stuck out here miles from anywhere and miles from any friends, it isn't mine!'

Dennis Cooper tried to be conciliatory. He said mildly, 'I think you exaggerate a little. We're one of the busiest National Trust centres, with many thousands of visitors each year and the extensive staff which reflects that. There are friends to be made here, if you care to make the effort.'

Alison sniffed derisively. Dennis admitted to himself reluctantly that she had a good range of sniffs, able to express a variety of emotions. All of them were negative, and the derisive sniff was one of her most effective, conveying contempt without ever straying into a snort. Alison followed it with a voice in a matching dismissive tone. 'Friends? If you mean people like your Lorna Green, then no thanks! Dry as a stick women with pretensions to be historians aren't my idea of friends. Why you choose to let her walk all over you is quite beyond me.'

She sniffed again, needing no words to convey that this time her contempt was for her hapless husband rather than the absent Ms Green. Dennis sighed again, as if in counterpoint response to her sustained nasal fugue. 'When you interrupted, I was trying to explain to you that we have to take into account that Lorna Green and the other guides who help here are unpaid volunteers. She gives valuable service during the hours when Westbourne is open to the public; we simply couldn't operate without her and the thirty other people who come in and work without payment. I have to be mindful that these people are not paid lackeys but enthusiasts for what we do here. The fact that they are unpaid allows them a certain latitude when it comes to expressing an opinion. I have to be more patient with voluntary helpers like Lorna Green than I might be with paid employees.'

Alison's face set into the sullen lines she always adopted when she did not want to confront logic. 'You're too bloody patient, if you ask me. You're allowing yourself to become a bloody doormat!'

Dennis bit back the comment that he hadn't asked her and finished his second glass of Merlot appreciatively. It was a good wine, as were the others in his small cellar. The restaurant bought excellent wines in bulk and he was allowed to purchase whatever bottles he wanted at cost price. It was a small but very welcome perk of the job and it helped to make life here more comfortable. But Alison Cooper wouldn't want to be reminded of that at the moment. He ate his strawberries and cream in silence, then pronounced the quality excellent. His wife nodded, but did not smile.

Five minutes later, they sat awkwardly opposite each other in the lounge, with the evening birdsong floating agreeably outside the open window on the heavy summer air. Dennis eased himself back into his leather-studded armchair and said sincerely but unthinkingly, 'This is the life!'

Alison glared at him for a moment before she spoke, her hostility apparent in every bristling line of her still-attractive figure. 'Some life, with your nearest cinema and your nearest decent shops forty miles away!'

She rose to her full height, walked slowly across the room, and turned on the television as if pressing the trigger of a gun. The strident theme tune of *EastEnders* was followed by the even more strident voices of the denizens of the soap in strenuous argument. Alison Cooper's bottom hit her chair like a battering ram. She arched her body and her attention away from her husband and domesticity and towards the raucous melodrama of the box.

From nowhere at all, the thought came to Dennis that sex tonight was unlikely. His dignity did not allow him a final sigh. After a sour smile, he rose and left the room in silence.

The gardens soothed him, as they always did. A summer

evening was the best time of all. This was one of the great gardens of England, which to Dennis meant one of the great gardens of the world. Whilst all the visitors wandered where they wished during the heat of the day, you had this wonderful place to yourself in the evening. All the sections were beautifully tended, whilst you didn't need to pull a single weed yourself. In the evenings, you lived here like a king, or a duke at the very least. There was not a breath of wind, but the air was cooling now, after the warmth of a perfect day. The sun was setting, a crimson orb touching the summit of the hills to the west, purpling the whole of the sky around it.

Heart of England, this was, in every sense you cared to interpret the phrase. The great battles of the Wars of the Roses, which had shaped the medieval future of the land, had been fought not far from here, by the waters of the Severn at Shrewsbury to the east and Tewkesbury to the south. The great battles of the civil war which had finally established the mother of parliaments had been at places like Worcester, a few miles to the north. And the last great invasion of the land, led by the prancing dandy romanticized as Bonnie Prince Charlie, had been quashed fifty miles north-east of here at Derby.

And now, on this so peaceful summer evening, after the stresses of the day, the crowds were gone and he had the best of all English gardens to himself.

Yet Dennis Cooper was wrong in that. He was not completely alone here, after all. He was wandering slowly through the series of 'garden rooms' which was Westbourne, moving deliberately slowly to calm his racing mind, when he heard the metallic sound of hedging shears. An irregular, clipping sound, which meant that this was a manual, not a powered, shearing. A sound which was more appropriate than machinery on this still, quiet evening.

He moved cautiously towards the noise of the shears, coming eventually upon the sight he had expected. A slight man stood with his back to Dennis as he entered the white garden. The man's head was on one side, considering carefully the effects he was securing with his shears upon the topiary bird in front of him. Dennis watched the work for a moment before he said softly, 'It's true what they say then. A garden's never quite perfect to the people who work in it.'

The slim shoulders jumped with the shock. Jim Hartley turned with a smile towards the familiar voice. 'I was so wrapped up in what I was doing that I'd no idea there was anyone else around.'

He looked even younger than his thirty-four years. Indeed, when he was enthusiastic, Jim always looked quite boyish. And at Westbourne, he was enthusiastic for most of the time. Although it was over a year now since he had been appointed head gardener, he often said that he still couldn't believe he was in charge of what was in his opinion the greatest garden of all.

There had been many raised eyebrows and some dissent at the time. The National Trust is a conservative organization, even though it strives, sometimes a little desperately, to move with the times. No one had queried James Hartley's qualifications and competence, but some had thought his experience could not possibly be wide enough for this plum horticultural appointment. Dennis Cooper had been one of the men who had pleaded his cause. Hartley had worked at Kew and at the Royal Horticultural Society gardens at Wisley. He was hard-working, enthusiastic and had strong references from all who had employed him.

Dennis was glad that he had spoken up so strongly for the youngest candidate when they were interviewing, because Jim Hartley was emphatically a success. He had moved into the long, low cottage reserved for the head gardener with his wife and two small children and quickly become one of the keys to Westbourne's ever-increasing popularity with the public. The existing glories were being consolidated, whilst some of the hitherto slightly neglected and peripheral areas of the gardens were being developed. Jim was a 'hands-on' gardener, not just a supervisor. You saw the work of his hands as well as the plans of his mind wherever you moved in the grounds.

There were twenty years between them, but Dennis Cooper felt very close to Jim Hartley. He sympathized with the younger man's attitude, where everything was a challenge, but a challenge he was confident of meeting. Dennis had been like that himself in his younger days, he fancied. Now he watched over Hartley's development almost like a father, quick to defend, anxious to praise.

He said with a smile, 'You do quite enough during working hours, Jim, without coming out here in the evenings.'

'Oh, I don't mind this. It's a pleasure, not a chore. And it needs to be done carefully – I'm not much good with the public looking on and making comments!' As if to reinforce his words, he stepped forward to the bush and made a sharp cut with the end of his small, specialist shears, sharpening the bird's beak and giving it an interrogative look, as if it was conscious of other events in this small, intimate section of the garden. It was almost like a painter stepping forward to his easel and making some tiny but telling stroke on a canvas, emphasizing his mastery of the medium.

'I didn't know that you listed topiary among your many skills,' said Dennis appreciatively.

'I don't. That's why I have to do it very slowly and without being observed. Jack Fisher usually takes care of the clipping here, but he's got shingles and will be off for a fortnight. And the public deserve to see the place at its best – they pay enough for the privilege!' Jim Hartley still thought it amazing that the public should turn up in such numbers and pay so handsomely to view his work.

'But you should be at home with the children, reading bedtime stories and so on.' Dennis, who couldn't remember much reading to the son who had long grown up and departed, was rather vague about the duties expected of a modern father.

'The meeting seemed to go all right this morning,' said Hartley, as if anxious to change the subject.

Dennis, who had chaired the meeting of the resident staff and the two representatives of the voluntary guides and helpers, had almost forgotten that Hartley had been present. Avowedly not a committee man, the head gardener chose to stay silent and observe, unless he was called upon directly for his views. 'Yes. I'm sorry if you felt you could have been better employed in the gardens. But meetings are necessary to keep everyone informed of what's going on and make sure we're all pulling in the same direction.'

'Yes.' There was a pause, whilst Jim Hartley wondered whether he should really say anything more. 'I thought Lorna Green went on a bit.'

Dennis smiled. 'She did, I suppose. That's Lorna's way. But we have to bear in mind that she gives us a lot of her time and is entitled to her opinion. It's better that she says what she thinks rather than keeping it bottled up.'

'I suppose so.' Jim, having sized up the needs of another topiary bird, leapt forward and made another small but telling incision. 'All the same, I expect there are moments when you could cheerfully kill Mrs Green!'

Dennis Cooper smiled benignly, then uttered another meaningless cliché about it taking all sorts of people to make up an interesting world. It was a remarkable coincidence, he thought as he continued on his evening stroll. Two people as different as his wife and Jim Hartley had suggested within an hour of each other the death of Lorna Green.

It was a good thing that the lady herself couldn't hear such shocking suggestions.

TWO

The lady in question was in fact very busy with quite different concerns.

Lorna Green was contending with that fiercest of contemporary ogres, senile dementia in a loved one. Her mother was eighty-four now. Until a year ago, Barbara Green had been a lively and vigorous octogenarian. She had done her own shopping, argued her corner with any political canvasser who had the temerity to knock at her door, played swift and imaginative bridge with three ladies who had once been her golfing companions.

It was just a year since the doctors had mentioned that sinister word Alzheimer's. The symptoms were there, in a mild form at present, but the tests had confirmed it. No, it wasn't possible to forecast the speed of development. Many people passed away peacefully without suffering really serious mental decline. In others, deterioration was rapid. There was much more they could do to keep the worst at bay, with the drugs now available.

Nevertheless, Lorna should now keep a close eye on her mother.

It wasn't meant to be a message of impending doom, but it rang like one in Lorna's ears. The answers to her questions confirmed it. Yes, someone should be in the house with Mrs Green. Not all the time; not at present, anyway. Lorna gave up the flat she had been renting and moved back in with her mother. It was what the people from Mrs Green's church thought a spinster daughter should do, even in the twenty-first century. Her mother still attended the high stone church where her daughters had been christened.

Lorna wasn't a churchgoer herself. She was pretty sure that she was now an atheist rather than an agnostic, and her mother's decline seemed to be confirming that for her. It was so relentless, so cruel, so illogical. Nor was Lorna a typical spinster, if there was any longer such a creature. She had never married, though she had come close to it on two occasions. She had never been promiscuous, but she had undertaken by her count four serious relationships, where she had lived with a man for two years or more. That none of them had ended in the formal ties of marriage had been her choice, on three of the four occasions. Perhaps she expected a little too much of her men, or perhaps she had simply not been the best of choosers.

She had never wanted children and she didn't miss them now. She declared that forcefully to anyone bold enough to raise the subject. Some listeners felt that the lady did protest too much, but had more sense than to voice the thought.

Lorna had a degree in history from the University of Birmingham – one of the older and more respectable universities, she assured anyone who cared to listen. She didn't approve of these modern, tin-pot institutions, which should never have been allowed to call themselves universities. All they did was add to the lengthening lists of unemployed graduates, with their degrees in media studies and sports science and even less suitable subjects for higher education. These opinions received a good deal of support from her contemporaries, except for the occasional moments of embarrassment when she propounded her views to parents unfortunate enough to have their children in attendance at these dubious institutions.

Lorna had greater concerns than embarrassment at this moment. Her mother's long grey hair was flying round her head, though Lorna had combed and brushed it for her before leaving for her meeting at Westbourne Park. A shorter style would be better when the hairdresser called next week, if she could persuade Barbara to accept it. The television was blaring loudly through a children's programme, though her mother did not seem to be following it. Lorna turned the volume down to a level which would allow her to think. The old woman looked at her resentfully, but said nothing.

Lorna forced a smile and tried hard to relax. 'Did you have a chat with the Meals on Wheels lady today?'

'No. She didn't have anything for me today. She was in such a hurry that she didn't even apologize.'

Lorna looked at her for a moment, but her mother's attention had returned to the television set. She went back along the hall and into the kitchen. A plate of cold casserole lay on the table, with a knife and fork untouched beside it and the gravy congealed at the edges. Barbara had forgotten to eat again. You had to get her through the first mouthfuls and then she'd carry on. But the Meals on Wheels lady wouldn't know that and she had other dinners to deliver.

She went back to the sitting room. This place was far too big for the two of them, but she couldn't face persuading Mum to move and then enduring the agonies of selling and packing. She had always rather despised material comforts, but now she missed the convenience and modern fittings of the neat flat she had forsaken to come here

Barbara Green was sitting staring at the television, her forehead frowning her resentment that she could not follow the excitements of the child actors.

Her daughter said gently, 'Jean did leave your meal, Mum. You forgot it.'

Barbara turned her head and looked at her intently. 'It'll do for your Dad when he gets in. He likes stew, does Wally.'

It was this strange mixture of comprehension and nonsense which she found most hard to deal with. Lorna looked hard into the lined, familiar face and said quietly, 'Dad's dead, Mum. Wally died eight years ago.'

Her mother looked at her for a moment sorrowfully. Then she spoke as if the fifty-three-year-old woman beside her was a child in plaits. 'He'll be in presently, just you see. He's probably been kept late at work again.' She transferred her gaze to the television, rocking gently backwards and forwards on her seat.

It was only when Lorna had been sorting through his papers after her father's death that she had found the letters which showed that he had conducted affairs with other women. Barbara had always been very tolerant and very trusting about Wally's need to work far into the evenings a couple of times each week. Lorna wondered whether her mother had known nothing of his amours or whether she had chosen to ignore them. Now she would never be certain about that – unless of course Barbara let it out unwittingly in one of her musings about her husband. Lorna hoped she wouldn't. It seemed to her an invasion of privacy to discover through her illness things which her mother would normally have concealed.

Lorna felt suddenly weary. She went into the kitchen and sat down for two minutes. Then she rose and made a simple meal with sausages and new potatoes and carrots. She had learned to cook only what her mother would eat; it was very irritating to see Barbara turn away from dishes which had taken her hours to prepare. Barbara liked spaghetti bolognaise, but the eating of it had proved a disaster last time Lorna had prepared it. Today the old lady demolished the simple meal with apparent relish; presumably she'd eaten nothing since breakfast. Then she laid her knife and fork down neatly and said, 'Our Debbie's a good cook. Better than you.'

Lorna tried not to feel resentful. She had been her father's favourite, but Barbara had always favoured her younger sister. 'Debbie's four hundred miles away, Mum.'

Barbara nodded with a small, secret smile. 'Debbie's in Aberdeen. Looking after my grandchildren.'

Lorna was about to say that they were grown-up now and had left home. But what was the use? She bit back the explanation and said merely, 'That's right, Mum. Debbie's a long way away.' But she was a naturally precise person – positively anal at times, her best friend had told her – and it came hard to her not to correct the old woman's facts.

Probably that's what she should have done in the meeting this morning, bitten her tongue and held back the words. Dennis Cooper had obviously been put out when she had corrected him on the history of Westbourne Park. It had meant a loss of face for him, in front of his staff. And she had gone on a bit; she could see now that she had enjoyed correcting Dennis and embarrassing him in front of others. Initially, she had merely been anxious to have the correct facts established, so that the eight people in the meeting wouldn't go away with false information.

All the same, she could see now that she had been insensitive. Dennis Cooper had been careless, not harmful. There had been no need to make him look a pompous twit in front of his staff.

Lorna Green watched her mother toying with her strawberries, pushing them around her dish instead of eating them. Eventually, Barbara dropped her spoon and a long splodge of cream shot out across the clean tablecloth. Lorna would put it in the washing machine, as soon as she'd stowed her mother safely back in the sitting room. Perhaps the time was coming when she'd have to give up tablecloths. She'd already abandoned them for breakfast and lunch, but she'd kept them for the evening meal; they were a symbol of the civilized life which was ebbing away from her mother.

For the first time, Lorna wondered whether the strain of the strange, loving battle she was conducting in her home was affecting her conduct outside it.

At Westbourne Park, Hugo Wilkinson was nothing like as exhausted as Lorna Green. At fifty-five, he was a couple of years older than Lorna, but he had energy to spare.

It was a curious life, being the head chef with responsibility for the kitchens at Westbourne, but over the three years Hugo had been in post, he had grown used to it and found that the work suited his present needs.

The clientele, for a start, was very different from that of the fashionable restaurant by the Thames he had left to come here. Older and more polite, which was good. Much more conservative in their choice of dishes, which was not so good. After finding that his more adventurous items had few takers, he had been forced to revise his menus for the premier restaurant at Westbourne Park. But the place was licensed for weddings and other functions, which gave him the occasional chance to spread his catering wings.

The oddest factor about Westbourne for a chef was the change in working hours. Like most men of his calling, Wilkinson had grown used to working at top pressure through hot and frantic kitchen evenings and not arriving home until after midnight. The odd working hours had helped to destroy his marriage, he told anyone who asked him about his private life. It was a useful ploy; people usually nodded their heads sympathetically and did not press him any further about the real reasons.

At Westbourne, with its opening hours of ten to six, the peak period was in the middle of the day; the restaurant was invariably full at lunchtime during the summer months. You worked intensively for four hours or so. Then you were less stressed as people came in for teas. During the evening, when most chefs were dealing with temperamental staff, high emotions and colourful language, you could relax. On a summer evening like this, you could enjoy the gardens in tranquillity, or even enjoy a game of croquet on the Theatre Lawn.

Croquet wasn't a hobby of Hugo Wilkinson. Nevertheless, he often went out on to that great lawn with its raised grass stage, where outdoor performances of Shakespeare had once disturbed the wildlife. He was always delighted when he heard the shrill voices of Jim Hartley's sons. The head gardener was trying to introduce Sam, eight, and Oliver, six, to the joys and mysteries of cricket, and Hugo would join in as an extra fielder and underarm bowler whenever he was free. He'd no children of his own and he'd never enjoyed cricket much at school, but with a tennis ball and children of this age, he was a valuable addition to the ranks.

Tonight, there was no cricket or croquet and Hugo Wilkinson was indoors and restless. It seemed a pity to waste a still and perfect summer evening, but he was waiting for a phone call. It was one he couldn't take on his mobile in the grounds. They'd agreed not to use mobiles, because you needed to be certain that no one else could overhear the conversation. You couldn't be too careful; secrecy needed to become a habit. That had been drummed into them by the man who'd been in this from the beginning and they were all happy enough to accept it.

Hugo watched a little television, read a few pages of his thriller, put in a couple of clues in his crossword, but found he could settle to nothing. The last glimmers of light were seeping away from the western sky when the phone shrilled in the corner of the room. Five past ten, his watch told him. He was across the room and lifting the receiver as the second rings began.

'Wilkinson.'

'It's there now.'

'Thank you. It will be well received.'

This was the code that was agreed between them, when the leader had emphasized that brevity was essential. The line went dead immediately. It all seemed a little silly and melodramatic, Hugo thought, as he stared down at the phone. It was like some Masonic ritual, though he had never known the Masons to favour brevity. He'd been a member for a few years before deciding that the arcane ceremonies had little to offer him. There weren't many Masons in the world of haute cuisine, so that he'd enjoyed few companionable handshakes and no advantages in the promotional stakes.

He hadn't realized how tense he'd been, until the call brought him satisfaction and relaxation. He went over and turned on the computer which stood on the small desk at the side of the room. These were the times when it was best to live on your own. You didn't have to dive like a rat for cover when anyone else came into the room. You didn't have to wait for hours or even days to indulge yourself.

You could go about your business and pursue your little hobbies undisturbed.

Whilst Hugo Wilkinson fretted and waited for his phone call, Detective Chief Superintendent John Lambert was thoroughly enjoying the long summer evening. That did not mean it did not contain moments of tension, because he was on the Ross-on-Wye golf course.

He was partnering Detective Sergeant Bert Hook whom he had introduced to golf, despite this sturdy son of Herefordshire's declared contempt for a game he had previously declared appropriate only for toffs and the seriously deranged. They were playing in the second round of the club's knock-out fourball competition. And thanks to Lambert's steadiness, Hook's high handicap, and a little luck, they were winning.

That was satisfying, for they were playing against a cagey and experienced farmer from the Forest of Dean and one of the club's bright new talents, a young Glaswegian called Alex Fraser, who played off a handicap of two and was proving every bit as good as that implied. Alex was slightly built and looked even younger than his twenty years. Whether because he was a little in awe of the older men around him or whether because he wished to concentrate on his golf, he didn't say much. He was perfectly polite, but responded mainly in monosyllables, even to his partner from the Forest, who was no great conversationalist himself. But the excellence and accuracy of his striking compelled a respectful silence in his three companions.

Hook had been a sturdy Minor Counties cricketer for almost two decades and was now rapidly improving at golf. Although he still held a seventeen handicap, he had holed several crucial putts on the outward half. Lambert, who played off eight, had not looked like a single-figure man at that time, but two pars on the tricky tenth and eleventh showed his quality. The pair were two up when they came to the twelfth tee.

The twelfth at Ross is a picturesque short hole, played over a large pond which is alive with roach and bream. The pond stretches invitingly in front of the tee, but finishes well short of the green. Only an absolute novice or an absolute mishit would deposit a ball in the water.

Bert Hook's ball disappeared with an impressive splash into the very middle of the still and inviting pool.

'Bad luck!' said his farmer opponent automatically.

'Bad bloody shot more like!' said Hook dismissively, slamming the offending club back into his bag.

'It can happen to anyone,' said John Lambert consolingly. The fact that he said it through clenched teeth rather took away from any consolation Bert might have felt. He was left to meditate on the truism that there are very few shots in golf, good or bad, that do not please someone. No doubt his two opponents had been extremely gratified by this one.

Lambert teed and addressed his ball carefully, then dispatched his six-iron shot into the middle of the green, some four yards behind the flag. He accepted the congratulations of the other three modestly and gave Hook a reassuring smile. Bert for some reason thought of it as admonitory; no doubt his attitude was influenced by the ripples still visible upon the previously still waters of the pond.

Alex Fraser pitched and stopped a gentle eight-iron six feet below the flag, watched Lambert nurse his putt carefully down the hill to the side of the hole, then struck his own putt confidently into the middle of the hole for a two. Back to one down.

The Lambert/Hook partnership halved the tricky thirteenth, then the long par-four fourteenth, where they both received shots. Fifteen and sixteen are two shortish par-fours, and the young Scot made birdies at both of them to put his side one up with two to go. It was not just Alex Fraser who was saying little as the players toiled up the long seventeenth which is agreed to be the most difficult hole at Ross. The police partnership had the advantage of shots here, and Lambert sank a curling eight-feet putt for an unexpected four to square the match.

The sun had sunk behind the Welsh hills to the west as the four contemplated the long descent of the eighteenth hole to the final green and the clubhouse. Lambert hit his drive a respectable distance and straight. Hook was too far left and could not reach the green with his second. The farmer found the trees on the right, but young Alex hit a three-wood to exactly the spot he had chosen on the fairway. After watching

Lambert bounce his ball accurately into the green, Fraser hit a short iron which stopped impressively within a few feet of the flag.

After the two lesser players in this little drama had failed, it was left to Lambert and Fraser to act out the final action. After ritual consultation with Hook about the line, Lambert crouched over his ball and dispatched it impressively to within a foot of the hole. The four was duly conceded. Then young Alex stepped up to his ball, glanced twice at the hole, and rolled his putt slowly into the heart of the hole for an impressive winning three.

With but minimal help from his older partner, he had secured victory for them against Lambert's impressive steadiness and Hook's huge handicap advantage. It wasn't until he stepped forward with a shy smile and removed his baseball cap to shake hands that they registered his most distinctive physical feature. His hair was the brightest red that either Lambert or Hook could recall in their now considerable experience.

Alex Fraser was as taciturn in the clubhouse as he had been on the course. He was perfectly polite, maybe even excessively so, but he said very little. Even when they questioned him with genuine interest about his Glasgow upbringing, he delivered only terse and colourless answers. It was understandable, thought Bert Hook. He was with men who were much older and with whom he had nothing in common other than golf. Bert said, 'I'm not used to the handicap system in golf. I've always played games where the better player or players were expected to win.'

Alex Fraser nodded and confessed that his greatest interest was in the club championship, where everyone played off scratch and the best player on the day did indeed win. But he hastened to say modestly that there were many better players than him and that he could never have made it as a professional. Then he subsided into silence again and sipped his beer contemplatively. As dusk deepened and the lights were switched on in the clubhouse, his hair seemed an even more startling red than it had done outside.

It was a most unexpected subject which suddenly brought animation to young Alex. John Lambert and the Forest of

Dean farmer shared an interest in gardening and Lambert, who had paid one of his regular visits to the National Trust gardens at Westbourne Park, was enthusing about the variety of the plants there and the fact that there was always something interesting to see, whatever the season.

Alex Fraser said suddenly, 'I work at Westbourne.'

He glanced at the three faces around the table, then down again at his beer. John Lambert realized with amusement that he was blushing. The redness emphasized the freckles around his temples. Lambert said, 'I didn't take you for a horticultural expert, Alex.'

'Oh, I'm not an expert.' Fraser looked even redder and more embarrassed. 'I've got a year's apprenticeship there. We didn't have a garden at home, but I worked in the Glasgow Parks Department and found I enjoyed it, so I wanted to learn more.'

'And are you doing that?'

'Oh, yes. We're not just cheap labour for weeding and mowing and hedge cutting, as I thought we might be. They let me try my hand at everything. I'm learning all the time and enjoying myself as well.'

He made that sound a combination he had never expected. He was genuinely animated by his enthusiasm for the work at Westbourne, as he had not been through the rest of the evening. He chattered happily and interestingly about his days at the great garden, until he stopped abruptly and said, 'Sorry. I must be boring you with all this.'

'Not at all,' said Bert Hook. 'It's good to find someone genuinely excited by their work.' He'd been careful to say 'someone' rather than 'a young man'. In Bert's probably biased view, too many golf club members were prepared to write the young off as an amorphous mass of trouble.

As he lay in bed that night, Alex Fraser reflected that he'd chatted easily to a Chief Super and a Detective Sergeant, without even being under arrest at the time. Most of his contemporaries in the great Scottish city of Glasgow wouldn't have believed that.

THREE

Alison Cooper was five years younger than her husband, but she considered that she was a good deal younger than that in terms of outlook and personality.

She wasn't prepared to be buried alive in the English countryside, for a start. When Dennis had first got the job of curator at Westbourne Park, life had seemed idyllic, but that had only lasted for a few weeks. She might be forty-nine now, but she was aware of the latest trends in popular music. Although she affected to deride the cult of 'celebrity', she perused organs of popular culture like *Hello!* and was as well acquainted with the doings of the Beckhams as she was the latest rumours and counter-rumours concerning the royal family.

And she had a lover. That was bang up to date: both a feminist assertion and a twenty-first century trend, she felt. Why should the men be allowed to have all the fun? Older and wiser women might have told her to beware of getting out of her emotional depth, but Alison wouldn't have listened anyway. She had never had much time for older and wiser women.

You shaped your own life and made your own mistakes, in her view. As she looked out of the window of the hotel in Stratford-upon-Avon, this lover didn't seem to be much of a mistake. This must be one of the most sought-after and most expensive rooms in this expensive town, she thought with satisfaction. You looked from the window straight across the wide waters of the river to the newly refurbished Shakespeare Memorial Theatre. There was a cross-section of people young and old on the terrace beside the river, as well as a steady traffic of boats large and small upon the Avon. This place teemed with life and she had a luxurious room from which to view it.

The en suite toilet flushed. Alison checked her hair again in the mirror. You had to make the effort; it was the least you could do.

Peter Nayland had also made the effort. His hair was carefully brushed forward to minimize the effects of its thinning and receding. His small moustache was immaculately trimmed. His face was a little florid still, but that should surely be taken as a token of the ardour of his recent lovemaking. If the odour of his aftershave and his deodorant was a little strong for Alison's taste, it must surely be a compliment to her that he chose to return so fragrantly to her presence.

Alison gave him a smile, then turned for a last look out of the window. She wouldn't tell Peter, but she'd never stayed in a room or a hotel quite as well appointed as this one. He came and stood behind her, sliding his hands round her waist, letting his head rest for a moment on the top of her hair. It was a surprisingly slim waist. He pressed his thighs against the back of her thin fawn trousers, feeling the curve of her bottom, comfortable with the intimacy of his sated lust. He said softly into her ear, 'Watching the world go by?'

She turned her head a little, brushing her lips against his cheek. 'I was savouring the view of the river, the boats, the theatre, the people. Trying to fix it in my mind for ever.'

'Glad you approve my choice of hotel.'

She wondered how much the room had cost him. She'd have known the exact cost, if this had been Dennis. He'd have made sure of that. But then it never would have been Dennis. A room like this wouldn't have been 'value for money'. But you shouldn't even be thinking about your husband, when you were with another man.

Money didn't matter to Peter. He had clubs in Birmingham and other businesses he didn't care to detail to her. Fair enough: she was more interested in spending his money and having a good time than knowing where it came from. That made her shallow, she supposed, but she wasn't going to feel guilty about that. There was a kind of honesty in recognizing yourself for what you were and living out your life as that person.

Alison said softly, 'This is so perfect I'm loath to leave it.'

'We don't have to, you know. I can make a couple of phone calls and—'

'We do, my darling. I must get back home and take up my other life.'

'Whatever you say, pet. You're the boss here.'

She wished for a moment that he'd argued a little harder to keep her here. And perhaps she should take exception to his Geordie habit of calling her 'pet'. It had shocked her at first, but now she found she rather liked it, just as she rather liked the fact that his father had been a riveter in a Tyneside shipyard, when such trades had still existed. It seemed to give a respectable base to Peter's dubiously achieved affluence.

She glanced once again at the river and the theatre and sighed. Then she turned to face him and slid her arms round his broad shoulders. 'There'll be other times, won't there?'

'Of course, there will, Ally.' He kissed her on the lips, his mouth firm and experienced. She found herself wondering how many other mouths those lips had touched in his fifty-five years – she had no wish to think of that, but the human brain is a complex and unpredictable organ.

She glanced unwillingly at her watch. 'I must go. I'll be late as it is.'

They went down together. She waited at a discreet distance whilst he checked out and settled the account: she had no wish to know how much the night here had cost. In the car park, her white Fiat Uno looked very small beside his maroon Jaguar. She reversed out quickly and confidently; men liked a woman who was competent behind the wheel, whatever jokes they made about women drivers. She waved to him, threw him the best and most mischievous of her smiles, and drove quickly away.

Peter Nayland watched her until the small white car disappeared, then opened the Jaguar door and sat down heavily on the driving seat. He hadn't criticized that wimpish husband of hers. He knew from experience that it was better not to cast slurs upon the husband you hadn't seen and never meant to see. And Alison had done a good demolition job herself on Dennis.

All the same, if things developed as it seemed they could do, he might have to do something about Dennis Cooper.

At Westbourne Park, Dennis Cooper looked at his watch. Five minutes until they opened to the public; he smiled as he caught the buzz of conversation and laughter from the other side of the high wooden gates. Opening them was a little like ringing up the curtain at a theatre, on a scene which altered slightly and subtly with each passing day.

He found Jim Hartley completing his mowing of the area they called the Wilderness, where visitors were encouraged to picnic. As always when the head gardener left it ready for occupation, the area looked far too trim and well cared for to be called a wilderness. That term came from the man who had initiated and developed this great garden, who regarded any area not crammed with plants, preferably new and interesting, as a wilderness, waiting to be tamed and colonized with new horticultural introductions.

He was a pioneer with vision, imagination and energy, the original owner. He had also amazed his gardeners by his seemingly unlimited funds. But he had also had the single-minded, blinkered vision of the pioneer, with its refusal even to consider other points of view than his own. Not for the first time, Dennis admitted to himself with a rueful grin that the quiet American with the will of steel must have been a very irritating man at times. No wonder his mother had threatened to cut him off from the family riches.

Dennis asked Jim Hartley how the latest children's activity sheets for the garden had gone down with Sam and Oliver. They had taken to using those two boisterous boys as guinea pigs for their efforts to make Westbourne lively and interesting for youngsters, for whom gardens had no obvious and immediate interest. 'Not bad,' said Jim, with the grin which came automatically when he thought of Sam and Oliver. 'Some of the things they were supposed to discover were a bit difficult for a six-year-old, but Olly was all the more pleased when he did get there. I've already got three or four suggestions for when we reprint at the end of the season.'

'I'll need to chat to you about the apprentices in the next week or two.'

'They're all doing quite well. No slackers and all willing and able to learn.'

Dennis suspected the young men wouldn't dare to be anything else, in the face of Hartley's own enthusiasm and commitment. He allowed himself a rueful smile. 'That's good to hear, Jim, but it gives us a problem. It looks as if we'll be able to take one of them on to the permanent staff at the end of the season, but no more than one. National Trust finances won't run to it.'

They went through the ritual of complaint about the unfairness of life, about the success of Westbourne being used to shore up other, less visited properties, about unseen moguls who expected you to maintain high standards with thinly spread resources. Hartley eventually said, 'We develop more and more each year here. They can't expect us to extend the acres under cultivation and maintain our standards without the staff to do it.'

'And they'll say we're getting the extra member of full-time staff for exactly that reason. You know the score.' Both men nodded, content to grumble about the mysterious 'they', aware that their moment of protest was over and their sights reset. You indulged in a little harmless whinging, then you got on with the work and enjoyed it, in this perfect setting. That was the British way. By way of closure, Dennis Cooper said, 'How's young Alex Fraser getting on?'

'Well enough. No, he's doing better than that, if I'm honest. He's got the poorest qualifications of all our present trainees, but I'd say he's the most intelligent and the most determined. That makes him a quick learner.'

Cooper nodded. 'He's got the toughest background. I suspect he truanted from school for a lot of his last few years. It was something of a gamble to take him on, in view of that. I'm glad he's making the most of the opportunity.'

Jim hesitated. He didn't wish to run the young Scottish lad down, because he liked him and was delighted with the man's love of plants and the propagation of them. But you had to be fair to the others as well as Fraser. 'The only fault I'd find with him is that he's not much of a team player. He takes on anything I ask him to do without complaint, but I find it better to use him on individual tasks. He's not as good when he's working in a group. But that might come with time.'

Cooper nodded thoughtfully. He wandered away to the edge of the gardens as the first influx of the day's visitors flowed into the popular areas. Near the southern boundary of the property, he found Alex Fraser at work with a scythe beneath ornamental trees. He was stripped to the waist, but there was no mistaking the fiery red hair which marked Fraser off from his peers. He watched him swinging the scythe rhythmically, the naked torso and the ancient implement moving almost as a single unit, the long blade cutting the lush grass with surprising swiftness round the boles of the trees.

'You've got the knack of that quickly!' Dennis said as the scythe reached the last tree and its handler prepared to move on to the next section of his task.

Fraser jumped a little at the comment. He had been so absorbed in the rhythm of his task, so dedicated to the movement of man and scythe as a unit, that he had been totally unconscious of any other human presence in this quiet place. It took him a moment to realize that this was not a member of the visiting public, who often felt the need to compliment him upon his work, but the boss himself. The big boss, the man who controlled the careers of even men like Jim Hartley.

Alex managed a smile as he said, 'You get the hang of it, eventually. I'd never even seen a scythe afore I came here. You have to get your whole body moving with it, to get the best out of it. You sort of let the blade control you.'

Cooper looked at the widely spaced handles, polished smooth by decades of use by long-departed hands. 'I'll take your word for that. I've never even tried to use a scythe.'

For a moment, he thought Fraser was going to offer him the use of the implement. Then he grinned and said, 'There's no need, is there? You've got other things to do.' Though exactly what bigwigs like Cooper did had always been a mystery to Alex. Took decisions, he supposed. But you couldn't do that all the time, could you?

Dennis said as casually as he could, 'Like it here, do you, Alex?'

Fraser was always suspicious when bigwigs used his forename. When people had done that in the home, there had usually been something bad coming up. 'S'all right.' Then, realizing that he should have grown out of this teenage surliness, he made an effort. 'It's better than all right. I'm enjoying the work here even more than I expected. Better than I ever thought I could.' He realized that this might be one of his rare chances to talk to the top brass, the person who made decisions. He wasn't stupid, and he also realized that he should be making out a case for himself. 'I'm glad of the chance I was given, Mr Cooper, and I want to make the most of it. I like the work here.'

Alex wondered if that sounded too much like arse-licking. But he wasn't used to sucking up and the chance had come to him unexpectedly. He said desperately, 'I'd like to work here permanently, if there was any chance of that. But I don't suppose . . .' His voice trailed away miserably and he wondered if he'd said too much.

'Out of my hands, that, Alex. All depends on the funds available to the Trust at the end of the year.' Cooper delivered smoothly the answer he had ready for anyone who mentioned permanent employment. He leaned a little towards Fraser, looking at the green of the trees above his head even as he spoke almost into the young man's ear. 'With a bit of luck, we might be able to take one of you lads on, in due course. But there can't be any promises as yet.'

He wasn't saying more than he should do. He'd say the same to any of the other apprentices, if they pressed him about the possibilities of work here. There was nothing wrong with encouraging a little healthy competition among your workers, in Dennis Cooper's view.

Cooper went back to his office, dictated a couple of letters, and then slipped back for a few moments to his house in the grounds. It was good to be able to shut yourself away from the crowds in the privacy of your own thatched home when Westbourne was at its busiest. He'd have coffee with Alison and welcome her back. His wife would be pleased to see the place so busy. Maybe he'd start to rebuild a few bridges, if she was in a receptive mood.

Alison wasn't there.

He made his own coffee and munched a biscuit savagely as he glanced at his watch. It was silly to allow yourself to get so upset. It wasn't as if he was afraid for her safety. She was a good driver and she wouldn't have been involved in an accident. But when they'd been young, she'd always been a stickler for punctuality. She didn't seem to have much sense of time, these days.

You could be on top of things in your job, but you couldn't always control things in your private life. He contemplated that bleak truth as he walked over to the window of the bedroom and stared out at the heads of the crowds. The heads moved as busily as ants in the quadrangle near the entry point, where the toilets, shop and restaurant diverted people away from the main purpose of their visit, the gardens. He saw the head and shoulders of Hugo Wilkinson hurrying towards his kitchen at the rear of the main restaurant. He didn't like Wilkinson, who could be truculent and sometimes seemed to question his authority as the senior person here. But the man certainly knew his job. He might need something outside his work, something from the man's private life, if he was to bring Wilkinson to heel.

It was high time he was back at work. He checked his face in the mirror; it was important that you projected an air of calmness when you were in authority. He was descending the stairs when he heard the key turn in the lock.

Alison looked startled when she saw him standing before her in the hall. For a second, something near to panic seemed to freeze her familiar face. It was the most fleeting of moments, so brief that afterwards Dennis was not sure that it had occurred at all. Then she said, 'This is a surprise! I thought you'd be much in demand, with all these visitors pouring through the gates. Have you time for coffee?'

'I've had my coffee. I was planning to have it with you. You're later than you said.'

'Yes. I'm sorry. Carrie kept me talking.'

It was clipped and nervous on both sides. Dennis wondered why that should be. 'I thought she had to be at work at nine.'

'She does. I think she must have made herself late, talking to me. Then I took longer than I intended to get my things together. I left a top behind last time. I wanted to be certain I had everything in my bag.'

She lifted the sports bag she used for her overnight things

in front of her – as if it were evidence, he thought. He said stiffly, 'I expected you back earlier.'

'The traffic was bad. Especially on this last section, through the lanes. That took me a lot longer than I expected. Does it matter?'

'No. You missed having coffee with your husband, that's all. No big deal.' He forced a smile, feeling a little ridiculous.

'That's all right then.' She stepped forward and gave him a peck on the cheek. 'I'll be here at lunchtime, if you can get away.'

He glanced at her sharply, then nodded, forcing himself to relax. As he went back to his office, he wondered why she hadn't mentioned the traffic first as the most obvious cause of her late return from her friend's house.

In the house he had left, Alison Cooper slid the dress she had worn to the theatre on the previous night swiftly back into the wardrobe.

It was the hottest day of the summer so far and a Saturday. Everyone predicted the biggest attendance at Westbourne Park this year. The restaurant was already busy. By one o'clock, there would be a queue at the door, with visitors waiting for early diners to vacate their tables.

Dennis Cooper, who didn't like Hugo Wilkinson, had thought he would need to investigate his private life if he was to find anything to undermine him. The man was highly competent and reigned supreme in his kitchen. Yet ironically, it was in that kitchen that Hugo was about to provide him with just the sort of transgression Dennis had thought unlikely.

In retrospect, it was the classic situation for trouble in a kitchen. Hugo should have been ready for the problem and he should have dealt with it capably. He had handled much worse incidents in his previous post, where a demanding clientele had expected not only quality but swift service for the high prices they paid by the Thames. But surely chefs were expected to have short fuses; wasn't it almost a condition of the job? Their staff should not only expect abuse, but take it in their stride.

The warning signs were there for all to see. Two of the unskilled but necessary kitchen workers had called in sick; Hugo was sure that one of them at least was swinging the lead, but there was little he could do about that. He set to work with the staff he had and tried hard to keep ahead of the game.

The pressure built as he knew it would as midday approached and the dining room filled up. Most of the meals were served plated, so that the waiters had little to do at the tables. The pressure was in the kitchen. They needed to dish up quickly to allow people the illusion they were eating a leisurely meal. That is one of the paradoxes of restaurant service. People need to receive their food as soon as is possible after they have ordered it, so that they can eat without haste and yet still be finished in time for the tables to accommodate a second sitting.

That is where the profit comes from; more than in any other business, the number of bums on seats dictates profits, as Hugo explained carefully to each new member of staff he took on. There was more stress than usual today. The highest number of diners who had eaten in the restaurant this year were being serviced by what was little more than a skeleton kitchen staff.

Hugo Wilkinson worked fast himself, as he had always been able to do. He almost enjoyed the pressure, hearing his decibel levels rise as the tempo increased and he yelled at his staff to keep up with him. There was excitement and satisfaction in showing that you could work at ever-increasing speed without losing any of your competence. Those nearest to him admired the spectacle of a professional operating at the top of his form.

At twelve thirty-five, there was a clash in the doorway between a waiter leaving the kitchen with a full tray of main courses and a waitress returning from the restaurant with a full load of used crockery. One of the oldest and commonest of accidents, and one which should never occur in a smoothly running operation, as Hugo had repeatedly told his workers. A huge crash of filthy plates in the doorway, screams and stifled recriminations in the kitchen, a ragged, friendly cheer from the patrons of the restaurant. Nothing too boisterous: the patrons of the National Trust are not given to rowdiness.

There was indeed much sympathy for the two young people

involved from the tables nearest to the disaster, but it meant that one of the precious kitchen staff had to be spared to clean up the mess as quickly and unobtrusively as was possible in this catering Hyde Park corner. Two of the entrées had ended on the floor, resulting in even swifter movements from Hugo to replace them. There was a rise in the volume and intensity of industrial language amidst the other noises in the kitchen.

In this situation, it could have been anyone who became the unfortunate focus of the chef's attention. It was in fact a young Asian man who had only been taken on three weeks previously. He was methodical but slow. He felt he could not speed up without losing the method he had been taught. In fact, he became slower rather than faster under pressure. The process would have interested a psychologist, but head chefs are not interested in the workings of the mind in a frantic kitchen.

'Shoab! For God's sake move your arse!' Hugo yelled at him.

Shoab tried to speed up, but the hands and fingers which were entirely reliable when he moved at his own pace began to make mistakes. He felt he was the centre of attention, found himself watching his shaking hands as if they belonged to someone else. The hands faltered, dropping the cabbage he had just strained on to the floor. Other hands, swifter and more dexterous than his, swept up the green mass and flung it in the bin. He said he was sorry, several times, but no one had the time or the space to acknowledge him.

Shoab gave extra care to his next task. He drained the peas and beans competently, taking care to allot exactly the right share of them to each plate. The waitress stood by patiently, glancing at her watch, understanding that if she rushed this novice things would only get worse. She slid each plate on to her tray the moment it was ready, glancing at the calmer and more ordered scene in the restaurant as the door swung open and her colleague re-entered the kitchen, yelling out the orders he had taken for dessert courses.

This was the point at which Hugo Wilkinson lost all patience and hurled a phrase he should never have used at the wretched Shoab. It was racialist and it was uttered at the top of his voice. Even in the chaos and frenzied movement of the overheated kitchen, most people stopped what they were doing for an instant, as if a film had faltered and frozen this larger than life moment upon a screen.

It was but an instant. Then things moved again, as if the film had resumed its running. Hugo had shared this moment of truth with everyone else around him. He knew as everyone knew that he had overstepped the mark, even in a world where excess was expected and permitted under stress.

He could not possibly have known at that time how far the effects of his outburst would carry him.

FOUR

On Monday morning, Lorna Green ate her breakfast slowly, sitting in the conservatory at the back of the big house. She looked out with a mind full of memories at the lawn where she had played as a child. She had already helped to dress her mother and measured out her cereals in the kitchen. She acknowledged to herself with a little flush of shame that she had come out here to get away from Barbara. She needed a few moments to herself with *The Times* and her own thoughts.

Twenty minutes later, she looked at her watch, scrambled hastily to her feet, and went indoors to install her mother in the sitting room. 'There'll be tennis on later, Mum. I'll leave the set ready for you.' Lorna Green set the remote control on the small table at her mother's elbow. 'All you have to do is press this button and the tennis should come on for you. This afternoon, that will be. After Jean's delivered your meal at lunchtime.'

Barbara Green looked down at the remote control. For a moment she was puzzled. Then she gathered herself and said with exaggerated dignity, 'I'm not a child you know. I'm quite capable of arranging my own viewing.'

'No, of course you're not a child. I was only trying to

help.' Lorna tried not to think of the number of times she had returned to find children's programmes blaring loud and unheeded whilst her mother stared at the wall or through the window. 'Anyway, if you want it, just push that little red button.'

Her mother looked at the button as if seeing it for the first time and nodded sagely. 'I'll do that.' She looked up into her daughter's face, as if anxious to fix a stranger's image in her mind. 'Going out to the shops, are you?'

'No, Mum. I'm going to Westbourne Park. You remember, the beautiful gardens? The ones which are arranged like separate rooms? You used to enjoy going there. Perhaps we'll go again, when it's quieter.' Yet in that moment she realized with a searing, shocking certainty that Barbara would never go there again.

'Wally does the garden.'

'He used to, Mum, when he was alive. Dad was keen on his garden, wasn't he? Fred comes in to help us with it now. You like Fred, don't you?'

But Barbara Green's face had set into that mask-like expression which meant that she had shut her ears to any words which might be confusing or unwelcome. Lorna sighed and gathered her things together for her day at Westbourne Park. She always took her notes on the history of the house and the gardens with her, though she never needed to refer to them nowadays. The National Trust depended on voluntary helpers like her for its very existence. Probably she now knew more about Westbourne Park and its past than any living soul, she thought.

That idea brought her considerable satisfaction as she drove beneath green canopies of leaf from oaks and beeches which arched over the road. She liked this time of the year, when growth was burgeoning but the leaves were still new enough for nature to display a seemingly infinite range of greens. She felt the tension drop away as she drove the blue Corsa through the Cotswold lanes. It was only when she was away from her mother that she realized the strain she was enduring. Some day it would all become too much and she would have to find a retirement home for Barbara. But she refused to think about that at the moment.

Dennis Cooper was giving one of his introductory talks to a group of visitors when she arrived at Westbourne. 'This site was once a muddy field on a draughty hilltop. Six hundred feet up in the northern Cotswolds is not the obvious place to choose for a great garden experiment. Nevertheless, Westbourne is now the gardening jewel in the National Trust crown. Indeed, it was the first place to be acquired by the NT purely for its garden, in 1948 . . .'

Cooper became more self-conscious when he saw Lorna standing at the back of the hall. But most people in his audience thought he spoke with authority and confidence. They were surprised when the clear female voice spoke up behind them as he concluded. 'Just a couple of points, Mr Cooper. Our American founder did indeed fight in the 1914–1918 war, as you indicated. But this was not his first military service. He became a British citizen as early as 1900 and fought for Britain in the Boer War in South Africa. And in the Great War, he was injured not at Mons but at the first battle of Ypres – one of one and a half million casualties there. That is important, because it was during his convalescence that he began his researches in the Royal Horticultural Society library. His great bible was *The Art and Craft of Garden-Making* by Thomas Mawson.'

'Thank you, Lorna.' Dennis spoke with measured neutrality, then forced a welcoming smile. 'Ms Lorna Green is one of our most willing and energetic voluntary helpers at Westbourne. She helps us on three days a week and she is, as you can probably already appreciate, very knowledgeable on the history of our gardens.'

It was not until an hour later that Cooper called Lorna into his office. He said to his PA, 'Ros, make sure that we're not disturbed for ten minutes or so, please,' and shut the door carefully himself.

He gestured towards the chair he had set in front of his desk and then turned and stared out of the window for a moment. Lorna sat down carefully, feeling as she had done long ago when she had been called into the headmistress's study as a sixth-form prefect. Perhaps he was going to discuss policy with her. There was a tray with a coffee pot on it upon his desk, but he had not asked for another cup.

Dennis turned abruptly from his consideration of the scene from the window and came and sat down opposite her. He put his hands on the edge of his desk and contemplated her for a moment. She wanted to break the silence, to reduce the tension she suddenly felt in the room, but she sensed that it was not she who should speak first.

He said, 'How's your mother?'

'Getting worse. I think I shall need to get someone in to sit with her, when I come here.'

'I'm sorry about that.' He sought desperately for something less trite, came up only with, 'She used to be so sharp.'

Lorna smiled for the first time. 'She was. She never quite approved of you, did she?'

His own smile was awkward, embarrassed. He hadn't wished to go here, but he seemed to have led the way himself. 'I only met her a couple of times.'

'It wasn't really you, you know. It was her generation. She didn't approve of people living together outside wedlock.'

He wanted to say that they'd never really lived together. They'd each kept their own bases and met whenever they chose. Admittedly, that had been quite frequently, for a couple of years. He said lamely, 'It's a long time ago.'

'Yes, I suppose it is. Why didn't we get married, Dennis?'

She spoke as if that had been a puzzle to her for many years. He frowned, staring down at his desk, at the handsome ornamental stand for ink and pens which he never used. 'Let's not go over old ground, Lorna.'

Part of her wanted to say 'No, let's do just that!' But her decorum just held. She said sadly, 'Mum wouldn't know you now.'

'I'm sorry about that. Lorna, I wanted to—'

'And now you're married and settled, and paid handsomely to live in a place like this. You've landed on your feet, Dennis.'

'Yes. I'm conscious of that. I've been very fortunate.'

'Sex all right, is it?'

'Lorna, we really shouldn't be—'

'We were good at that, weren't we? Good together, I mean. I often wonder why we let what we had go. I expect you wonder too, sometimes. Well, to be completely honest, I rather hope you do. That's no more than vanity, I suppose.'

He glanced at her. She was animated, when he had wanted her subdued. She was dictating the direction of their conversation, when all the rules said that in this office he should have been in easy control. She was still an attractive woman, but he mustn't tell her that. He had a sudden vision of them years ago in the bed in his flat, uninhibited, joyous, caring nothing for others in their happiness with each other. Lorna had never been one to play by the rules, in the old days.

Dennis Cooper thrust those days resolutely out of his mind. 'We've moved on, Lorna, all of us. It's best that we leave the old times behind us, sweet as they were. I called you in here about a different matter altogether. Whether you realize it or not, you've been undermining my authority.'

She did not immediately respond. For a moment, she looked very tired. He was suddenly, belatedly, sorry for her. Then she said quietly, 'I have a respect for truth, that's all. I like to see it observed.'

He was uneasy, wondering how widely she meant that to be understood. He said, 'I know that you have a great knowledge of this place and its history. I respect that. But you must see that when you correct me on minor matters, as you did last week in committee and this morning in front of visitors, you diminish my position as leader here.'

'I see. I thought you were a bigger man than that. I thought you'd want the proper facts to be stated.'

He saw how set her face looked, sensed that he needed to help her out of this. 'I do respect the truth, just as I respect your knowledge and your enthusiasm for the correct facts. But when it's a matter of detail, it confuses people rather than illuminates. People like to see the man in charge of Westbourne as just that.'

She looked him full in the face for the first time in several minutes. 'A matter of detail. I see. Well, I shall bear that in mind in the future. Thank you for putting me right on this. Is that all?'

'Yes. Except that if your mother's becoming more of a burden, we can cut down your hours here.'

'Yes. I'm sure you could. But that will not be necessary, thank you.' She rose, moved to the door, then turned to look at him again. He wondered what she was going to say now, whether there would be some bitter final thrust from this woman whom in another life he had loved.

Instead, she looked at him for seconds which seemed to stretch, with both of them as motionless as if they were fixed in a painting. Then she gave a little nod, turned on her heel, and left without another word. She closed the door behind her as quietly and carefully as he had done at the beginning of their meeting.

Jim Hartley found gardening the best of all escapes. Once you were pruning or mowing or hedge-cutting, you gave all your attention to the precision required to secure the right effect. That made you forget the troubles in your private life.

Digging was best of all. You worked yourself into a steady rhythm, efficient but not too fast – those who went bull-at-a-gate at their digging were soon panting and unsteady. More importantly, their work was poor; you quickly became ragged and uneven, if you didn't maintain an even pace. There wasn't a lot of digging at Westbourne, because most of the ground was already thickly planted, but today was an exception.

They were creating a new bed for perennials. Jim would have a major say in exactly what was eventually planted here, but a final decision wouldn't be taken until the end of the season. He had some firm ideas on the subject, but he was keeping them to himself at the moment. Meantime, the plot had to be marked out precisely and double dug. Then the soil would be analysed and compost and animal manures applied to the new surface, ready for planting in the autumn.

Jim Hartley had pulled rank and told his staff that he would initiate the digging himself. There was no such thing as a menial task in the garden, he always told his workforce: there was simply good work and bad work. Everyone should be prepared not just to try his hand at anything, but to master whatever skill was needed. Jim was secretly proud of his digging. He also knew that if the boss was prepared to take on anything, the rest of the gardeners were in no position to pick and choose which tasks were allotted to them.

He had already dug his first set of sods and his first trench, transferring the turfs and the soil by wheelbarrow to the other end of the plot, where they would be used to fill in the final trench. Now he was putting the next set of turfs face down in the trench he had created and covering them with the soil which had been beneath them. Double digging; men had treated virgin ground like this for centuries and still found no more effective method of intensive cultivation. It was slow and demanding, but it was effective. And he liked the feeling that he was continuing a tradition, that he was doing what many thousands of anonymous labourers had done in centuries long gone.

He worked steadily, finding the rhythm he had sought from the outset, hearing his breathing becoming steadier after the panting which had accompanied his creation of that first and very necessary trench. He was well under way now, settled into the pattern of the work. Now the activity itself rather than the labourer seemed to dictate the tempo. He felt it in his shoulders and his arms, in the steady turning of his waist.

'You all right there, boss?'

He started violently, almost crying out with the shock. He had been even more deeply engrossed in the digging than he realized. A slim shape stood motionless between him and the sun, little more than a dark outline until his eyes refocused upon it. The Scottish lad, Alex Fraser, the apprentice who was so keen to learn that he sometimes seemed a little too enthusiastic to be true. Perhaps he realized that Hartley could not immediately comprehend his presence here, at the lower extremity of the gardens, for he said, 'Ye told me to come here at ten. Ye said I was to take over the digging.'

Alex never stepped out of line, always did his best in whatever task he was given. But he never called Hartley 'sir', as most of the other juniors did. Jim liked that in him. Jim nodded now. He asked if the Glaswegian had done this before and was told he had not.

'It's simple enough.' Jim explained the principles of double digging, emphasized that although it was slow and demanding, it was by far the best method of getting a deep tilth in new gardening ground. He demonstrated as he spoke, enjoying his own proficiency in the task, finding himself out of breath as he combined instruction with labour.

He climbed reluctantly from his latest trench. 'Don't rush it, or you'll need to keep stopping. Cultivate a slow, steady rhythm; that's good for the ground as well as for you.'

Jim Hartley left the young man with the bright red hair concentrating fiercely upon his simple task and moved reluctantly back into the activities of the established gardens. Over the multiple hedges of Westbourne, he looked towards his cottage and the problems that it held for him.

Six hours later, Jim Hartley's wife collected her two children from school. That's how she was defined nowadays, she thought, that's how people thought of her: as someone else's wife.

Julie Hartley wasn't looking forward to the birthday party to which the children had both been invited. To Julie's mind, a school day was quite taxing enough, without the added excitements and tensions of a gathering like this afterwards. Children's parties should be held at weekends or not at all, in her view. To hold one on a Monday evening after school was asking for trouble. There would be childish quarrels and tears before this one was over, if she was any judge.

She had a point. But Julie was not widely noted for her optimism.

She was a pretty woman with long black hair; her dark brown eyes seemed alert to everything around her. She smiled readily, but rarely at length; there seemed always something brittle in both her amusement and her approval. When she had been in college, few of her contemporaries had envisaged her as a wife and mother. She had seemed then too independent and spirited to settle into quiet domesticity before she had made her mark in the world. Of the several men who had passed in quick succession through her life in those days, the least likely candidate for permanency had surely been Jim Hartley. The fresh-faced, powerful young man couldn't discuss books or films or art or even television, and he had a passion for horticulture which seemed to most of the young people in Julie's set quite bizarre.

Yet the marriage seemed to have worked. And Julie, against all expectations, was quite certainly a splendid mother. Sam was eight and Oliver was six now; they were boisterous, happy boys, comfortable at home and doing well at school. To all outward appearances, the once mercurial Julie had settled happily into family life, accepting its challenges and coping well with its inevitable problems.

To all outward appearances.

The party was a huge success, despite Julie's earlier fears for it. The birthday boy's parents were richer than anyone had realized before this day. They lived in a huge modern house with three acres of grounds and a large swimming pool. On this broiling-hot day, the pool was the star attraction. Released from the disciplines of school, the boys – there were no girls at this celebration, on the strict instructions of the eight-year-old at its centre – splashed, screamed and flung balls and rubber rings to each other in joyful ecstasy.

There was no restriction on the decibels here, because there were no neighbours to disturb. There was that most important of childish requirements for happiness, infinite space. The adults were at hand to control over-excitement and excess, but in this environment there was surprisingly little of either. There were inevitably a few clashes and a few falls, even the occasional tear, but the injured were too eager to rejoin the party to grieve for long, especially with male pride at stake.

Julie Hartley watched her boys happily among the communal chaos, saw how well they fitted in with their peers, and wished suddenly and heartily that she could do the same. In the midst of this noisy and unthinking euphoria, she wondered bleakly how her own situation could ever be resolved.

Peter Nayland tried to see the humour of his situation. He was sure that others would, if he was ever fool enough to reveal the facts of it.

It was a strange thing to feel so vulnerable, when you were surrounded with all the trappings of power. Like all men who make fortunes by dubious means, Nayland had assembled around himself the muscle to repel both his rivals and the enemies inevitably made as he became successful. It was like the Swiss Guards around the Pope, he thought; you gathered a small group you could trust, who knew that their mission was both to display your power and standing and to enforce control whenever it was needed.

Peter liked the Swiss Guard comparison, for he had a lively sense of irony. He was an intelligent man, despite the dubious businesses he operated; the idea of the unthinking thug at the head of an enterprise had always been anathema to him. You needed to be well organized, whatever the source of your wealth. You needed to be aware of the competition. You needed to know your markets. You needed to be able to anticipate trends, to foresee what would be popular in two years' time as well as currently.

Wasn't it Sam Goldwyn who said that no one ever went bankrupt through underestimating the taste of the public? One of those movie moguls, anyway. Well, in Peter Nayland's view, no one had ever gone bankrupt through exaggerating the depths to which human sexual tastes could sink. That philosophy, combined with the absence of any sense of morality, had stood him in good stead over the years.

Yet today he felt vulnerable. Not to any threat from his enemies or his rivals, but to a totally unsuspected sentimentality he had discovered within his own being. He called it sentimentality in an attempt to despise it and thus control it. Sentimentality was mawkish and maudlin and could be easily dismissed.

Love was something else altogether. Nayland had a vague idea from his early youth that love was something you should cherish. Ever since he had watched her drive away from him after their last meeting in Stratford, Peter Nayland had been fighting the gnawing suspicion that he might be in love with Alison Cooper.

He'd had plenty of women over the years. He'd even felt quite close to a few of them, without ever considering setting up house with them for the long term. Nor had Ally the sort of Hollywood looks which would blind a man to reality and let his penis rule his brain. She was attractive enough, with her neatly cut dark-blonde hair, the blue eyes which were rarely without a twinkle, and the small, attractive nose which lifted just a little at the end. She'd kept her figure; not only did she curve in the right places but she made you want to stroke those curves. He smiled even now at that thought.

And she was good in bed, was Ally. They were good together. But Peter had been good with others in his time. With the power and money he had now, he could summon women twenty years younger than Ally to his bed – a succession of them in a variety of shapes, if sex was all he wanted.

But Ally gave him more than that. And some unsuspected adolescent streak lurking still within Peter Nayland made him proud of his feelings for her. He might move through sordid channels to make his money, but he was capable of higher sentiments in his own life. He would show those people who thought he was a crude and ruthless money-maker that he was more than that. But first he would show it to himself.

There were certain obstacles, of course, but nothing which couldn't be easily overcome. He buzzed his PA and asked her to let Chris Horton know that he wished to see him at three p.m. today. Horton wasn't part of his muscle, nothing as crude as that. He was an expert at acquiring information on other businesses and the people who ran them. Because of Horton's researches, Nayland went into any meeting better aware of the strengths and weaknesses of his rivals, equipped to strike wherever they were most vulnerable, if negotiation did not secure what he wanted.

When Horton came into his office, Peter Nayland sat back comfortably in his chair. Love would be preposterous in this context. He wouldn't declare such a weakness to this subtle and efficient man. He said almost casually, 'I want you to find out all you can about a man called Dennis Cooper.'

Horton nodded and made a note of the name. It was not familiar to him and the boss did not volunteer anything to help him. He looked up and said, 'Where does this man work?'

'Cooper works at Westbourne Park, the famous gardens. He lives on the site. He was appointed by the National Trust to run the place and exercise a loose control over other Trust properties in the area.'

If Chris Horton was surprised, he was too practised to show it. 'Any other details you can give me?'

'Nothing more at the moment.' It was all he had been able to pick up from Alison; most women didn't want to talk about their husbands when they were with a lover. 'I'm relying on you to provide me with that, Chris.'

He gave him a smile of encouragement, and Horton, a small man with a narrow, inquisitive face, gave him a brief, almost conspiratorial grin in reply. 'Usual stuff? Sexual preferences, shagging away from home: financial peccadilloes; lies told or facts concealed in applications for posts; tax evasions?'

Peter nodded. 'Anything that you can dig up. You might find this one more difficult than most. On the face of it, Cooper's a pillar of rectitude, operating in a blameless area. A highly meritorious area, some might say. But he'll have his weaknesses. All of us have.'

Horton looked down at the name and the brief notes he had already made. The smile he offered this time was more malicious, in line with the assignment he had been given. 'You're right. Even pillars of rectitude have their weaknesses, sir.'

'And they crash to the ground even harder when they're exposed. You've got the idea, Chris. But work discreetly. I don't want this man to know that he's being investigated. He doesn't even know that I exist, as yet.'

'Right you are, sir. It might take a little longer to gather material without his knowing we're after him. Should I give it priority?'

'Yes. Top priority. Let me know as soon as you have anything useful on him.'

Chris Horton nodded and left. He wondered why Nayland wanted to dig the dirt on a man like this. Quite different from the people he usually worked on. All the same, if Peter Nayland had him down as an enemy, he wouldn't like to be in this Dennis Cooper's shoes.

FIVE

Hugo Wilkinson was thirty-eight, a head chef with a wealth of experience. But he felt like a schoolboy as he waited outside Dennis Cooper's office.

He had come ten minutes early for the appointment. He planned to say that he needed to be away quickly to ensure that the serving of lunches in the restaurant went ahead smoothly. That would show that he was conscientious.

It turned out to be a bad tactic. He was left waiting on his chair in the outer office for the full ten minutes. Whilst Cooper's PA worked busily at her PC, Hugo became increasingly nervous. He wasn't used to nervousness, not in his working life. His hobby caused him plenty of anxiety, but that was another matter altogether.

Chefs were powerful people, and head chefs the most powerful of all. Whatever the official pecking order in a hotel or restaurant, everyone knew that if the head chef walked out the enterprise would be threatened with chaos; his departure would be followed by a plethora of customer complaints. Head chefs were allowed, even expected, to be temperamental creatures. They were given more rope than other employees.

All this passed through Hugo Wilkinson's mind as he sat on the upright chair in the outer office, crossing and uncrossing his legs. But he remembered his father telling him when he was no more than thirteen that if you gave some people enough rope they would hang themselves. He had an uncomfortable feeling that he might have used his position to hang himself. You had to be more politically correct when you worked for the National Trust than you did when retained by a private employer.

It seemed to Hugo warm and airless here, though the PA in her white blouse and others who arrived and departed seemed cool enough. Everyone who came into the room gave him a curious glance, though none of them spoke to him. Here was another aspect of this business, which he had not considered previously. The junior staff who entered and left this busy anteroom would be surprised to see him here, would speculate to their fellows about seeing the head chef waiting like a schoolboy outside the headmaster's office. He told himself that they would merely think he was waiting to confer with Cooper about budgets and menus, but that didn't seem to help much.

He was sweating hard when Cooper eventually called him in. The curator did so with a professional courtesy, betraying no sign to any curious watcher that this senior employee was in trouble. His expression changed once the door was closed and the two men took their positions carefully on either side of the big desk. The curator studied him for a moment before he said, 'As I told you when I asked you to come here this morning, I have received a complaint. Complaints, in fact.'

'He's quick to take offence. He doesn't know how a kitchen—'

'Complaints from the public, Mr Wilkinson, not the man you insulted. Two visitors came to my office on the day. There have been three written complaints since then. There may well be more.'

Hugo licked his lips. He knew he hadn't a leg to stand on here. He needed to make the best plea of mitigating circumstances he could and then get the hell out of here. 'We were short-staffed and under pressure. These things happen.'

'These things should not happen, Mr Wilkinson, whatever the circumstances. Do you dispute the facts of the case?'

This perpetual use of his title and surname was disconcerting him. Ever since he'd moved in here, he'd been 'Hugo' to Dennis Cooper. Now the man was behaving like an old hanging judge preparing to put on his black cap. Hugo wanted this over and done with. He would do anything to accelerate that process. 'No, I don't dispute the facts. I called Shoab Junaid a "fucking coon". I should not have done that.'

He looked up to see Cooper's reaction, but the curator gave him no relief. Cooper's face was set in stone. He studied his man as dispassionately as if he had been a specimen under a microscope. Eventually he said, 'Can you repeat for me the full sentence you used?'

Hugo swallowed. 'Yes. I believe I said, "For God's sake move your arse, you fucking coon!"'

Cooper nodded coolly. 'That tallies with what I have heard from others.' He leaned forward, earnest and unsmiling. 'You're not stupid enough to think you can get away with this sort of thing.' It was a statement, not a question.

'I was stupid enough to say it.'

'True. I find that disturbing. You'd better give me a full account of any extenuating circumstances. I know at least one complainant has sent a copy of his letter to me to the Chairman of the National Trust. I may have to account for my decision to him. Perhaps to Prince Charles, if news of the incident reaches him as our president.'

'You're really training the big guns on me, aren't you?'

'You trained them upon yourself, Hugo, when you used those stupid words.'

At least they were back to 'Hugo'. And Cooper seemed to be admitting he'd been no more than stupid. 'I appreciate that. I've already said I was stupid. But you don't think of the repercussions when you shout something in a red mist of fury.'

'But you should do, Hugo. In most respects, you have easier conditions here than in your previous post. As you've pointed out yourself on occasions, you don't often operate far into the night and the standard of cuisine expected is not as high as Michelin three star. But you are working in a more public context than you have ever done before. When you took employment with the National Trust, you accepted that. You should have realized that a lapse like this could have far-reaching consequences.'

Hugo Wilkinson was suddenly sick of the man and his scoldings. He'd taken a step down professionally when he came here. He could get other jobs, if he needed to. 'Look, Dennis, if you're going to sack me, stop pissing about and get it done. I won't be short of offers, if you want me out of here.'

'You might not find the offers you anticipate. Prospective employers are sure to ring me up to find out why you left here. Are you in fact saying that you wish me to terminate your employment here?'

There was a long pause, whilst Hugo strove to control his

anger. His palms felt very damp. 'No. I'm happy here. I can do the job and it suits me. You haven't had any complaints about the quality of the food or the way I run my kitchen.'

'No. But you're sitting in that chair today because of your own actions, not anyone else's. And you shouldn't have any illusions about this. It is a more serious complaint than someone finding your steak isn't tender or your broccoli is overcooked.'

'We were three short on staff, on a day when we served more meals than any other day so far this year. Shoab Junaid was very slow when we needed speed. Everyone else was operating at maximum capacity and he was holding things up. I'd already told him twice to get a move on. What I said was over the top, but I was under extreme pressure.'

'It was racialist, Hugo. You might get away with obscenities under the stress of that situation, but not racialism.'

'I know that. I know the law. I've already admitted I was stupid.'

'The question any barrister would ask in court is what this says about you. Did you reveal the real Hugo Wilkinson in a moment of stress? Is the racialist in you concealed only by a thin cloth of courtesy which is ripped apart by a bit of pressure?'

Hugo knew what he had to say here. 'I've asked myself that. My answer is that I'm not a racialist. I was looking round for the most violent words I could find to stir the man into action. I picked the wrong ones, that's all.' He'd no idea himself whether this was correct or not, but he knew it had to be stated.

'Does Mr Junaid intend to take the matter any further?'

'No. I've told him that I lost my temper under pressure and spoke without thinking. I've apologized to him and he's accepted that his speed of work was unacceptable and a contributory factor in the incident. We're working together amicably again.'

It was more or less what Shoab Junaid had said to Dennis Cooper when he had spoken to him on the previous day. He seemed a willing if limited worker, more anxious about keeping his own job than about exacting retribution from Wilkinson.

Cooper reached forward and moved his pen minimally on the desk in front of him. 'If what you said represents your real attitude, Hugo, you'd be better getting out now. Neither we nor you can afford any repetition of the incident.'

Hugo knew now that he was not going to be told to pack his bags and get out. His relief was more overwhelming than he had ever expected it to be. He must say the correct, contrite things now. It would soon be over, if he ate a little humble pie. 'There won't be any repetition. I can guarantee that.'

'There mustn't be, Hugo. I shall send you a formal written warning about this incident, which will state among other things that any recurrence will mean immediate dismissal. A copy will be placed on your file.'

'I understand that.'

'I hope you do. And I hope we can put this happening behind us and never discuss it again.'

He stood up and Wilkinson followed suit, realizing that the meeting was at an end, hesitating awkwardly for a moment as he wondered whether the curator was going to shake his hand.

Dennis Cooper sat still for a long time after the head chef had left his office. He pondered whether he should have raised his other concern with Wilkinson, but decided that he had been right not to do so. This was a formal reprimand and a formal warning about a serious incident in the man's working environment. It wouldn't have been appropriate to raise anything else.

Cooper unlocked the top right-hand drawer of his desk and made a note in the small notebook he kept there. He'd need more than mere suspicion, to raise anything as serious as what he suspected.

Most of the younger gardening staff at Westbourne thought Alex Fraser was a loner. In his first few months there, he had been quite prepared to foster that impression.

He'd never had to think about company in Glasgow. The gang had seen to that. But when he'd moved south into an alien world, he'd chosen to keep himself to himself. That had been the advice of the only social worker for whom he'd had any respect, the man who'd hauled him out of trouble and then helped him to keep out of it, in the teeming Scottish city where he'd spent his turbulent adolescence.

'Keep your nose clean and join a golf club. The English will like that,' Ken Jackson had said, after he'd helped him to get the apprenticeship at Westbourne. He'd smiled when he'd said it, almost smirked. Golf was a very odd thing for Alex Fraser to have in his armoury. Even in Scotland, where golf cuts across the class divisions much more than in England, a lad of Fraser's background didn't often get near a golf course, unless it was for theft or other mischief.

Five years ago, when Fraser was fifteen, someone at the council had thought it a good idea for some of the boys in care to attend a golf clinic at the neighbouring municipal course. The tuition was subsidized by the golf authorities, who thought it was a splendid idea to introduce youngsters to their game, so it was very cheap. No doubt that appealed to council staff perennially in pursuit of economies. The slight young man with freckles and ginger hair spoke very little, but he showed a talent for the game unexpected by him as well as those who controlled his life. Ken Jackson persuaded the authorities to buy Alex a yearly ticket for the municipal course; at least one of their charges would be safe from the multiple temptations which beset youth in their great city. The boy improved rapidly, and his fiery red hair made him recognizable from great distances on the fairways, so that his excellence was apparent to all observers.

When Fraser moved to that strange country called England and that strange district they called the Cotswolds, Ken Jackson had made a few phone calls and arranged for him to join the Ross-on-Wye golf club. Alex's low handicap secured him immediate entry; every golf club was anxious to have young players of his standard. It was a course set in beautiful country, with the Malvern Hills splendidly visible and scarcely a house in sight. That in itself was strange for Alex Fraser, who had never played on anything but a public course surrounded by housing.

But the strangest experience of all was belonging to a private golf club. Alex Fraser was still tackling the arcane mysteries of etiquette and precedence that this involved. Perhaps because it was so different from any experience he had ever had before, he was secretly rather enjoying it. The English gentry at play revealed more of themselves than they ever suspected to the shrewd young observer from north of the border. He found it both amusing and instructive. He'd even played a couple of weeks ago with a detective chief superintendent and a detective sergeant, and he'd actually enjoyed it. What would the lads in Glasgow have made of that?

Alex had taken to riding his battered little motorbike down to the club on summer evenings. Once there, he would either team up with someone for a few holes or hone his considerable skills on the practice ground. He was fit and well fed through his work at Westbourne and hitting golf balls even further and straighter as a result. 'Keep out of trouble and join a golf club' had been good advice from Ken Jackson.

If only he had held to it, life might have continued serenely for Alex Fraser.

It was Tom Bracey and Matt Garton, the two local apprentice gardeners, who persuaded him to go into Cheltenham for the night. Matt's brother was having his twenty-first birthday party; a room had been set aside for the celebration in one of the pubs near the centre of the town. It would be a laugh and a good piss-up. They'd arranged a lift to Cheltenham with one of the other gardeners and they'd share a taxi back. A responsible way to end a riotous night.

'But I'm not invited,' Alex Fraser objected.

'Don't matter,' said Matt in his confident West Country accent. 'Our Jake won't mind us being three instead of two, and after an hour no bugger will give a shit!'

Secretly, Alex was pleased to be asked, to be included as part of the group. He wasn't a natural loner. Besides, he'd never been to Cheltenham. He knew its reputation as a quiet spa town, the haunt of retired army colonels and ageing ex-pats. Vicarage tea party this place would be, compared with the Gorbals on a Saturday night.

All the same, he couldn't get rid of a strange feeling that he was doing the wrong thing. He decided he'd better take certain precautions, even though it was odds-on that they'd never be needed. 'Be with you in a minute,' he called after the others. Then he slipped back to the tallboy in the corner of his tiny cottage bedroom and opened the bottom drawer. He moved the socks aside, stared for a moment at what was beneath them, and slipped it into the pocket of his jeans.

In the early evening, Julie Hartley watched the three apprentices drive off with the older gardener in his car. The lads looked spruced up and excited, as if they were anticipating a lively evening. She wished for a moment that she could spirit fifteen years away and be back at that age, when everything seemed new and vital, and life had stretched invitingly before you as a challenge.

She smiled as she heard Oliver's shrill voice. She rounded the end of the hedge and found her son holding the tennis ball above his head in both hands, celebrating the catch he had just unexpectedly held. 'You missed it, Mum! I caught Dad out!' he said. Then he flung the ball as high in triumph as his six-year-old body allowed him to do. It was no more than a few feet in the air, but no doubt it seemed much higher to him.

Jim Hartley smiled at his wife and Hugo Wilkinson invited her politely to join in the game. 'We can always use another fielder, though you'll have to be good to catch it like Oliver.' Sam, who was pacing out his run with the intense seriousness of an eight-year-old as he prepared to bowl to his father, directed her imperiously to field at mid-on.

'Sorry, chaps, I'm not available. I have to go out.' Julie turned towards her husband's interrogative face. Jim stood looking a little ridiculous with the boy's bat which was so much too short for him. 'I'm sorry, but Sarah left some library books in the car when I gave her a lift home. I've no idea when I'll see her again, so I'd better take them round. Shan't be long. Read you a story, boys, if Dad doesn't keep you out here too long. Bye!'

And she was gone as suddenly as she had appeared. The smile disappeared abruptly from her face as soon as she was out of sight. She was appalled at how easy she had found it to lie.

It was no more than three miles, but you couldn't rush it, with the narrowness of the lanes and the innumerable blind bends. These roads had been designed originally for horses and carts. She glanced impatiently at the car clock. It was after half past seven already. She mustn't stay long. She really shouldn't have come at all.

Julie Hartley rapped hard on the door of the cottage, felt the familiar, absurd surge of pleasure as she heard the steps inside, then saw the surprise on the fresh-skinned face as the door opened. She followed Sarah inside, scarcely waited until they were in the living room to seize her shoulders and turn her. She kissed her, first gently and then more fiercely, running her hands up and down over the familiar shoulder blades, sliding her hands under the blouse on to the smooth skin beneath it.

The pub in Cheltenham was much noisier than Alex Fraser had expected. The party had its own room, but to Alex it quickly became an overcrowded box. As things got rowdier it seemed that everyone except him knew everyone else in the room. He was an interloper, and he shouldn't have come here.

He went out to the Gents, then tried a door in the corridor and found himself outside, in a little courtyard behind the building. It was almost dark now, though above the wall he could see the purple of the western sky where the sun had set. It was probably private ground here, but he was doing no harm, was he? He just needed a few minutes in the open air, a little period to gather his resources together. Then he would paste on his determined smile and rejoin the boisterous celebrations he could hear twenty yards away.

'You with Matt Garton?'

The voice came from the shadows behind him, near the door he had used himself to get here. He hadn't heard it open and shut to admit the mystery newcomer. Alex turned to look at him, his hand automatically in his pocket, feeling the reassuring touch of metal. 'What if I am?'

The newcomer stepped forward. Alex was pleased to see that the mystery man looked younger than he was himself. More to the point, he seemed even more nervous. 'I got stuff for Matt. I can't take it in there.' He flicked his head backwards, towards the noise from the private room.

'Why not?'

The youth looked shocked by such a question. 'Too public, ennit?'

'What do you want with Matt?'

'Don't want nuffink. I'm delivering gear.'

'Gear?'

Alex looked blank, but the man didn't believe his bafflement. 'It's all paid for. I promised him delivery tonight. You gotta give it him for me.'

He produced a small package, tightly wrapped in a plastic bag from a supermarket, and thrust it into Fraser's hand. 'Ask no questions and you'll be told no lies.' He set his finger against the side of his nose in a gesture he had obviously executed many times before. It made him look ridiculous, as if he was guying a much older man.

Alex broke the tension with a little laugh. The finger on nose gesture reminded him of Fagin; he had seen only the Fagin of *Oliver!* and not Dickens' older and darker creature of the London stews. Disturbed by this unseemly mirth, the youth flashed his hand from his face to set it on top of the package Fraser held in his hand. 'You just deliver, or it'll be the worse for you, mate. Understand?'

Alex could see the zits on the youth's forehead, could smell the foulness of his breath. 'You do your own deliveries, mate. You wait here. I'll send Matt out to you, if he wants to come.'

But the man was gone, back into the darkness whence he had come, closing the door behind him with a crash. The noise made Alex realize for the first time that they had spoken in whispers throughout their strange, unsatisfactory exchange. He looked at the small package in its innocent-looking covering. Drugs, probably. That Matt was a young fool. He'd tell him so when he gave him this. He slid it into his pocket and took a last look at the top of the wall and the faint light of the dying day at the top of it.

It seemed even noisier and hotter in the room where Matt's brother was having his party. It was too crowded for Alex to get anywhere near Matt, who presently made a drunken speech about the twenty-one-year-old's life to date amidst much hilarity. Alex, despairing of making contact in a room now very packed, mouthed, 'I've got your package' at Matt over quickly moving heads, but he wasn't sure whether Matt had got the message or not amidst the prevailing raucous confusion. He couldn't hand it over here, in any case. He'd keep the little parcel in the pocket of his jeans until they were safely in the taxi at the end of the evening. He'd give Matt a bollocking for being stupid at the same time.

Meanwhile, he might as well relax and join in the mirth and the celebration. The party moved towards its conclusion with a number of drunken toasts and ragged cheers. Alex didn't know most of the people involved, but he raised his glass obediently. It was a reaction encouraged by Matt's sister, who seemed to have taken a fancy to the fresh-faced young Scot with the fiery hair. She embraced him enthusiastically after each toast. He got the message and roared his approval of these people he did not know, being rewarded by kisses and ever more fierce embraces with each name they toasted.

He accepted a chaser with his final pint, downing the whisky and beer and wiping his mouth with a flamboyant gesture. Then he wrapped the enthusiastic young female body around himself and the erection hardening beneath his jeans. The Cotswolds seemed now a splendid place, and Cheltenham not so fusty after all. His companion was wrenched away from him with bawdy admonitions by her family. She pressed a scrap of paper with her phone number upon it into his palm as she disappeared with hand held high towards him in a final gesture of affection. He hadn't even known her name was Lisa until he glanced at the paper.

He was back with Matt Garton and Tom Bracey as they shot through the pub exit and into the street, propelled like corks from a bottle by the crowd behind them. A shoulder brushed hard against his face, almost bursting his nose with the force behind it. He was still trying to decide whether the collision had been deliberate or accidental when he felt friendly arms pulling him back into line. At the same moment, he realized that there was another ragged line of men opposite them. A line mouthing insults, yelling the obscenities calculated to cause offence and propel his side towards the violence of a gang fight.

Alex glanced automatically behind him, then at the faces set in vicious hatred on the other side of the narrow street. They were outnumbered by approximately two to one. But there was nowhere to flee. They'd have to fight, have to reach the end of the street before there was any escape. He calculated the odds. It would depend how much real hatred was here, how far this went back. If there was the kind of psychotic violence which surrounded some of the Celtic–Rangers clashes, there'd be serious damage done to flesh and bone here.

Not to Alex Fraser, if he could help it. His hand flew to his pocket. The fingers of his right hand slid into the knuckleduster he had put there at the beginning of the evening. Soft as shit, these southern Sassenachs. They wouldn't know what a real battle was about. His face set in hard, thin lines. The time for shouting was past: he wouldn't waste breath on shouting.

He was partly right about the Sassenachs. The charge when it came was not as coordinated as many he'd met in Glasgow. But this was a gang fight all right. Most of the people beside and behind him were members of the Garton and Bracey families and they had fought this opposition before. This wasn't his fight. But no one on either side was going to recognize that. He'd involved himself by attending the party, by his very presence in this narrow, hate-filled street.

As if to confirm the fact, he heard one phrase among the multitude that were being flung across the narrowing space between the sides. 'Get the fucking carrot-head!' a squat youth with tattooed arms yelled. Alex fastened upon this man as the sides fell upon each other, dodging a clumsy blow from the muscled forearm, driving his own fist hard into the side of the stubbled jaw. He felt the crunch of metal on bone, saw the blood spurt. Then the scream came, later than expected, and the body went down.

There was no time to relish individual victories. Arms were flying all round him, friend and foe merging as men caught each other round the throat and reeled about the street. He registered a couple more blows, driving his armoured right fist this time into the bodies of his adversaries, hearing with delight the sounds of the pain he was inflicting. It was primeval stuff, with survival the only aim and staying on your feet the only victory. He had no idea how his side was doing, though he saw a couple of other small victories which gave him hope.

Then he saw what he had feared from the first. A flash of metal in the dim lights of the street. Knives! One at least, and there would surely now be others. The blade he'd seen was within two yards of him. Then the man beside him went down, the breath rasping from him with the sound of a bursting tyre, and Alex knew that he must be next.

Alex faced the man, saw eyes wide with bloodlust within a foot of his own, saw the fillings in a mouth yelling words he did not hear, saw the hand with the knife in it rising to strike, as clearly as if he was watching a film in slow motion. And in that moment, when the action seemed to be arrested, he saw his chance. He drove the knuckleduster on his right hand hard into the man's belly button, then into his face as the body doubled in agony and the knife clattered on the tarmac beneath them.

The noise was deafening now, crashing about their ears like a physical, hostile force. Alex shut it out. The din was a distraction, when you needed your concentration to be at its sharpest. You didn't know where the next challenge would come from, but you had to be ready for it, if you wanted to survive. He didn't know if they were winning, but he had hope now. He'd downed two of them, hadn't he?

It was because he'd shut out the noise that he didn't hear the urgent wailing of the sirens. The police vehicles were at the end of the short street, cutting off all escape, before Alex Fraser realized they were there. He was fighting furiously, with eyes only for his physical survival, so that he went on a little while after others had ceased and begun sliding sideways to try to evade arrest.

He heard a man shout, 'Get the redheaded sod!', saw the sergeant's stripes upon the blue of his arm, wondered furiously if he would ever be marked by anything other than the colour of his hair. He dropped his hands in time to avoid the charge of resisting arrest. Don't give the bastards the excuse to hit you.

The old code was back with him, as if he'd never left it. He flinched now, where he had not done in the fury of the contest, anticipating police blows to his body and arms as they shouted the words of arrest in his ear.

But there were no blows. Just rough hands on his arms, then the crowded inside of the police van, the journey which flung you hard against the others in there with you, the sudden dumb horror of charges and detention. They set his possessions on the desk and made him sign. He stared for a moment at the money, the little package in its plastic supermarket wrapping, the unused handkerchief, the knuckleduster with blood thickening darkly upon it.

The cell with its windowless walls looked depressingly familiar. As the small hours of the night dragged through, Alex Fraser felt stone cold sober and very depressed. He couldn't quite work out how he had come to be here. Hadn't he vowed that he was finished with all of this?

SIX

At the same time as Alex Fraser was partying and fighting, Hugo Wilkinson was attending an altogether quieter and more cautious gathering.

He couldn't make his mind up until the last minute whether to go. He was still shaken by his interview with Dennis Cooper. He wasn't used to being carpeted and threatened with dismissal; in fact he couldn't think it had ever happened to him before, even in his younger and wilder days. What made it worse was that he had deserved every word of it. However humiliated he felt now, he had brought it all upon himself when he had yelled his racialist words at that dim Asian boy.

He'd felt all right immediately after the interview with Cooper, because he'd been working; busy kitchens didn't allow you much time for reflection. But as soon as he'd returned to his own room, gloom had overtaken him again. He wasn't pleased with life in general, and he certainly wasn't pleased with himself.

He played cricket with Jim Hartley and his kids until their bedtime approached and stumps were drawn. When young Oliver missed with his final extravagant swipe and saw the bowler, his brother Sam, leap joyously into the air, all four of them trooped indoors. But after the sunlit innocence of their play with the tennis ball on the Theatre Lawn, Hugo couldn't settle in his room. When it was almost too late, he drove swiftly out of Westbourne Park and set his course for Bristol.

The depressing Victorian house had high, narrow windows and high, shabby rooms. He was almost the last to arrive. Their host waited in the hall, gruffly greeting each of his visitors. For the second time that day, Hugo Wilkinson made to shake hands, when that was not the gesture expected. This man and the one who stood silently behind him in the sombre hallway were vetting guests, not welcoming them. This was not the sort of gathering where you fussed over visitors; here, any newcomer had to be announced in advance, with an existing member of the group to vouch for him.

Hugo put his tenner in the dish by the door and went into the big room at the front of the house. There was still daylight outside, but the long velvet curtains were carefully drawn and the lights were on. Fourteen men conversed in low tones. There were no women here; the only woman who entered this house came once a week to clean. Three or four of the men acknowledged Hugo, but there was little warmth in their greeting and just as little in his acknowledgement. Everyone was trying to behave as if this were a normal gathering, yet everyone knew it was no such thing.

'It's like Freemasonry without the joy and the laughter,' said Hugo's neighbour dejectedly. He made it sound as if he'd been exiled here for some transgression.

Hugo could think of no rejoinder save, 'I've never been a Mason. I've always had to work in the evenings.' Until now, he thought. Until I got the chef's job at Westbourne Park. I wonder how much longer I shall be there. He wondered why he told that small, unimportant lie about never being a Mason. Perhaps dishonesty came naturally here.

His neighbour didn't react to the remark. The natural follow-up would have been to ask what sort of work Hugo did, but you didn't pry into people's lives here. That made conversation stilted and difficult, as was evidenced all over the room. Everyone held a glass of wine, but most of the men sipped cautiously, as if they feared a loss of control. They talked about having to drive home, but their real fear was that they might reveal more of themselves than they wished to do whilst they were here.

Hugo had been told that the group numbered a circuit judge and a senior civil servant in line for a knighthood among its members, but he had no idea who they might be. Nor could he identify them as he glanced surreptitiously about him and sipped his wine. Everyone wore a suit and a tie, everyone seemed to carry a muted air about him, despite the effects of the wine and the eventual attempts of the man who lived here to introduce a little bonhomie into the proceedings.

Another man, the one who had stood behind the householder in the hall, took over what might have been termed the business section of the meeting. Whether he was the natural leader or merely the man who knew more about the workings and the secrecies of computers than anyone else was not clear to Hugo, who was still a fairly new member of this strange company.

The man said he hoped they'd all received their latest 'instalment', the word he used for the material Hugo had inspected and enjoyed on his laptop a week earlier. There were murmurs of assent and approval, but no real congratulations. The speaker promised them more and better in a fortnight or so, then asked if they would be interested in material from abroad. It was a vague word, 'abroad', but everyone in the room knew the countries which were the likely sources of this material.

One man said he liked more local stuff, preferred to support home industries, and there was a tiny rumble of amusement at this sour little joke. The man who had offered them the foreign material pointed out that it was cheaper and safer than the home-produced product. He did not take a vote on the matter – they never did that – but he sensed he had the approval of the majority and passed on. They would receive their next 'instalments' in three or four weeks. Their funds were adequate at the moment, but they might in due course need bigger contributions to take advantage of the opportunities which were increasingly available to them.

It was like a bleak version of a sports club meeting, Hugo thought. He'd known reports like this at the cricket club he'd belonged to years ago, though there'd been laughter and jokes and teasing there as well. There were one or two embarrassed murmurs of thanks and a relaxation of tension when the man finished speaking. This was the time when the conversation should have livened up and the decibel level risen, but neither happened.

It wasn't long before men began to glance at their watches and make their excuses to leave. Hugo waited until six people had left, then spoke briefly to the householder and slipped out himself. He walked the two hundred yards to where he had parked his car without meeting a soul. They were asked to leave their transport at a distance. It was all designed to preserve the anonymity they craved, to avoid drawing attention to themselves and their common interest.

Hugo Wilkinson drove very quietly, so that his journey back to Westbourne might occupy quite a long time. He wondered how many others dispersing from that meeting felt the self-disgust which was now seeping like a noxious gas around the inside of his car.

Alison Cooper reversed her car into the parking space outside the hotel in Broadway. She knew she was already late, but she had an obscure feeling she might want to get away quickly. Extramarital affairs made you like that. You felt vaguely guilty, even during the days when you were not together. You also felt you had to be prepared to move quickly in any emergency.

Peter Nayland was already here. She paused for a moment beside his red Jaguar, setting her hand briefly upon its warm bonnet. Then she turned and went into the hotel.

Peter was sitting at a table in the reception lounge. He had a whisky in front of him and a gin and tonic lined up for her. He struggled to his feet as he saw her, but she motioned him immediately to sit. You didn't draw attention to yourselves, when you were meeting like this. She gave him a brief, nervous smile, then sat down and sipped her gin and tonic. For a moment, it was as if they were meeting for the first time.

'You look as lovely as ever.'

She gave him a brief, impatient smile. 'You didn't bring me here to tell me that.'

'No.' Peter Nayland didn't know how to go about this. He'd never done it before, never expected that he would ever do it. 'Thanks for coming.' He flicked his forefinger automatically across his neatly trimmed moustache, resisted the impulse to run his hands over the hair he had combed forward so carefully in the cloakroom when he had arrived here.

'I can't stay the night. It was difficult enough to get away.'

'No, I understand that. Not that I wouldn't want you to, my darling.' He reached out and ran his fingers down her forearm when he used the endearment. It was cheap and tired, but most of their tensions dropped away with the touch and the word.

She felt the stirrings of sexual desire, of the wish to live the life this man represented for her. She said more tenderly, 'What is it, Peter?'

This was the moment, Peter Nayland thought. She'd asked the question which would determine the rest of his life. It must be the fear of rejection which was making him uncharacteristically awkward. He could suddenly see himself and Ally from the edge of the room. Was what he was planning ridiculous? He said abruptly, with the words tumbling from him in a rush, 'I want to make this permanent. I want to live the rest of my life with you and with no one else. I never thought of it like that when we started, but now I do. I want to know if you feel the same. I want to know if there's any chance for me.'

He was staring at the small round table with the drinks upon it, concentrating on delivering his message, unwilling to look into her face and see rejection there. Peter Nayland, controller of a business empire, a man who dealt smoothly and contemptuously with dangerous rivals and the threats of the law, reduced by the love of a woman to uncertainties he had not felt since his adolescence.

Alison Cooper understood a little of his discomfort, but not all. She was too shocked to think clearly. She said stupidly, 'I never expected this. I need time to think.'

'Of course you do, my darling.' He reached out, put his hand on top of hers. He could look at her, now that he'd stated his ridiculous desire. 'I've sprung it upon you. I've had time to get used to the idea, and yet it still seems strange to me. But I mean it. The one thing I'm certain of is that I mean it.'

She could feel him looking at her as she sipped her drink, uncrossed her legs, searched for any movement which could postpone a decision on this. Eventually she gave him a small smile and said, 'It's flattering, isn't it? To have a man like you say he wants to pair up with me for the rest of our lives.'

'It doesn't feel like that. You could pick and choose among men.'

And so could you among women, she thought. You treat me decently and you have all the money any woman could want. I'm forty-nine and I'm not stupid enough to think money and having whatever you want aren't important. She started to her feet and said irrationally, 'I'll get us some more drinks.'

She refused his attempt to pay; it was suddenly important to her that she asserted this small independence. The two minutes at the bar were useful to her; she gathered her resources and her thoughts together. She gave him a small, grateful smile as she set the drinks down carefully on their table.

He said, 'Sherlock Holmes used to speak of two-pipe problems. This one is obviously a two-drink one!'

She reached across and put a hand on his. 'I'm not opposed to the idea, Peter. At the moment, I'm bowled over by it! I'm very flattered and very pleased. And I think I love you. I haven't allowed myself to think long term until now, that's all.'

'I haven't any ties. I've been divorced for years.'

The implications were obvious; she had to consider her marriage. She nodded slowly, trying to pick her words carefully, to say nothing which she might later regret. But eventually she said slowly, almost reluctantly, 'My marriage to Dennis is dead, really. We've both been preserving the forms of it, for the last few years. It was convenient, for him in particular, to be married. The National Trust is a very conventional organization.'

'Then leave him. Come and live with me. That's the only decision that really matters. We can sort out all the details of where and how once we've decided that.'

'Dennis won't like it.'

She'd said 'won't', not 'wouldn't'. He felt his experienced heart leap a little at that, and this time he was glad that he could still feel like a teenager. He said quietly, 'What Dennis Cooper wants doesn't matter, if the marriage is dead.'

'He won't agree to a divorce. He'll fight us all the way.'

'He's the least of our problems. If you agree to live with me, I can handle Dennis.'

'I must get back.' There was no reason for that, if she was going to finish with Dennis. But she needed desperately to be on her own.

In the car park, she was glad she'd reversed the Fiat into its space. They embraced beside it, holding each other hard, for the first time not caring how publicly they displayed their love. Then she leapt into the small white car and drove swiftly away, not trusting herself to look again at him.

She was almost back at Westbourne before she wondered quite how Peter Nayland proposed to deal with Dennis.

Alex Fraser didn't have a watch. After the early summer dawn, the hours stretched slowly as he sat in his cell, contemplating the bleak facts of what had happened to him. Twice the small flap near the top of the door was slammed aside and a dispassionate eye assessed him. The noises and shouts from other parts of the station grew in number as the morning advanced. After what seemed to him many hours of daylight, he was given toast and a mug of hot, sweet tea. Then he was left alone for at least another hour to meditate upon the error of his ways.

It was a relief when he was released from his cell and led up stone stairs to a small, windowless room. At least something was happening at last. He was one step nearer to getting out of the nick. He looked round at his new surroundings and recognized them immediately. This was an interview room. He'd been in similar ones in Glasgow and this wasn't very different; he realized now that every nick must have them.

There was a single powerful light in the ceiling, out of reach of vandalizing fists. The walls were sage green and recently painted, no doubt to cover the obscene graffiti of previous occupants. There was a small, square table, fixed to the floor to eliminate its use as a weapon. On the opposite side from where he sat, there were two chairs identical to the one he occupied. A cassette tape recorder was ready for use.

Alex was slightly disappointed that he wasn't in one of those rooms with one-way glass, where you couldn't see out but other pigs could see in, observing your behaviour and listening to your answers. But you couldn't expect rural areas like this to be up to speed with the great cities of the realm. He listened to the dull sounds of movements on the floor above him, wondering if the interrogators were deliberately leaving him here alone for a while to soften him up.

When they came, the opposition consisted of a uniformed copper and a taller, thinner man in plain clothes. This man studied him without speaking for a moment, then slipped a new cassette into the recorder and announced their ranks and names, along with his as the subject of the interview. He didn't register any information other than that this interview was beginning at 10.07. The constable in uniform said practically nothing in the minutes which followed, but his eyes never left Alex Fraser's face.

The thin-faced man relaxed after his formal iteration of ranks and time. Alex couldn't thrust away the thought that they'd be well into the working day at Westbourne. His absence would leave a gaping hole which he would eventually have to explain to Jim Hartley. He told himself that he needed to think about things here, not there. But the human brain, or at least his human brain, was obstinately uncooperative.

The plain-clothes sergeant eventually said with some relish, 'Well, Mr Fraser, you've landed yourself right in the shit here, haven't you?'

'It all happened very quickly. I was involved before I knew it was happening. It wasn't my fight.'

He'd blurted out all his mitigating circumstances arguments at once, much too quickly. He should have waited for the point of maximum effect. He knew in his bones now that this wasn't going to go well. Grey-suit said, 'You must have been really pleased to find yourself a serious rumble at the end of the evening. You'd gone prepared for it, hadn't you?'

'No. I nearly didn't go at all. I didn't know the people there, apart from Matt Garton and Tom Bracey. I work with them. At Westbourne Park. We're apprentice gardeners there.' He threw the name of the gardens in as weightily as he could; it must surely be some small evidence of his respectability.

'You did work with them, Mr Fraser. It's doubtful whether you'll be resuming work at Westbourne after this. When the people there hear that you went out looking for violence last night, I can't think they'll be impressed.'

'I didn't go out looking for violence. It was a twenty-first birthday party. I nearly didn't go at all.'

'Doesn't tally with the facts, that, Mr Fraser. You went looking for violence. Maybe you began it yourself. The evidence is there for all to see. You took a dangerous and unlawful weapon with you. To whit, a steel knuckleduster of the most vicious sort.'

Alex didn't know that there were various types of knuckleduster, some apparently less vicious than others. It didn't seem the moment to voice that thought. 'It was just a last-minute precaution. When you've had nights out in the Gorbals, you tend to take precautions. You have to look after yourself up there.' To his dismay, he heard the last statement emerge with a ring of pride, as if he was denigrating these southern softies.

Grey-suit said grimly, 'Yes, we know about your past history of violence. It will no doubt be taken into account when the judge is passing sentence.'

Alex said desperately, 'I shouldn't have taken the knuckle-duster. I realize that now.'

'Indeed you shouldn't, Mr Fraser. There's a man with a broken jaw and another with fractured ribs who will bear witness to that.' The plain-clothes officer wasn't sure yet how serious the injuries were in this affray. But he'd use the details to intimidate this young thug. No one was on oath yet.

Alex couldn't see a way out of this. Perhaps he should have demanded a brief from the start, but he'd hoped it wouldn't come to that. 'Look, we weren't the guilty parties. We didn't start it. All we did was enjoy a twenty-first birthday party in a private room. It was boisterous and noisy, but it didn't cause any trouble. That came when we came out of the pub, when we were ready to go home after a good night. We had a taxi organized, Matt and Tom and me.'

'But by that time you were pissed and looking for a fight. And you found one for yourselves immediately, when you spotted a rival gang.'

'No! We weren't meaning any harm to anyone, and then we found these buggers waiting for us as we came out of the pub.'

'And promptly set about them, rather than finding your taxi and departing.'

'We'd no choice. They were waiting for us in the street. They had us cut off. And not a bloody pig in sight to keep order and prevent violence.'

For the first time, Alex saw the uniformed man smile in unison with grey-suit, and knew that he'd made a mistake. He said hopelessly, 'I shouldn't have taken the knuckleduster. I realize that. But we were the innocent parties in this. They set upon us. We had to defend ourselves.'

Grey-suit smiled, registering his victory before moving forward. 'What do you propose to tell us about your attempts to sell drugs, Mr Fraser?'

'Sell drugs? I've never dealt in my life. I'm not even a user, never mind—'

'You were found with a considerable quantity of class A drugs on your person. Are you now trying to suggest they were planted upon you?'

For a wild moment, Alex was tempted to take up that suggestion, to claim that the filth must have slipped the stuff into his pocket as they flung him into the van or led him into the station. But he sensed that such lies would only infuriate them and make them throw everything they could at him in the way of charges. He said dully, 'No, they weren't planted.'

'So who's your supplier?' Grey-suit couldn't disguise his eagerness.

'I don't have one.' He realized he couldn't leave it at that.

'Those drugs were passed to me. I was supposed to hand them on to someone else. No money changed hands.'

Grey-suit looked at the uniformed man, then back into the pale, lightly freckled features beneath the fiery red hair. He sighed theatrically. 'Surely you can do better than that, son. You wouldn't even believe that yourself, if someone tried to sell it to you.'

Alex had an uncomfortable suspicion that this was true. His tale sounded like fiction, even in his own ears. And very unconvincing fiction. 'It sounds daft because it's true. If I'd made something up, it would have been more convincing than that.'

Another elaborate sigh. 'Would it, indeed? Let's pursue this fairytale of yours for a minute or two, then. You had in the pocket of your jeans cocaine rocks with a retail value of around five hundred pounds. Who was going to be the grateful recipient of this valuable little package?'

'I can't say that. I'm not a grass.'

Grey-suit gave him a withering smile, then turned a more affable one upon his uniformed companion. 'The man seems to be admitting these drugs were for his own use, Constable. Criminal offence in its own right. Perhaps we should just throw the book at him for that and have done with it. We've wasted enough time on the little slug, if you ask me.'

Whilst the uniformed man grunted affirmatively, Alex wondered desperately what he was to do. He couldn't grass on Matt Garton, not if he had to go on working alongside him in the gardens. But these men said he wouldn't be doing that, even though he desperately wanted to. He took a decision. 'I was to pass the package to Matt Garton, who works with me. The drugs were already paid for, which was why no money changed hands. The package was handed to me when I went out for a breath of fresh air at the back of the pub, after I'd been to the Gents.'

Uniform made a note of the name. Grey-suit continued to look at Fraser contemptuously. 'Describe the man who supplied you.'

'He was young. Younger than I am. And he was nervous. I don't reckon he's been dealing for long.'

'Oh. This man with no experience thinks he can recognize a new dealer when he sees one, Constable. Perhaps we should consider recruiting him to the Drug Squad.' They both chuckled inordinately at this suggestion. Then grey-suit said sternly, 'You will be returned to your cell now. We shall decide later in the day exactly what charges to proffer. Probably you will then be released and told not to leave the area without informing us.'

They were gone as abruptly as they had arrived, leaving him to contemplate a future which seemed to become bleaker with each passing hour.

SEVEN

Westbourne Park, despite the ever-increasing numbers which move around the house and its acres, remains for the residents a very private home.

It is a quiet, cheerful place before ten a.m. At this time, the resident staff, particularly the gardeners, get on with their work without an audience. Once the gates open at ten, the workers who come in daily to staff the shop and restaurant and to act as guides take up their posts and are fully occupied. But they leave with the public at six o'clock. Westbourne then becomes once again a quiet and private place.

Alex Fraser, released after his grilling in the police interview room at Cheltenham, was grateful for the peace and the privacy of Westbourne. He hadn't enjoyed the inevitable interview with Dennis Cooper which his conduct had caused, but he tried not to think about that. He threw all his energy into his work in the gardens. He didn't talk much with the men around him, though he was well aware that Matt Garton had been taken in for questioning after Alex's revelations about the cocaine package.

No one accused him, but he was aware that the other young men who worked alongside him in the gardens watched him now with a new reserve. Never the most articulate of groups, they nevertheless made him feel now that he was an outsider. His accent and background had always set him apart; now the fact that he had been forced to reveal Garton to the police as a drug user made them even more cautious about him. Alex didn't much mind this; he felt shaken and he needed to regroup, to decide what he was to do about his future.

He was unaware of the main cause of his isolation amongst his fellows, though it should have been obvious to him. They did not blame him for releasing Matt's name to the police, accepting that he had had little option when under such pressure. What compelled a mixture of fear and respect was his performance in that fight which had been forced upon him at the end of the evening. Any man who not only possessed knuckledusters but took them on an innocent night out warranted caution. Any man who inflicted the damage which Fraser had inflicted upon the opposition merited a certain awe.

Unlike the other apprentices, Alex read each night as he collapsed with a pleasant lassitude upon his bed. He was reading a book about the Battle of Britain, about those young men of his age who had saved the nation in 1940 and 1941. He was excited by the descriptions of those dogfights against blue summer skies, with the fate of a nation at stake. But it was the first time he had read about the 'phoney war', those strange months before the dogfights, when everyone waited for carnage and invasion and very little in fact happened.

The quiet week between his night in the cells and the defining event at Westbourne seemed afterwards to Alex Fraser to have been his own 'phoney war'.

Like many young men in crisis, he thought himself much more the focus of other men's thoughts than was in fact the case. The other people around him were busy with their own lives. The Westbourne workers struggled with their own problems, which were unknown to the young man from Glasgow with the fiery red hair and the fiery red temper. In some cases, their dilemmas were even more serious and life-changing than those confronting Alex Fraser.

It was at the end of this strange hiatus that the weather broke. After four weeks of warm, dry nights and long, sunny days, the rain came late in the afternoon on Sunday, July the third. The gardens were packed with visitors and all the facilities of Westbourne Park were strained. The man giving his talks about the history of the gardens found that he had his biggest ever audience, so that those on the fringes missed much of what he said. Sales were high in the plant shop and in the National Trust shop by the courtyard. There were patient queues throughout the day outside the toilets.

It was heavy and humid, and by noon the sun had disappeared behind menacing grey clouds. The atmosphere grew increasingly airless and sticky during the afternoon. As the skies darkened, children grew fractious and tearful, the ceiling fans in the restaurant seemed scarcely to move the air, and visitors began to hurry back to their cars, casting anxious eyes at the sky in anticipation of the downpour everyone now knew was inevitable.

The thunderstorm was impressive. Lightning forked vividly down black clouds and the thunder cracked loud on its heels, rumbling impressively away into the distance. Then an eerie, expectant silence stretched for a few seconds before the next and even fiercer outburst. The deluge when it came fell in vertical rods, forming swiftly into rivulets over the parched earth. The heavy spattering of the downpour eliminated all other noise save the Wagnerian bursts of thunder.

The storm lasted in all for some six hours. The rain became intermittent, but each time that it seemed it was over there was a renewed short, heavy burst, as if nature was rebuking those who chose to venture forth before the drama was concluded. Eventually the lightning ceased to dazzle the sky and the thunder growled away to the east. By the time the rumbling ceased, natural darkness had fallen over Westbourne Park.

Its residents looked out of their opened windows and smelt the fresh green of vegetation as the great garden offered its gratitude for the rain. They settled down thankfully for a good night's sleep in this newly buoyant atmosphere. Only the occasional note of a screech owl disturbed the warm silence of the summer night.

The dawn chorus of birdsong woke Matt Garton. Usually he slept far too heavily to be disturbed by it. This day it seemed as if even the birds were rejoicing in the mini-monsoon which had for a few brief and precious hours irrigated Westbourne. Matt lay on his back for a while and congratulated himself upon the simple fact of existence. He relished the exhilarating sound of the birds; he relished the first rays of the sun amidst the coolness of the new morning; he relished anew being young and being alive.

He had heard the previous day that he was not to be charged with the possession of a class A drug. The police were content with a caution. The truth was that he was far too small a fish to be worth pursuing. He had not been dealing. He was merely a user and this was a first offence. They had given Garton a week to consider the error of his ways and the need to amend them, then informed him that on this occasion he was lucky.

It was an immense relief to him, for all that he had behaved with a brittle bravado amongst his fellows. His joy had only increased when his tentative enquiry elicited the news that his fellow-offender Alex Fraser had as yet heard nothing from the police about what action they proposed to take against him for his violence on that fateful night. Matt felt guilty about his pleasure, but he supposed it was a normal human reaction. And Fraser had after all shopped him to the fuzz, hadn't he? He was surely entitled to remember that. The fact that he would have done exactly the same if the circumstances had been reversed scarcely occurred to him. Matt Garton was not a deep thinker.

He lay for a while with his hands behind his head, running his fingers through the thick black curls of his hair, staring contentedly at the ceiling whilst he listened to the birdsong spilling under the eaves of the old cottages where the apprentices slept. Presently he eased himself from the sheets and slid into the jeans and tee shirt he had discarded on the previous evening. Quarter to six. Plenty of time for a stroll before he showered and faced the new working day.

He crept quietly down the stairs and out into a perfect morning. Everything looked and smelled very fresh after the prolonged downpour. The dawn chorus was long over now, but the birds piped exultantly still, as if celebrating the fresh green of nature's response to the rain. Matt sniffed the air appreciatively, rubbed his hands together for a moment, then moved out to look with new eyes at the gardens which had hitherto been a source of employment rather than aesthetic delight to him.

He had never really walked round the place with a visitor's eyes before. In the perfect peace of the early summer morning, he saw exactly why people made long journeys to see what he was looking at. Even the water lilies seemed better for the rain, turning their flowers to the eastern sun as if seeking to display their freshness. The leaves and buds on the shrub roses in the rose walk were quite definitely greener and fuller after the storm. In the white garden, the white flowers and silver leaves which gave the place its name were surely purer in form and colour than when they had stood over parched earth twenty-four hours earlier.

He moved on through the red borders, brilliantly vivid in the early morning sun, exulting now in having this magnificent place to himself, looking with newly opened eyes at the glories he had helped to tend. He paused for a moment between the twin gazebos at the end of the Long Walk, gazing down the neatly mown grass between the hornbeam hedges to the distant wrought-iron gates and the Cotswold landscape beyond them.

It was a wonderful privilege to be alone in such a place – if you could call it alone, when birds sang all around you and invisible wildlife rustled occasionally in the longer grass. It was the first time in his young life that Matt Garton had enjoyed that thought. He wandered on, following the stream which ran through the lower and wilder part of the garden. You could hear the stream rushing cheerfully now, flashing bright where it rattled over tiny falls in its stony bed. Yesterday it had been no more than a silent trickle; today it seemed not only to have a new life of its own but to be bringing life to the area around it.

He wandered on into the lowest area of all, the one they called the Wilderness. Next month he would be planting bulbs here, scattering them first over the turf to give a natural effect, then using the special tool to take out a core of soil to set the bulbs at the correct depth. He'd seen the blaze of colour the daffodils and narcissi and scyllas brought here in the spring; now he would be making his own contribution to that picture.

He'd never been to the very end of the garden. He realized that with a little flush of shame. He'd put that right now; he'd stroll to the end of the Wilderness and then walk back towards the house between the hornbeams of the Long Walk. It was the first time he'd appreciated the gardens as a work of art. He was really enjoying having this magnificent creation to himself on such a glorious morning. He must do this more often.

He followed the busy stream down through the Wilderness to the southern extremity of the garden, stopping for a moment to watch a thrush singing a celebratory hymn to the heavens. He was amazed at the speed with which the sun was climbing against the unbroken blue of the sky to his left. He was about to turn back towards the house when he saw the thing he could scarcely believe.

It was so utterly wrong in this context that he thought at first he must be imagining it. He wanted to turn away, to break into a run, to flee in panic back to the cottage and his awakening friends, to a world which was safe and familiar. Yet his eyes would not follow the urgings of his other senses. They remained obstinately fixed upon the thing which was within five yards of him. The thing which was so utterly wrong in what he had thought was a perfect world.

A foot, perfectly still. Harmless in itself, but totally out of place here. Shattering the joyous and innocent world which had enveloped Matt Garton during his early-morning stroll. He moved slowly, reluctantly, towards it. The horror seemed to seep along his limbs with each grudging, inevitable step.

The foot had a sturdy brown shoe upon it. Not the gardening boot which a worker here might have worn. Not the trainer which was the leisure wear of a gardener off duty. These thoughts ran swiftly across his brain when he did not want any thoughts at all. There was a trouser leg of good quality above the boot; cavalry twill, he thought, though that was a material he'd never worn himself.

Matt Garton paused, then stepped forward quickly, as if his discovery would conclude some macabre game of hide and seek. It was the man who controlled all this. The man who controlled the future of Matt Garton and most of the other people who worked in this perfect place.

Dennis Cooper lay with his sightless eyes wide open, glinting brightly and reflecting the light of the sun he would never see again.

EIGHT

Chief Superintendent John Lambert wasn't good at meetings. In the modern police service, you needed to be, once you reached his rank. Indeed, some chief supers seemed to positively enjoy meetings.

But Lambert was a dinosaur among the higher ranks, in that he hated sitting behind a desk and directing operations. He was much happier investigating cases on the spot, much more efficient when meeting and questioning the people who were involved in a crime, whether innocently or otherwise. Despite affecting to despise modern technology, he made effective use of it whenever it was appropriate, recognizing that national as well as local registers of crime made vital contributions to the solution of serious offences such as fraud, rape and murder.

But John Lambert was at his best worrying away at serious crimes, especially suspicious deaths. Those around him, including his chief constable, had long since recognized that; they allowed this particular senior detective a latitude which they would not have accorded to a younger and less experienced man. Even amidst the bureaucracy of the modern police service, success makes its own rules, and Lambert had been notably successful over the years.

The CID section at Oldford police station was happiest when Lambert was in pursuit of villains. During quieter periods, when his attention turned from the wider world outside to the narrower one of Oldford police station, he asked penetrating questions of his juniors. At such times, he demonstrated that when he chose to he could play the lesser games of office as efficiently as those which surrounded life and death.

On this particular Monday morning, he had emerged from his meeting with the chief constable filled with a righteous energy. Already he had made queries about the use of the overtime budget and the expenses claims of two detective sergeants. People were scurrying to justify themselves. CID men moved out into the community to pursue mundane enquiries about stolen cars and missing husbands; this was a good time not to be around the station.

Detective Sergeant Bert Hook, who had recently graduated as an Open University BA and was thus a local police curiosity, had been Lambert's bagman for many years now and knew him better than any other man. He pronounced the scurrying activity his chief had set in motion in the CID section as a 'necessary evil', a reminder that life was not always smooth and that perhaps it shouldn't be so.

Under questioning from the uniformed desk sergeant, who was observing this commotion in CID with wry amusement, Hook suggested that the only thing which would quell it was 'a good juicy murder'. Not that anyone wished for any such thing, of course; that would be morally reprehensible. In the meantime, Bert had quietly checked his own claim for expenses.

At that very moment, as if responding to a cue, John Lambert marched quickly through the door behind them. 'Ah, there you are, Bert! Time to stop your gossiping and get moving. We have a suspicious death on our hands! At Westbourne Park, of all places, amidst the roses and the lilies and the crowds of elderly, respectable National Trust visitors! Ten to one it's murder; I can feel it in my water! Chop chop, lad!'

Hook had long since ceased to be a lad. He looked at the desk sergeant, allowed his stolid features an inappropriate wink, and followed his chief through the swinging doors with a quickening pulse.

The whole of Westbourne Park might have been declared a crime scene, with the public denied access. But it would have been difficult and no doubt impractical to cordon off such a huge acreage for very long. Lambert, who had made several visits to Westbourne and knew the gardens well, instructed that the tract known as the Wilderness should be out of bounds to visitors and staff for an indefinite period. This was itself a large area for the detailed search normally conducted at the scene of a crime. Nevertheless, any evidence which might later be vital to prosecution or defence must be discovered and retained before even workers' feet trod here again.

Death has its own ghoulish attraction. When Lambert and Hook arrived at the entry to the Wilderness, a group of middle-aged and highly respectable National Trust visitors were standing beside the blue-and-white ribbons which delineated a scene of crime. There was nothing to be seen save the comings and goings of the police and their civilian acolytes, but this staid audience lingered here, staring at the foliage of the innocent trees and speculating about what was going on beyond them.

What they now saw was senior men donning the white overalls and plastic foot-coverings designed to prevent the contamination of a crime scene. The grass was still damp after the deluge of the previous day, though the parched earth had drunk it eagerly and left no puddles. The two large men followed the narrow, descending path which had already been delineated by white markers, so as to minimize the effect of feet upon the crime scene.

It was obvious from the first that this was murder. The body lay exactly as it had when Matt Garton had discovered it three and a half hours earlier. It was at the southern extremity of the property and its sightless eyes gazed still at that sun which could never damage them. Lambert knew the civilian scene of crime officer well from previous cases. He gave him a quiet good morning and stood motionless for a few moments, as if death compelled this homage, even from those used to seeing it in its worst forms.

Then he moved the few yards to look down upon the corpse and said, 'Do we know who it is?'

'Dennis Charles Cooper. The man in charge of this place.'

Lambert allowed himself a slight moue of distaste. The deaths of men or women in authority were almost invariably more complex to investigate than those of lesser mortals, where the number of suspects was usually much smaller. He looked at the neck of the corpse, at the broken skin and the livid, darkening weals, and said dully, as if it was no more than a formality, 'Almost certainly murder.'

'I'd say there's no doubt of it. The pathologist is over there, waiting to speak to you.'

Lambert left Hook to talk quietly to the SOCO team about what they had found so far and went across to the edge of the clearing, where the pathologist was speaking to the photographer, who had also finished his work and was waiting to depart. The pathologist was a thin, intense man with a small, neatly trimmed beard. Lambert and he were well used to each other's idiosyncrasies. In answer to the chief super's unspoken query, he nodded and said with apparent satisfaction, 'It's murder all right.'

Homicide brought novelty and excitement into his dull routine, as it did for CID officers. Lambert smiled grimly and said, 'Manual strangulation?'

'No, not manual. Some kind of tourniquet was used.'

The first setback. Manual strangulation would almost certainly have meant their killer was male, because of the strength required against a victim fighting for his life. 'The throat didn't look as if a wire had bitten into it.'

The pathologist shook his head. 'The murder instrument wasn't a wire, or even a rope. Your tourniquet in this case was something broader, nearly an inch wide. Probably two centimetres, now that we've all gone metric. I say tourniquet because it was probably thrown round the throat and tightened from behind. The width doesn't much matter, once someone is twisting it tight on a helpless victim. Whatever was used hasn't been found at the scene.'

And won't be, thought Lambert. It was probably miles away by now. Or perhaps at the bottom of the Severn. He glanced back towards the body. 'I presume he died here.'

'Almost certainly. He's quite a heavy man, so it would need two or three people working carefully to dump him here without leaving any evidence. There are no track marks from a vehicle here. And your people will confirm that there's no sign at the scene of the corpse being dragged to where it lay.'

They had the where and the how of this death. The when

was almost invariably the most difficult of the three key questions to establish. Lambert gave a sour smile to that thought before he said, 'Any idea of time of death?'

The pathologist's answering smile was equally wry. They were both professionals, both conscious of how wily defence lawyers could make fools of the incautious. 'The usual qualifications, John. I'll be more precise when I've had him on the slab. If you can find when he last ate, the stomach contents may give us something reasonably exact. In the meantime, I can tell you from rectal temperature taken at the scene and other factors that he hasn't died in the last few hours.'

'So he's been here overnight?'

'Almost certainly. His clothes were wet on top, but even wetter underneath. That would indicate to me that he died after the fiercest rain in yesterday's storm, but before at least one of the heavy showers which fell during the evening. That's the best I can do for you at the moment.'

'It's more than I expected. Did he put up a fight?'

'Again I might be able to tell you more after I've got him stripped. At the moment, I'd say he was caught off guard. There's no immediate evidence of skin or hair under his nails, but a microscope sometimes gives us more than we expect. I'll give it priority. You should have my report by tomorrow.'

Murder as usual jumped the queue. Lambert took a last look at what had yesterday been a man and today was no more than a CID puzzle, then left the scene.

In the house of the dead man, there was a curious contrast between the uneasy silence within and the unheeding noise of the public outside. A tray with two used cups and saucers and a teapot sat on a low table. An unread newspaper had slipped to the floor and not been picked up. From the windowsill, a black-and-white cat stared at the two strangers with wide-eyed enquiry, then jumped down and strode disdainfully from the room with tail held high.

Alison Cooper's dark-blonde hair had strands out of place and her face was very white, accentuating the pale blue of her eyes. She wore no make-up and was plainly on edge and in shock. But that was natural enough.

Before Lambert could even introduce himself and Hook, she said, 'I've only known about this for two hours. Will I have to identify him?'

'In due course, that would be the usual procedure. If you find it too much, we could probably get someone else to do it.'

She nodded but said nothing. He wasn't sure which option she was agreeing to, but he let that go for the present. He said, 'I'm Chief Superintendent Lambert and this is Detective Sergeant Hook. We appreciate that this is difficult for you. We shan't keep you for any longer than is necessary.'

She looked at Hook's square, reassuring features, then back at his senior. 'You're old for a policeman. I'm sorry, I shouldn't have said that.'

Lambert smiled, trying to loosen her tension. 'You're observant. That's a quality we try to encourage among the people we talk to. And you're quite right. I was given an extension beyond the usual retiring age a little while ago by the Home Office.'

She gave a high-pitched giggle, which rang loud in the quiet room and showed how nervous she was. 'I expect that means you're very successful.'

'We always speak to the surviving partner first in the case of a suspicious death.'

'Yes. I suppose that means I'm the prime suspect. That's what you call it, isn't it?'

'Did you kill Mr Cooper?'

'No. Why would I have done that?'

Lambert could have reeled off a variety of possibilities. Instead he said, 'In the case of domestic disputes, the partner is often the killer. This does not look like such a crime. We speak to the surviving partner first because he or she is the person likely to know most about the victim. About his habits, his friends and his enemies. We have to form a picture of a victim who can no longer speak for himself.'

'Yes. That makes sense. I've never been involved in anything like this before.'

'Then let me tell you a little about what happens. We need you to tell us anything you can today. Then, when we've spoken to other people and learned a little more about the circumstances surrounding the death, we shall probably ask to speak to you again. That will be in a few days' time.'

'Unless you've got someone for it by then.'

'Unless, as you say, we've made an arrest by then. When did you last see Mr Cooper?'

'Yesterday morning. Before the storm began.' She spoke wonderingly, as if it felt to her more than twenty-four hours ago. Perhaps the fierceness of the downpour had made her think in terms of biblical floods.

'Where were you last night, Mrs Cooper?'

'Is that when he died?'

Lambert had never taken his eyes from her face; it was part of his job to study her every reaction. She was a suspect until it proved otherwise, despite his efforts to put her at her ease. Now he gave her a small smile and said, 'This will be over more quickly if we and not you ask the questions, Mrs Cooper.'

'Sorry. Last night I was with my friend.'

'Name, please.' Hook's first words sounded almost apologetic.

'Carrie. Carrie North. She's an old school friend. We've kept in touch over the years.'

'And what time did you return here last night?'

'I didn't. I stayed the night at Carrie's. I didn't get back here until ten o'clock this morning.' Alison watched the sergeant record that in his swift, round hand. Her absence seemed somehow more momentous, more damning, when it was written down.

She thought Hook would ask her more; she had this image of him pinning her squirming to the paper, like a small crab which had to be prevented from scurrying away. But it was Lambert who said quietly, 'Is that something you do often? Staying away overnight, I mean.'

'No.' The denial had been immediate and unthinking, as if he had accused her of some awful, damning thing. She pulled herself together and said more reasonably. 'I've done it a few times recently. Carrie lives alone and always has her spare bed made up. As she says, it's safer not to drive when you've had a few drinks, and we tend to enjoy a bottle of wine when we reminisce about old times.'

'If you have any idea who might have killed Mr Cooper, you should tell us about it now. Even the slightest suspicion is worth voicing at this stage. We shall treat anything you say here in the strictest confidence.'

It was a chance to divert attention away from herself. But her brain would not work when she most needed it. After what seemed to her a long pause, she said woodenly, 'When you're in charge of things at a place like this, you're bound to annoy people. I expect Dennis did that. I kept well clear of what he did at work, but I thought he was a fair man. He must have made some enemies among the staff. I'm sure there are people with grievances, real and imaginary. But I can't think of anyone who would have wished to kill him.'

It was delivered with a strange evenness, almost like a prepared statement, thought Lambert. She seemed curiously detached. But the shock of a sudden and violent death affected people in all sorts of ways. He said quietly, 'How would you describe the state of your marriage, Mrs Cooper?'

How direct they were! It seemed years since strangers had made anything more than small talk with her and she didn't feel prepared for this examination. She forced a smile. 'That's a brutal question, with Dennis lying dead outside. But I'll try to be objective. I'd say that our marriage was about average, whatever that means. The first flush of young love was over, as you'd expect. I'm forty-nine and Dennis is – was – fifty-four. We got on well enough. He was very interested in the job here and very dedicated to it.'

'And you weren't quite so happy at Westbourne?'

How quick the man was! Her first instinct was to deny it. But it was better to dispense the truth, when it could not harm you. She said, 'I'm not so dedicated to the country as Dennis was. I recognize that this is one of the great gardens of the nation, as our brochure puts it, but living on the site can be claustrophobic, especially when you're not employed here. I like to get away sometimes, to see people like Carrie, who works in a completely different environment. But Dennis realized that and understood it. We got on well enough.'

'I see. Well, I think that's all for the moment. As I said, we shall probably need to speak to you again in a few days. In the meantime, you will naturally go on thinking about who did this awful thing. If any thoughts on the possible culprit occur to you, please ring this number immediately.'

She stared at the card with the number of Oldford CID section on it for a full minute after they had gone. Then she fumbled in her bag for her mobile phone. 'Carrie? It's Alison . . . Yes, they've just been here and talked to me . . . No, not as bad as I expected, but they said they'll need to speak to me again in a day or two . . . Yes, that's right. Carrie, I'm afraid there's one more favour I need to ask of you . . .'

NINE

It was early afternoon now. Still only a few hours since the tapes had been thrown round the serious crime scene at Westbourne. But news travels fast across the countryside, and bad news fastest of all.

The announcement of a suspicious death at Westbourne Park had been made on the radio at lunchtime. By the time Julie Hartley arrived at the house of her lover, suspicious death had been swiftly translated to murder. Sarah Goodwin opened her door, took one look at Julie's animated features, and ushered her hastily within. They kissed, then held each other tightly for a little longer than usual. Eventually, Sarah released herself gently and said, 'I shall make tea for us. Then you can tell me all about it.'

When she returned with two beakers and a plate of flapjacks, Julie was examining the drawings she had left on the table. Sarah stopped for a moment in the doorway to study her, with her long dark hair touching the edge of the table and her brown eyes studying the drawings intently. It was the stillness, the capacity to become completely absorbed in what interested her, which had first drawn her to this woman, who was in most of her actions so swift and spontaneous.

Now, when she should have been full of her own sensational news, Julie Hartley was suddenly immersed in how her lover had spent her morning. Sarah Goodwin was an internal designer, still making her way in a competitive world, existing by word-of-mouth recommendations rather than any extensive advertising. The décor and furnishings she had been working on all morning were different from anything she had done before and correspondingly more difficult and challenging.

She would have been embarrassed had her sketches received such attention from anyone else, but Julie was different and privileged. Sarah realized with a shock that she was actually pleased to have Julie looking at her draft, when from anyone else it would have been an intrusion. She walked across, put the tray down on the unused leaf of the table, and said defensively, 'You won't like that. It's not your style at all.'

Julie looked up at her. With her back to the light and taken by surprise, she looked more mysterious, more beautiful than ever to Sarah. 'Who's it for?'

'It's an Asian lady who's moving into a big house in Edgbaston. She's very dark, very mysterious, with eyes as big as yours and even darker. And with an English husband who is totally smitten and fortunately very rich.'

'It looks very ornate.'

'It is. That's her taste. But everything balances; the colours are rich, but the curtains complement the wallpaper. The sofas they've chosen are very plain, but they'll sit well on the carpet and let your eyes appreciate the detail of the rest without being too dazzled. That's the idea, anyway.' Sarah was always rather diffident, as if she scarcely believed in her own talents; Julie was trying to change that in her. Sarah pulled her friend gently away from the table and sat her down beside her on the rather battered settee. 'For God's sake tell me what's been happening at Westbourne, before I burst with curiosity. Who's been killed and whodunnit?'

'The curator's been killed. The man in charge of the whole schimozzle. And no one knows who did it. The police are swarming round the place, but if they know anything they're not telling the likes of me.'

'How thrilling! And poor man, of course! But as I didn't

know him, I can't really grieve for him. What sort of chap was he?'

'Dennis Cooper? Jim could tell you more than I can – he worked for him and saw him day to day. He was always polite with me, but rather distant.' She paused for a moment, wanting to give more to Sarah than she would have done to anyone else, seeking to make even this strange and terrible thing a moment of intimacy for them. 'He tried to play the gentleman, but for me there was something a bit sinister about him.'

'How thrilling! And now he's dead.'

'And now he's dead. And I'm a suspect.'

'You? Surely not. Not if you hardly knew him. You're winding me up, Julie Hartley!'

Julie grinned. 'Perhaps I am, a little. But Jim said the police would treat everyone who lives on the site as a suspect, until they know a lot more about this.'

Sarah watched her put her tea down on the small table beside her, then flung her arms extravagantly around the slim, familiar shoulders. 'And I shall have to protect my precious darling from the nasty policemen and the maniac stalking the gardens of England!' Her teasing became a caress, and the caress became a kiss which lasted longer than either of them had planned.

Sarah wondered through her excitement whether they were kissing too much, whether they were so taken with the physical pleasure that it was distorting balance and diverting them from serious things. But that was always the way when your meetings were snatched and secretive. She would do something about that, in the months to come. As they eventually drew apart, she said breathlessly, 'Do they know about us?'

'Who? The police? They don't know about anything. They don't even know I exist, except as a name on a list.'

'Don't tell them! It's not their business. It's nobody's business but ours!'

If only that were so, thought Julie. It was all right a single woman like Sarah feeling that, but it wasn't true. This was Jim's business, and the boys' business. She was a married woman with a family and this thing had hit her like a bomb. But she didn't voice that. She nodded and said firmly, 'This is nothing to do with the police. I don't suppose they'd be interested, but I shan't tell them about us anyway.'

As if to remind Julie of her other life, the French clock which was the most valuable thing in Sarah Goodwin's house suddenly pinged three o'clock, forcing her to shuffle to her feet. 'I must go or I'll be late for the children. I'll keep you posted!'

And with a final, more hurried kiss she was gone. Sarah watched the red Toyota until it turned the corner and disappeared from view, then went back into the house and her sketches. She was suddenly beset by melancholy. She wondered for the first time what the long-term future of this affair was, whether she could stand alone and win against the powerful claims of family.

'I didn't think you'd come here. I thought you'd want to see me on neutral ground. Don't you set up what is called a murder room?' Hugo Wilkinson heard himself sounding defensive, but he'd been caught off guard by the arrival of the two plain-clothes policemen. He glanced surreptitiously around his small, neat sitting room, wondering if there was anything visible which they should not see.

Lambert caught the movement of his head and stored it away for future consideration. 'You're very knowledgeable, sir. Do you read crime fiction?'

Hugo did. He had also read enough of real crime to know that this was John Lambert, the man the local and even some of the national press chose to call a 'super-sleuth'. The man was older than he had expected. His face was lined and his hair, though still plentiful, was laced with grey. The dominant things about him were his grey eyes, which seemed to be seeing and recording more than they should and blinked very rarely in the exchanges which now followed.

The chief superintendent was tall and slim. His legs and arms seemed a little too large for the fireside chair in which Hugo had chosen to place him. The solid figure with the countryman's weather-beaten complexion whom he introduced as Detective Sergeant Hook seemed a more relaxed and less threatening figure. Hugo decided that he would address most of his answers to Hook, but this soon proved impossible. After a friendly nod when he was introduced, Hook said nothing for ten minutes, being content to record Wilkinson's replies whilst he studied him without comment. Hugo had been determined to behave with the bluff bonhomie of someone with nothing to hide, but he found the combination of the two men curiously unnerving.

He found himself speaking first, when he had intended to let them make the running whilst he took his time with his answers. 'I know nothing about this, you know. I'm as shocked as anyone by what's happened.'

'But you know something of the victim – probably quite a lot. Whereas at the moment we know almost nothing,'

'You've searched his office.' It was almost an accusation.

'Part of the team is searching it at this very moment. It takes a long time to study files in detail.' This time it was Lambert who made a challenge out of a simple statement. 'We may use his office as our murder room when we are satisfied that we have exacted all the information from it.'

But in the meantime, they've chosen to see me here, thought Hugo. Like most people with things to hide, he saw sinister intent in innocent and pragmatic decisions. He glanced again round his sitting room, which was tidy and anonymous, as he wished it to be. The computer stood like an accusation on the table beneath the window, but they surely couldn't know anything about that, could they? Almost everyone of his age had some sort of computer now.

Lambert broke into his thoughts by saying, 'You live on the site. You must have known Dennis Cooper quite well.'

'Not very well.' The denial had come automatically and too quickly. He tried to relax and justify what he had said. 'I scarcely knew him outside work. I haven't been here that long.'

'Almost a year. Long enough to get to know Mr Cooper, I should have thought, with both of you living on site.'

'It's a strange life, being a chef. You tend to be busy in the evenings, when other people are relaxing. It gives you a different sort of social life.'

'Yes, I can see that. But isn't the bulk of your work here

done at lunchtimes? That's when the visitors are using the restaurant, surely?'

'That's true enough. But we advertise widely. We're getting an increasing number of evening bookings which have nothing to do with visits to the gardens.'

'I see. How did you find Mr Cooper as an employer?'

Hugo wanted to say that his real employer was the National Trust, that Cooper had been his boss, but not the payer of his salary and retainer of his services. He sensed just in time that it would be pedantic and obstructive to take this line. 'He was fair; I think you'll find most people will say that. I haven't had many dealings with him, but from what other people tell me, he's – he was prepared to listen to whatever you had to say. I've known many owners of restaurants who merely issued orders and didn't want to listen to what you thought about them. It makes life difficult, when you're on the spot all day and they appear occasionally and only see part of the picture.'

'Yes. That sort of thing's not entirely unknown in the police service.' Lambert allowed himself a small, private smile. 'What sort of man was Cooper?'

He was leaning forward a little, as if inviting confidences, as if saying that stating the character flaws of your boss would be perfectly natural and expected. Wilkinson said stiffly, 'He was a rather private man – at least he was as far as I'm concerned. Perhaps I'd have got to know him better if – if this hadn't happened.'

'No doubt. But remember that DS Hook and I never met him at all. Anything you can tell us about his relationships with you and other people here would add to our knowledge.'

For the first time, Hugo paused and thought before he replied. They'd already told him that Cooper's office was being searched; no doubt officers in the team were already talking to Cooper's PA. These men would know, probably by the end of the day, about the contents of his file. It was better to tell them frankly that he'd been in trouble than to let them find out later and think that he'd tried to conceal it.

He said heavily, 'I said Cooper was a fair man and I stand by that. Ten days ago, he had occasion to give me an official warning about my conduct. He was perfectly entitled to do that; indeed, he probably thought he had no alternative. For my part, I accepted that I was in the wrong and we parted amicably.'

They were the phrases he'd been planning to deliver ever since the body had been discovered. He hadn't expected to be doing it quite as early as this. Lambert studied him for a moment without speaking. 'You'd better tell us what your offence was.'

'It was the kind of thing which happens often in a kitchen, but I'm not saying that makes it any better. You can't get away with these things nowadays, especially in a place like this. I used a racialist phrase to one of our employees.'

He hoped for an understanding policeman. Racialism had been common in city police forces once, hadn't it? Hadn't there been accusations of 'institutional racialism' against the Metropolitan police? But he was disappointed. All Lambert said in a carefully neutral voice was, 'We'd better have the full details of this, I think.'

'Well, we were short-staffed in an overheated kitchen and the restaurant was very busy. Everyone was stressed and under extreme pressure. We had a full restaurant with people waiting for their food and a lengthening queue at the doors.'

For the first time, Lambert's face creased with impatience. 'That's the mitigating circumstances plea. Tell us about the crime, please.'

'I shouted at a willing but very slow Asian boy. I think my exact words were, "For god's sake move your arse, you fucking coon!" It sounds terrible when I repeat it in cold blood in a place like this. It was over in a flash at the time.'

'I'm not interested in passing judgement, Mr Wilkinson. My only concern here is your relationship with Mr Cooper and how it was affected by this.'

Hugo felt relieved and more able to defend himself now that this was out in the open. 'He had complaints from the public and a couple of letters. I admitted immediately I was in the wrong. I've told the Asian boy that I shouldn't have used that phrase; he's accepted that and continues to work under my direction in the kitchen. Mr Cooper issued an official warning to me and that was the end of the matter.'

'You're sure of that? His treatment of this incident wasn't an enduring source of bitterness between you and Mr Cooper?'

'No. I freely admitted I was in the wrong and for his part he made it clear that the rules dictated that he had to issue an official warning. That was the end of the matter as far as both of us were concerned.'

'I see. In view of the public complaints, the incident must have been a source of considerable embarrassment to the man in charge here. You don't think there was any continuing resentment on his part because of that?'

Hugo swallowed hard and dug his nails into his palms. 'No. Dennis Cooper wasn't that sort of man.'

'I see. You will appreciate that we are trying hard to build up a picture of exactly the sort of man he was.'

'He was fair and balanced. He preferred to think about things rather than take action in a hurry. He wouldn't have survived long in a hectic kitchen.' Wilkinson gave a sour little grin at that thought. 'But I'm sure he thought that a measured approach was best for the job he did, and I dare say he was right. As I said a moment ago, I only knew him in a working situation.'

Lambert wondered how far that was true; it seemed to him that residents on a site would inevitably get to know quite a lot about each other outside working hours. He'd know whether he was right about that after he had spoken with others. He glanced at Hook, who said immediately, 'Where were you last night, Mr Wilkinson?'

'That's when he died, isn't it?' It's what an innocent man would ask, he thought. Hugo had determined on the question in the two minutes which was all he had to prepare himself for this meeting.

Hook said only, 'Very probably. Where were you between six and twelve yesterday evening, Mr Wilkinson?'

'I was in this flat. Things were pretty hectic in the restaurant at lunchtime, but I managed to get through without disgracing myself.' He glanced at both of them to see how they would react to his irony, but found them only grave-faced and attentive. 'It was a busy weekend and I was on my feet for most of it. I was glad of a rest – I think I might even have flaked out on my bed for a while.' He glanced automatically at the shut door to his bedroom. 'Perhaps middle age is setting in. I'm fifty-five. It was also raining very hard for a lot of the time – not the sort of weather to encourage a stroll in the grounds.'

He laughed nervously at this, but found the two men giving him only polite smiles in response. Hook, ball-pen poised over his notebook, said, 'So you did you not leave this flat at all between six and twelve midnight, sir?'

'No, I don't think I did. I'd eaten well at around three, when the restaurant is closed to visitors and those of us who have been supplying the meals eat a late lunch. I made myself a snack here at about eight, watched a little television, and enjoyed a couple of whiskies. I'm not a big drinker, but I like to finish off a heavy working weekend with a malt whisky, unless I'm going out.'

He wondered if they would ask him to name the programmes he had watched, perhaps even to give them some account of what they had contained. But Hook merely nodded as he wrote. When he had finished, he said unexpectedly, 'Was Mr Cooper the sort of man who made enemies easily?'

It was a chance to implicate others, to divert attention away from himself. But he hadn't had time to think about it. It wouldn't do to seem too eager. 'I don't think so. Why do you ask that?'

'For the obvious reason that someone has chosen to kill him. And because I've always found that the man in charge of things makes more enemies than most. He often has to take unpopular decisions which affect the lives and careers of those who work for him. Unless he's very good at his job, some of these decisions will be unfair or ill-advised. Even when they're not, they may be perceived as that by those who suffer from them; not many people are as objective as you claim to have been about being reprimanded.'

Hugo noted that 'claim to have been'. This man he had taken as Sergeant Plod was an opponent to be reckoned with, despite his appearance. 'Yes, I can see that. There were the usual rumblings you get about any boss. You're right when you say that people get very subjective when decisions don't suit them. But I wasn't aware of anything beyond that. It seems a big step from grumbling about your lot to killing a man.'

'Indeed it does. Is there anyone who can confirm that you were here for the whole of yesterday evening?'

'No. If I'd killed Dennis Cooper, I dare say I'd have made sure there was.'

His little barb drew no response beyond a single word in Hook's notebook. The DS looked at his half-page of notes for a second or two, then said, 'We'd like you to continue to think about this very serious crime. If anything occurs to you which might have a connection with it, please get in touch with this number immediately. Anything you have to say will be strictly in confidence.'

They left then, without pressing him any further. He reviewed what had happened and couldn't be certain whether this had been merely a routine gathering of information, as they'd implied when they asked to see him, or whether they regarded him as a serious candidate for murder. At least they hadn't asked him about his computer, which had stood like an accusation on the table a yard or two to the right of them throughout.

Indeed, they hadn't pressed him at all about his private life or about how he came to be working here. What he thought of as his hobby was against the law; the group wouldn't need to be so secretive about it otherwise. But he couldn't see how Lambert or Hook could possibly know about that. Probably they wouldn't even be interested.

They were only interested in murder, so he'd better give his full attention to that.

TEN

Lorna Green was not working at Westbourne Park on the Monday when the body was discovered. Tuesday, Wednesday and Friday were her days for voluntary work. She had arranged to take her mother to see some old friends in Monmouth. They'd been neighbours of the Greens for many years. Lorna remembered lying in bed as a child and listening to raucous laughter from downstairs after one of her parents' dinner parties. They'd been younger then than she was now; she could imagine her dad and Mr Williams being quite risqué in their prime, and the ladies being guiltily amused in a foursome when they might have felt the need to be disapproving in a wider public setting.

She was shocked to see how much older the Williamses looked. Harry was walking with a stick and Enid had the beginnings of a humped back. Her hands shook quite violently as she handed round cups of coffee. Because she had known them since she'd been a small girl, Lorna found it difficult to call the old couple Harry and Enid rather than Mr and Mrs Williams. When she forced herself to do so, she heard echoes of old people's homes and hospitals, where people were now addressed by their forenames whether it pleased them or not.

Things became easier as she chatted about her work at Westbourne. She now knew as much as anyone alive about the history of the place. And she found she was better with an audience of two than the large groups she often addressed at the gardens. She felt free here to stimulate questions and to feed in amusing anecdotes about the man who had founded the garden. It seemed to her that the owner had been rather a dull man, redeemed by his passion for plants and his vision of what Westbourne might become. She told them about his mother's frustration with the ways he was using the considerable fortune he had inherited and the rather comical spats between the two.

The Williamses were genuinely amused and plied her with questions, which kept her going for some time and relaxed all of them. Her hosts had been to the garden years ago; Harry unearthed an old brochure from the depths of his bureau and Lorna was able to tell them how the National Trust had developed the gardens in the last twenty years. She had some interesting tales of the first head gardener under the Trust, who had been a benevolent despot with his own ideas of what were the best horticultural practices. The ways in which he had been supported and occasionally outwitted by the Trust's representatives had seen some hilarious moments.

'I wouldn't vouch for the absolute accuracy of that!' she said, concluding a tale which involved water butts and sheep droppings. 'I dare say people have added to it in the telling, as happens with most of these stories.' Her audience agreed. Then Harry went off on an account of the eccentricities of their own gardener, who was a great help and a good worker, but also a law unto himself.

Lorna glanced at her mother, who was sitting very still on the sofa and staring unseeingly out of the window. It was an expression that had become familiar to her over the last year or so. It was the means by which Barbara Green extracted herself from surroundings she found bewildering and retreated into that strange half-world which only she understood. Her daughter sought desperately for forgotten fragments from the time when the Greens and the Williamses had been neighbours and Enid, realizing what was going on, joined in and helped her.

For a time, Barbara came alive, even contributing her own fragments of reminiscence, recalling the day when a gale had broken a clothesline and Enid's and Harry's smalls had ended up festooned round Barbara in her garden. Lorna had heard the tale many times before, but Enid and Harry seemed to have forgotten it, so she joined in the laughter when the story was concluded. She wondered how far the couple recognized her situation; they were undoubtedly helping things along as much as they could.

Enid Williams had planned a pleasant lunch for them, but it was a little ambitious for her diminished energy levels. Lorna cast aside the restrictions of her childhood and helped all she could in the kitchen. She was frightened that Enid would scald herself as she tried to drain heavy pans of boiling water containing new potatoes and other vegetables – she had prepared and cooked far too much for the four reduced appetites who were to sit round her table today.

Presently they were able to take the food on the trolley into the dining room, where Enid and Harry had set the table out beautifully with gleaming cutlery and cut glass before their visitors arrived. Harry emerged from the sitting room as he heard the trolley, looking thoroughly distressed. 'Your mum's using the bathroom, Lorna. I showed her to our downstairs cloakroom, but she insisted on going upstairs.' He was plainly very glad to have Lorna back to take over.

Lorna heard the Williamses conferring in muted voices in the dining room as she climbed the stairs. Her mother emerged not from the bathroom but one of the bedrooms beyond it. She had taken off her shoes and the lightly patterned cotton dress which had looked so well on her; she stood on the landing clad only in bra and pants. 'I can't find my nightdress anywhere!' she said accusingly to Lorna. 'And it's high time you told me which bed I'm to sleep in!'

Lorna fought down a sense of rising panic. 'You're not going to bed, Mum. It's the middle of the day and you're not at home. Put your dress back on and we'll go downstairs. Enid's got a nice lunch ready for you.'

'Enid? Who's Enid? I don't know any Enid.'

'Yes you do, Mum. Come on, I'll help you get dressed and we'll make your hair look nice, shall we?'

Barbara looked for a moment as if she would resist, but eventually she let her daughter take her into the bathroom and slide her dress over her thin shoulders. She sat on the edge of the bath, silent as a child, whilst her thinning grey hair was combed for her. Lorna took her hand and led her carefully downstairs to where Enid and Harry Williams stood anxiously in the hall.

The meal was a muted affair, with three people making stilted conversation and trying to disguise their glances at the fourth. Barbara seemed to have recognized her hosts, but no one was sure of that. She said little but ate steadily, downing the token helping of wine which had been poured into her glass at one swallow. The others pretended not to notice that the food had gone cold whilst it waited on the table.

They went into the lounge and Barbara sat in an armchair and closed her eyes. Lorna terminated the visit as swiftly as possible. It wasn't necessary to be polite. Everyone would now be relieved to have this over. She would phone the Williamses this evening, once she had Barbara safely in bed, and make her apologies. And the Williamses would say that there was nothing to apologize for and it wasn't her fault and how sad life became as you grew older.

Lorna was growing used to conversations like that.

She fastened the seat belt carefully across her mother and drove carefully, as Harry Williams had reminded her she must do under stress. She put Classic FM on for her mother, so that there was no need for either of them to struggle with words. When the *Radetzky March* was played, she sang her way wordlessly through the tune and tapped the steering wheel to the vigorous rhythm, but Barbara did not join in as she would once have done. Lorna thought that her mother must be asleep, but when she reached the M50 she stole a glance at her. Barbara was staring vacantly at the greenery flashing past.

In the hourly Classic FM news summary, Lorna Green heard that there had been a suspicious death at Westbourne Park.

Jim Hartley was determined to play this very straight. He knew he mustn't be obstructive, but he wouldn't give them anything he didn't need to.

He'd been in the boss's office often enough before – probably more than anyone else who lived at Westbourne, he reckoned. Dennis Cooper had always emphasized that none of them would be here without the gardens and said firmly that that made the head gardener the most important employee of all. As curator, he had the widest brief and the biggest responsibility, but without the gardeners no one would be employed. Jim knew that it was Cooper who oversaw the finances of the place, who decided whether the increased success and the greater number of visitors each year warranted an extra apprentice gardener, and he was happy that it should be so. Like most dedicated gardeners, he didn't want any involvement whatsoever in financial matters.

He conveyed all this to the chief superintendent and the detective sergeant when they'd asked him about his work here. They let him go on for longer than he'd expected, though he was a little disconcerted by the way they studied him intently whilst he spoke, as if his words carried greater weight than he thought they did. He felt like a racehorse in the paddock, being studied intently by the punters for any strengths or weaknesses which might prove significant in the race to come.

It was only when they sensed he was faltering that Lambert said rather abruptly, 'So how would you summarize your relationship with the murder victim, Mr Hartley?'

'Good.' His words had been running easily whilst he spoke of the gardens and his plans, but they threatened to desert him now, when he needed to speak freely and convince these shrewd men that he was innocent. 'He discussed all the developments quite frankly with me. We have a five-year rolling plan; we add a few new things each year, but they have to wait their turns.'

'Did you have many disagreements?'

'No. I can't remember us having a real argument.' Jim wondered if they would think that was too trite. He went back to his job details; he had studied them for so long before his interview that he still knew them almost by heart. 'I was involved in all the thinking and planning from the outset, you see. For instance, I said a few months ago that the rose garden was looking rather tired and suggested some of the modern disease-resistant shrub roses which might replace older ones that are failing. A lot of the planning comes directly from my suggestions. It was made clear to me when I was appointed that I was to suggest and plan the developments here, rather than be just a working gardener who implemented other people's ideas.' He knew he'd mentioned thinking and planning too much, but it had seemed important to him to make his point.

'What kind of man was Mr Cooper?'

Jim hadn't expected anything so vague. He felt as though they were studying him rather than Cooper when they asked things like that. Perhaps they wanted to know if he'd been harbouring some grievance against the dead man. He said stubbornly, 'We got on well, as I've just told you. I liked him.'

'Fine. But that doesn't tell me a lot about Mr Cooper.'

Jim endured a moment of panic. It seemed that everything he could say about Cooper's character would rebound on him and place him at the centre of this business, when he desired more than anything to present himself as merely a spectator watching events. 'I'd say he was rather a private man. It wasn't easy to get close to him.'

'Fair enough. But from what you've told us, you were closer to him than anyone outside his family.' Lambert saw a protest coming and pressed on. 'You met him more often, both for long-term planning and for day-to-day decisions, than anyone else who works here. You must have some ideas about his strengths and his weaknesses – was he a womanizer, for instance?'

'No. Well, not that I'm aware of. But I'm usually the last to know about things like that.'

There was a flash of bitterness here, which they noted for future attention. But at the moment they were concerned with what he could tell them about Cooper. 'By definition, a murder victim has at least one serious enemy. Usually we find a man who excites that sort of rage has more than one. We need all the help that people like you can give us.'

'Yes. I can see that.' Jim forced himself to stop and think. He'd been quite a bright boy at school and he'd passed all his horticultural exams without much trouble. He'd been pleased to find he could still write quite well when he made his reports about the gardens. But the spoken word was different; gardening wasn't a trade where you had to express complicated thoughts in words. He said carefully, 'Dennis Cooper didn't give away much about himself. But he liked to know everything he could about others. He certainly seemed to know what was in everyone's file.'

'Which was probably partly why he was efficient as a leader. You need to know the strengths as well as the weaknesses of your staff.'

'Yes. Dennis seemed to be more interested in the weaknesses.'

There, he'd said it. Blurted it out in a few words. It showed his resentment against the man, when he'd meant to keep everything bland and unrevealing. He'd no idea at this moment whether this was a good or a bad thing. Lambert seemed to be trying to reassure him as he said, 'It's much better that we find this out now from you than later from someone else. That way, we might have thought you were trying to conceal something.' He gave Hartley a grim smile. 'You need to enlarge a little on what you've just told us, I'm afraid.'

'He wanted to know everything about the private lives of the apprentices we took on. He said I was to inform him of anything irregular which went on. "Irregular" was one of his favourite words, I think.'

'Perhaps he felt a responsibility towards these young people who are still feeling their way into a dangerous working world. Perhaps with the ones living on site he thought he had a responsibility to supervise their development.'

'Perhaps. And when only one or two of them can be taken on to the permanent staff at the end of their training, you could say that he had a right to know everything to help his decisions. But more often than not he takes my recommendations anyway. When lads are on drugs or binge drinking, it shows up very quickly in their work, when that work involves hard physical labour. We're lucky here: we can pick and choose our apprentices. We don't get many bad 'uns.'

'Are you saying the curator had an unhealthy interest in the young men working here?'

'No, nothing like that! It was all perfectly proper. He just seemed a bit of an old woman when it came to storing away bits of gossip. Am I allowed to say that?'

Lambert grinned wearily. 'Probably not. But please carry on.'

'Well, it wasn't just the apprentices. Dennis Cooper wanted all the information he could get on the senior staff here, as well. He wanted to know where the chef went when he went off the site.'

'And did you tell him?' The grey eyebrows arched above the grey eyes in innocent enquiry.

'No. I couldn't if I'd wanted to, because I don't know. My family's enough for me to worry about. I keep myself to myself.'

'But you think the curator liked to pry into people's private lives?'

Hartley nodded slowly. 'He liked to know everything he could about people. I expect he'd have said that was just part of his job. The more he knew about people, the more accurately he could assess whether they were suitable employees. He's responsible to the Trust for everyone who's employed here. None of us has a job for life. Even the most senior of us are on two- or three-year contracts.'

'But you need continuity, especially in jobs like yours.'

Jim Hartley smiled. 'Of course you do. And personally, I don't feel in danger of being made redundant. But any organization which depends on subscriptions for its income can see it decline rapidly in times of recession, so the Trust has to be prudent.'

'Did Mr Cooper threaten people with dismissal if they didn't toe the line?'

There was a long pause, during which Hartley seemed to find the curator's carpet deeply fascinating. 'He didn't threaten me. I can't speak for other people.'

'You mentioned the head chef, Mr Wilkinson. Were he and the curator at loggerheads?'

'No. I just gave that as an example of how Dennis Cooper wanted to know everything that went on here. I suppose the chef sprang to mind because of something which happened a week or two ago. Hugo shouted words he shouldn't have used in the kitchen. Everyone got to know about that. But Mr Cooper had dealt with it. I don't think there was any residual animosity between the two of them.'

A good phrase. Unusual for a gardener, even a head gardener, Lambert thought. But perhaps he was being patronizing. He nodded to Hook, who said, 'Where were you last night between six and midnight, Mr Hartley?'

'That's easy. I was in my cottage. It was a pretty foul evening, with a thunderstorm which took a long time to rumble away and heavy showers as it went. Not the weather to tempt you out.'

'So you didn't leave the cottage at all between six and twelve?'

'No. It was the kind of weather where you're glad to have a roof over your head.'

'Is there anyone who can confirm this for us?'

He hesitated for a moment before he smiled. 'Well, there's the boys. I read Oliver a story – Sam reads his own nowadays.

They were asleep by about nine, but of course Julie could vouch for me after that.'

'And you for her, I suppose,' said Lambert with a humourless nod. Husband-wife alibis were notoriously suspect, but always difficult to break.

'Surely Julie can't be one of your suspects? She hardly knew the man.'

'We shall be questioning everyone who lives on site. At this stage, we cannot think in terms of suspects. We gather information and try to eliminate as many people as we can from the enquiry as we do so. But it is important that we speak to everyone here. They may have seen something or heard something significant. They may know things about the victim, about his likes and dislikes, his friends and enemies, which give us pointers. It is often people on the fringes of an investigation who give us vital information.'

Hartley's tanned outdoor features clouded as he nodded. 'I can see that. I hadn't thought about it before. I still don't think Julie will be able to help you.'

'So who do you think did this, Mr Hartley?'

He was shocked by the directness of the challenge. 'I've no idea. You shouldn't just consider people on the site. There are a lot of people who come in here every week to help us. It could be one of them. Or it could be someone else entirely – someone connected with Mr Cooper's private life.'

'It could indeed. Do you know of any such person?'

'No. I'm just making the point that we don't live in a vacuum. Even for those of us working in the gardens all day and living on the site, there has to be life outside Westbourne Park.'

'I take your point. But can you suggest anyone who doesn't live on the site who should have our attention?'

Jim Hartley studied the carpet in Cooper's office for several long seconds as he forced himself to go further. 'There's Lorna Green. She's a voluntary worker who probably comes in more frequently than any of the others. She knows more about the history of the gardens than anyone. She gives talks to visitors and answers questions.'

'And you think she also knows quite a lot about the man

who was responsible for Westbourne? You think we should talk to her quickly?'

'I'm not saying she had anything to do with this. She's not that sort of woman. But something she said one day made me think she's known Dennis Cooper for a long time – longer than any of us who work here. She might be able to tell you the sort of things about his past that you were speaking of.'

'Members of our team will be speaking to all the voluntary workers here. But we'll make Ms Green a priority. Thank you for the thought. We may need to see you again, when we know more about what happened last night.'

That was merely routine, Jim told himself. It was just his own confusion which made it sound like a threat.

Twenty-four hours after its curator had been murdered, a strange, uneasy quiet lay over Westbourne Park. Monday had been a fresher day after the storm, but cloud had covered the skies in early evening, so that the long summer day darkened earlier than might have been expected.

This was normally a quiet place in the evenings, after the visitors had left. But it seemed unnaturally so tonight. The birds had ceased singing early and it would be an hour or two yet before the first cry of the screech-owl was heard. The few children on the site had departed indoors as the daylight dimmed. Silence and stillness were natural here. But what had happened on the previous evening was known now to everyone who lived on site, so that the quiet seemed extreme and unnatural.

One man who lived here had been waiting impatiently for the twilight. The figure in leathers and helmet looked scarcely human as it moved stiffly through the gloom; the silhouette might have been some biped from another planet. Once the gauntleted hands dropped upon the steel of the handlebars, it took shape as a motorcyclist and became less threatening.

But the silence held, because the rider did not want to be discovered. He wheeled the small machine awkwardly from the shed and turned it towards the gates. For the last fifty yards, he slipped astride it and pushed it along awkwardly with his feet, anxious to be gone from here, but also to escape detection, though there seemed to be no one else abroad in this still and brooding place. Once he was through the staff entrance and on the lane, he kicked the machine into life.

Its small engine roared unnaturally loud through the silence, its lights blazed sudden and dazzling in the summer darkness. Then the rider was away through the lanes, a succession of moths flashing briefly in and out of the long beam of his headlight. All other concerns disappeared beneath the concentration needed to control his bike on this journey through the night.

The presence of the steel frame beneath him, responding to the movements of his body, was as reassuring as the surge of power when he reached a straight stretch of road and opened the throttle. You heard nothing but the sound of your engine, felt nothing but the rush of the cool wind past your ears. You saw nothing through your goggles save what your headlight gave you on these unlit roads. You were in your own world, master of your own fate, on a motorbike. Whilst you rode it and controlled it, it shut out all other concerns which had set you on this journey.

Alex Fraser settled low over the fuel tank for his long retreat through the darkness.

ELEVEN

'Thank you for coming in here so promptly.'

'It was no trouble. The rota has me on duty on most Tuesdays in any case.'

Lorna Green looked round Dennis Cooper's office, at the battered filing cabinet in the corner, at the long wood-framed window with the under-eaves of the thatch just visible at the top, at the big picture on the wall of the original owner's other great garden in the south of France. She wondered if she should pretend that she had never been in this room before. That would surely distance her from the crime. She reminded herself that as far as these men were concerned she was only an unpaid part-time worker and thus scarcely worthy of much attention.

She was torn between wanting to know exactly what the CID men were thinking and trying to prove she was quite remote from it. It wasn't in her nature to play down her importance, she thought wryly. You got to know yourself better as you grew older. Even the tragedy which was threatening to overwhelm her at home had taught her things about herself. She looked at the tall, intense man with the grizzled hair and keen grey eyes who had said he was Chief Superintendent Lambert, then at the burly figure with the weather-beaten face who sat quiet and observant beside him. She said, 'The other part-time workers and guides are being interviewed by members of your team. May I ask why I merit the top brass?'

Lambert pursed his lips, decided not to tell her that she was here to answer questions rather than to ask them. This exchange was voluntary and unpaid, like the rest of her work here. 'We were told you know as much about this place as anyone. That made you a good starting point.'

'But you're interested in a man who died here, not the place itself.' Some men thought they could get away with any sort of bland explanation, so long as they were speaking to a woman. And perhaps they succeeded, if they threw in a little flattery; she acknowledged to herself wryly that she'd been pleased when the chief superintendent had said she was the leading authority on Westbourne.

This man seemed to appreciate finding a woman worthy of his steel. He smiled at her as he said, 'We don't know yet whether this death is connected with its setting. But I can tell you that we were also told that you might know more about Dennis Cooper than most of the people who work here.'

'I'm sure that won't be true. This place is all about plants and gardening. As head gardener, Jim Hartley must know more than me about Mr Cooper, for a start. He was in almost daily contact with him, I think. Indeed, I'm sure all the staff who live on site have had much more contact with him than people like me, who come here two or three times a week to act as guides and give our little talks to the public.'

'You underestimate yourself, I think. The people who work

here tell me that you are both enthusiastic and very knowledgeable. They turn to you when they have questions they cannot answer about the history of Westbourne Park.'

Lorna was pleased, despite her resolution to be low-key. 'People exaggerate. But it's true I've always been interested in the history of National Trust properties. When you work here and talk to the public, there is every incentive to find out all that you can about Westbourne.'

'And in doing so you must have come to know the curator quite well.'

She wondered if her tendency to correct Cooper in public had been noticed and reported by others. Perhaps they knew about her recent confrontation with the dead man. She looked hard at Lambert, but discovered nothing from that lined, enquiring face. 'I think you exaggerate the importance of what I do here. I am part of a large group of voluntary, unpaid workers. We enjoy what we do and we make our contribution, but Mr Cooper had far more important issues to deal with than what we do.'

'Nevertheless, his files show that he was well aware of the vital part you play here. You knew Mr Cooper for a long time, I think. For many years before either of you worked here.'

It was dropped in almost casually, as if it were a matter of small importance. The shock was all the greater for that. She wondered how they knew, who had told them, whether Dennis had left behind some record of their time together. For an absurd moment, she even wondered if she might be mentioned in his will. She tried to force her racing mind back to what she should do now. She heard herself saying in a low voice she could scarcely believe was hers, 'Perhaps I should have told you that. I expect I would have, eventually. But one guards one's privacy. What happened many years ago had nothing to do with Dennis's death.'

'I think you should tell us all about it, rather than leave us to prise it out of you by questioning. If it proves to have nothing to do with this crime, as you say, there is no reason why it should go any further.'

She fixed her gaze upon the picture of the Riviera garden on the wall; it was important to her concentration that she should not look at these two strangers who were about to hear about the most intimate relationship of her life. 'Dennis Cooper and I were lovers, twenty years ago and more. It wasn't the only serious relationship I've had. It was quite certainly the most important.'

'Did he also feel that?'

'You'd have to ask him about that. But you can't now, can you? He said it was important. He behaved as if it was important, at the time.' She took a deep breath, determined to be the modern, detached woman she was, rather than the woman desperate to be a wife she might sound. 'I think for a while we both thought we'd marry, but that never happened.'

'And why was that?'

He was as quiet and sympathetic as a therapist, she thought. And no doubt just as anxious to have her speak frankly, but for his sake, not for hers. 'I can't give you a convincing answer to that. I'm not going to pretend I didn't want to commit myself, because at the time I did. It was Dennis who shied away from the bond of marriage. That's what he called it, the bond.'

She kept her tone even and her gaze on the picture, even at this moment when she had most reason to sound bitter. It was left to Lambert to prompt quietly, 'That must have been a time of great emotional stress for you. Perhaps for both of you.'

'It was for me. I can't speak for Dennis. There was nowhere else for our relationship to go, once we'd considered marriage and rejected it. We broke up and moved on. We didn't see each other for a long time. Not until he came here, in fact.'

'You were here before him?'

'Yes. But only just. I took early retirement – it was offered to me when my firm was taken over by an international company and I was quite happy to take a generous package. I've always loved this place, so I grabbed the chance to offer my services and come to assist here on two or three days a week. I'd been here for about six months when Dennis was appointed. It meant I had the man I'd thought I'd never see again as my boss.'

She'd got through it, more quickly and with less emotion

than she'd feared. She took her eyes from the painting and looked back at the keen grey eyes of Lambert and at the stolid man making notes beside him. She wondered what they were thinking. She'd been too preoccupied with her own account to take much notice of their reactions. Lambert said, 'Would you have come here to work, if you'd known he would be in charge?'

'I can't answer that, because things happened the other way round. I felt established here when I heard about Dennis Cooper's appointment. I didn't immediately resign, did I? I could have done that quite easily, as a voluntary worker.'

'Indeed you could. Perhaps you wanted to have access to your former lover.'

How gently he inserted his daggers! The grim smile she gave him surprised her quite as much as it did him. 'So that I could revenge myself on the man who had refused to take me to the altar, you mean? That's a pleasantly old-fashioned idea. I like to think I'm more a twenty-first century woman than that. I can assure you that I'd put my two-year relationship with Dennis Cooper well behind me and got on with the rest of my life once he was gone. I'm still not sure whether I welcomed his appointment here or not. I think at the time it seemed an interesting diversion.'

'So how did you get on with him, when he arrived?'

She smiled a small, private smile. She was going to consider her answer. She wasn't going to be stampeded into indiscretions by their directness. She felt in control of this. 'In public, we behaved as if we'd never met each other before.'

'And in private?'

'There was no "in private". That was the way Dennis wanted it. He was probably right: he didn't want to compromise himself or affect his position here.'

Lambert caught the tiny whiff of contempt; perhaps she was repeating his phrases rather than her own. 'But it must have been a temptation for you to do that. Or at least to have a little fun at his expense.'

It seemed a strange phrase to come from this very serious man. She would take it as a warning to her not to underestimate him. 'There were in fact very few opportunities to do anything other than act out our very different roles here. He was the most important person in a thriving enterprise; this is one of the NT's most profitable properties, with many thousands of visitors each year. I was an enthusiastic, unpaid, voluntary helper. We were at opposite ends of the pecking order.'

'So you didn't resume any private relationship?'

Again she paused, reviewing her options, deciding just how much she would tell him. 'No. There were few opportunities and it wouldn't have been appropriate. Dennis was as far as I know a happily married man, with his wife living with him on site.' She paused on that, so that they wondered for a moment if she would offer something more. But she said only, 'Both of us are different people now – sorry, I suppose I should say that Dennis *was* a different person. We had different lives and different responsibilities.'

'So you scarcely acknowledged to yourselves that you had a previous history, let alone to those around you.'

He made it a statement, and she saw DS Hook making a note of some kind. She could have left it at that, but her inclination to have things exactly right tugged at the edge of her mind. She smiled to show them how relaxed she was. 'I suppose it coloured our behaviour a little. I know a lot about the history of Westbourne and it is a place I have come to love. Dennis could be a little careless with his generalizations and he was never good with dates. I'm afraid I felt the need to correct him, on a few occasions.'

'In public?'

'I'm afraid so. It was rather naughty, I suppose.'

But this staid, fifty-five-year-old woman looked younger and more mischievous with the thought. She'd obviously enjoyed putting the man right in public. Lambert grinned conspiratorially at her. 'Did it go any further than that?'

'No. I was indulging one of my foibles. I like to have even small details correct. Anal, one of my friends calls me; she says I should become a proofreader. But I don't want people who've taken the trouble to listen to our little talks about the gardens to go away with incorrect facts.'

'And did this habit cause any serious tension with Mr Cooper?'

She should have been used to it by now, but she still found it strange to hear Dennis called 'Mr Cooper'. It made her think of bedrooms long ago and images which were much better wiped away. She said firmly, 'Oh no, nothing like that. I suppose I'm just acknowledging one of my own weaknesses. I should have learned long ago to let small errors pass me by.'

Lambert studied her ageing but still handsome features for a moment. Then he said, 'You obviously knew more about Dennis Cooper than anyone else we shall see, outside his immediate family. Who do you think killed him?'

She didn't show the resentment he would have expected. 'I've thought about that a lot since I heard about his death. I have to say I've no idea. I should think someone who lives on site. But being only part-time and voluntary, I don't know the residents well. Most of the gardeners I hardly know at all.'

Lambert waited for a couple of seconds to see if she would add anything more, then nodded at Hook, who looked down at his notes before he gave her a reassuring smile. 'Where were you on Sunday night, Ms Green?'

If she was shocked by the question, she didn't show it. Indeed, she answered immediately, as if she had been expecting it. 'I was at home throughout the evening and night. That includes the hours from six to twelve, which I believe are the key ones.'

So she'd conferred with others before she came in here. Well, that was to be expected. You couldn't prevent people who were helping you in a murder enquiry from talking to others – indeed, they were usually besieged with questions after they'd been interviewed by CID. Hook smiled encouragingly and said, 'We shall probably have a more exact time of death in the next few hours. In the meantime, is there anyone who can confirm that you were at home throughout these hours?'

Lorna looked for the first time unsure of herself. 'My mother could do that. But I'd rather you didn't ask her, if it could be avoided.'

'Why is that?'

'She has Alzheimer's. We're coping with it, so far. But she wouldn't be a reliable witness. She'd probably be confused. And that would upset her. She used to be so precise. One of the few things I've inherited from her, I suppose.'

Her voice broke a little on that thought, and they caught the merest glimpse of her life away from Westbourne. Lambert told her gently that if she thought of any detail which might help them then she should get in touch immediately.

Lorna Green nodded and left them, walking carefully from the office of her former lover, preserving her suddenly brittle composure until she could be alone again with her problems.

At three a.m., Alex Fraser stopped at the Tebay services to let the engine of the little Honda cool off. She was too small a motorbike for a journey of this length, really. But she had done him proud so far, speeding up the section of the M6 north of Birmingham which was notorious as the most congested stretch of motorway in the country, gliding almost alone through the night between the Pennines and England's highest mountains in the Lake District. He'd give her a rest before taking her over the long rise of Shap Fell and north into Scotland. He wondered why boats and vehicles were always female.

He climbed stiffly from the machine, easing himself from the crouch he had used for so long to make him part of a streamlined unit. The long-distance lorry drivers nodded a friendly greeting to him in the café, grinning a little at the vivid red of his hair as he placed his helmet and gauntlets carefully on the chair beside him. They didn't speak. They'd nothing against bikers, but their camaraderie was with the other men who drove their leviathans of the road huge distances across Britain and Europe. They exchanged notes about the weather and the roadworks which lay ahead of them, grumbled happily about the ridiculous expectations of employers who had never driven a twenty-ton load in their lives, and ignored the slim figure in black leathers.

Alex listened to them happily enough for half an hour and more, enjoying this glimpse of a tough world he would never inhabit. It was hot in here with his full leathers on, but he wasn't going to take anything else off. He wanted to be warmed right through, even overheated, before he tackled what everyone said was the coldest stretch of motorway in Britain. The bike missed a couple of times when he restarted it, as if it had settled down for the night and was unwilling to be disturbed. But when he revved it, it roared more evenly, and he moved away easily and steadily, back on to the motorway and his route north. 'Good girl!' he muttered to the gallant little machine, as if it had been a pony labouring beneath him.

Hours sped past. He was on automatic pilot, his speed steady, traffic non-existent save for the occasional heavy lorry he overtook. It was daylight and he was exhausted when he stopped at the greasy spoon on the outskirts of Glasgow. He had to lever himself off the bike and it took him several seconds to stand fully upright. This must be what it was like to be old, he thought. He reeled unsteadily towards the lights and the food, righting himself and moving more easily after a few yards, as his balance came back to him.

The noise and the unexpected brightness of the lights hit him almost like blows as he pushed open the door. But it was all right. Everyone here was occupied with his own concerns and none of them with him. They gave the black-clad figure with the fiery red hair and the helmet in his hand a glance, then got on with their own conversations. This wasn't rural Gloucestershire, but one of the great cities. It wasn't the habit here to take too great an interest in the business of strangers. Curiosity could be positively dangerous. Alex Fraser loved his work at Westbourne and wanted passionately to retain it. But at this moment he felt that he had returned home.

That feeling was almost shattered immediately. In his fatigue, he nearly ordered a 'full English' breakfast, realizing just in time that the term would mark him as a Sassenach, maybe even a traitor, if they picked up his accent. But he bit back the words and five minutes later sat looking appreciatively at bacon, egg, sausage, tomato, baked beans and brownies, with two slices of toast on a smaller plate and a mug of strong tea by his right hand.

He hadn't realized until now how hungry he was. He didn't believe fried food could ever have tasted so good, or hot tea so welcome. The owner came and cleared the plates left by others, grinned at the young Scotsman's compliments to his cuisine, and asked him how far he had travelled. Two minutes later, the big man set down a second mug of tea and removed the shiningly empty plates.

Alex was overcome by the warmth of his surroundings and the food he had so sorely needed. He loosened the zips on his leathers and allowed himself to relax. He felt almost at peace with himself, for the first time in many days. His belly was full and he felt a delicious fatigue. Perhaps things weren't so bad, after all . . .

It was two hours later when the morning rush eased and the proprietor came out from behind his counter. He stood for a moment looking down at the fiery red of the head which lay so still and quiet upon the table beside the half-full mug of cold tea. He was surprised how clean the hair and the scalp were, how white was the small patch of neck which protruded from the leathers, how innocent and childlike the thin features looked in sleep.

Reluctantly, he bent and shook the young man's shoulder, noting how thin and wiry it felt beneath the leather. It took him a few seconds and a more vigorous jolting to rouse the sleeping traveller. Fraser returned abruptly to consciousness, springing like a warrior roused to confront his enemy. The big man in the apron stepped back and said, 'Easy, lad, easy! You've had a couple of hours' rest. Time now to be on your way.'

For a moment Alex stared blankly at his assailant. Then he looked round at his surroundings and slowly comprehended where he was. He said, 'Thanks, mate. Two hours, you said? You're right. It's time I was away.'

He stood up unsteadily, then gathered his gauntlets and his helmet carefully. Like an old lady with her shopping, he thought. He couldn't remember ever feeling quite as stiff as this. But he was all right once he'd moved the few steps across the floor and out into the welcome coolness of the day.

He'd expected sun, but the sky was grey and a thin drizzle

fell steadily. He could see the ghostly outlines of tall buildings through the mist. He stood still for a moment and studied them, getting his bearings before the last stage of his journey. The silhouettes looked ominous in the gloom, making Alex feel very small. Behind them lay the wide black waters of the Clyde, flowing steadily through the industrial heart of the great city.

His bike wasn't where he'd left it. He saw it quickly, though. It lay three yards from where he had parked it, but on its side, with the throttle grip almost touching the huge tyre of the lorry beside it. Someone had tried to pinch it, but given up the struggle when the lock frustrated him and the bike slid from beneath him.

Welcome home, Alex Fraser.

TWELVE

Julie Hartley was plainly very nervous. Her eyes darted quickly round the curator's office, then did the same circuit again in reverse, as if she was reluctant to look at the two CID men who had summoned her here.

They noted her anxiety with a certain pleasure. People who were on edge often made mistakes, often revealed more about themselves and others than they meant to do. But Lambert and Hook were too experienced to think it implied any connection with the death which was their only concern. Apart from hardened criminals, involvement in a murder enquiry was a new experience and often an uncomfortable one for most people. It made many of them nervous and apprehensive.

The two CID officers had introduced themselves, but then said nothing further whilst the seconds stretched and Julie completed her survey of the room. She spoke eventually, as they had known she would. 'I've never been in here before. Never warranted the boss's attention.'

'But he wasn't your boss, was he?'

'No. No, he was nothing to do with me, really. But he was

Jim's boss. And when you live on the site and you know he controls it, you feel as if he's in charge of you as well.'

'I see. Did you resent that feeling?'

'I've never thought about it before. I suppose I did, a little. But that wasn't Mr Cooper's fault, was it?' She smoothed the dress she had put on specially to come in here. She had grown used to trousers and the dress felt strange; she felt an absurd wish to cover her knees as she faced them.

The tall man who had said he was called Lambert had a long, lined face and grey eyes which never seemed to blink. She felt those eyes were recording her every movement and storing up the information for further use. He now said calmly and directly, 'Did you like Mr Cooper?'

'I didn't like or dislike him. I didn't know him. You should ask Jim that – he saw him nearly every day.'

'We already have, Mrs Hartley. And now we're asking you. Surely as a resident you knew him a little, even if that was outside his work.'

Julie wondered if they were playing cat and mouse with her, whether they knew all about her conversation with Cooper last week. It might be better to set it in front of them now, before they could say she'd tried to deceive them. She must cool down and think clearly. She decided that there was really no reason why they should know anything about that. 'We spoke occasionally. You're bound to meet sometimes in the gardens, once the visitors have left. I've got two boys who are out and about on most evenings, in the summer. It's a wonderful place to bring up children.' She mouthed the platitude everyone seemed to throw at her about the boys. It was surely a safe thing to say.

'So you met him informally in the gardens. What did you think of him?'

'I rather liked him, I suppose. Look, I suppose I did know him rather more than I said I did just now. We've been to his house and he's been to ours. The residents tend to get together for an evening about once a month, especially in winter when things are less hectic. Just a glass of wine and cheese and biscuits or canapés, things like that. Strictly informal. But there are usually a dozen of us at these gatherings, so you don't get to know anyone particularly well. And I was always conscious of Dennis being Jim's boss, so I was rather careful about what I said. You don't get to know anyone very well when it's like that. Sorry, I'm going on for too long.'

'On the contrary, Mrs Hartley, you've explained what went on rather well. I'm sure the information will be valuable to us as we speak to other people who are resident here. Who do you think killed Mr Cooper?'

She gasped. 'I've no idea.'

'But you must have thought about it. I'm sure you've discussed it with Mr Hartley.'

'No.' The denial was prompt and vehement. Her pale, oval face coloured a little beneath her long dark hair. 'We've hardly had time for that. When you've boys of eight and six to be aware of, life is pretty hectic. You don't get much opportunity to discuss things.'

But there had been time last night, once the boys were in bed, thought Lambert. He wouldn't push the matter, until he knew more about the Hartleys and more about others. He couldn't see at the moment why this woman should be so jumpy; she had no reason he could see to be so. But she was certainly on edge, and she remained so when Hook asked where she had been on Sunday evening.

'Between six and twelve, you say? That's a long time to account for. Well, I got the children to bed. That would account for the time up to nine o'clock. And it was still very wet on Sunday night, wasn't it? Heavy showers, even after the thunder. So I expect I was at home all the rest of the evening.'

Hook's eyebrows rose high on his normally placid face. 'Surely you can remember clearly enough, Mrs Hartley? This is only the night before last.'

'Yes, I'm sorry, I'm scatterbrained as usual.' But she didn't look at all as if that was her normal mode. 'Yes, of course I was in the house for the rest of the night.'

'Your husband said you were. He said you could vouch for his presence there.'

'And he's right. Of course he is. We were both there all night. I don't know why my mind went blank. And Jim's my alibi, isn't he?'

Lambert said with a hint of irony. 'In view of your admittedly disturbed state of mind, it's possible that significant facts may occur to you in the next day or two. Please contact us immediately if anything does.'

She stood, smoothing down her skirt again, behind her this time. For a moment, it seemed as if she might speak again, but then she nodded abruptly and left them.

'I had to see you. A phone call wouldn't have done. I'm not much good on phones, even now, when we all have mobiles.' Alex Fraser was rid of his leathers, washed and shaved. His fresh face looked healthy again beneath the fiery hair, though his slim body carried a tenseness which he could not shake away.

Ken Jackson was the only social worker whom Fraser had ever really respected. He'd met him as a sixteen-year-old, known him for three years, and in that time Jackson had rescued his life. Ken wouldn't have put it so dramatically and he'd have given the credit for his reform to the young man himself. But Alex knew the truth of the matter. That's why he'd had to see him now, rather than talk on the phone. Jackson was a father figure, he supposed. He'd never had a father.

Jackson found the beginning a little awkward, as father and son might have done after months away from each other. He'd brought the boy – his charges remained boys well into manhood, for him – back to his own house. He'd sensed as soon as he heard Fraser's strained voice on the phone that Alex wouldn't want curious eyes noting his presence in the council offices and speculating about the reasons for his reappearance.

'How are you getting on at Westbourne Park?'

It was stiff, conventional, ridiculous, in the way that opening exchanges sometimes are between people who've been close and then lived apart. Alex Fraser said equally stiffly, 'All right. I like it there. You said I would.' Then the strength of his joy in the place broke through and he spoke more quickly and naturally. 'More than like it, Ken. I love the work at Westbourne. I'm learning all the time. I can make something of myself there, the way you said I could.'

Jackson nodded and smiled, his own tension dropping away as he heard the new tone in Fraser's voice. 'You can and you will, Alex. You're interested in plants and you have a talent for them. You didn't expect that and I didn't expect that. But thank God we found out about it.'

Alex smiled that small, secret smile which people found so attractive in him. He was wondering why people who didn't believe in a God still invoked one; he knew that Ken Jackson wasn't a believer. 'It's because I want to go on working there that I'm here.'

Jackson's face darkened. He rolled the end of the sleeve of his sweater back an inch on his wrist; it was a movement Alex had forgotten, but now recognized. It was a thing Jackson did to gain him a few seconds for thought. 'There's been a murder at Westbourne, hasn't there? Is that why you're here?'

He'd come straight out with it. The fear that had been haunting him in the two hours since Fraser's strained voice on the phone had told him that he was in Glasgow. But to his great relief Alex said, 'No.' He thought for a moment. 'Well, it might be, I suppose. The place is swarming with police. They make me nervous, the police.' He'd not called them filth or fuzz or pigs; that was a kind of deference to Ken Jackson. The sort of deference you might have given to a father.

'I can understand that. Still, it might not have been a good idea to just piss off. Draws the attention of the CID, you see, when you disappear from the scene like that.'

'Don't you want to talk to me?' Fraser was instantly not just disappointed but prickly and aggressive.

'Easy, Alex, easy. I wouldn't have you sitting in my own front room if I didn't want to speak to you, would I?'

Fraser looked round the small room he had hardly registered before, with its family photographs, its prints of the Alps, and in pride of place its picture of Ken on the Matterhorn. In his preoccupation with his own concerns, he'd forgotten how keen Jackson was on mountaineering. 'No, you wouldn't. Thank you for bringing me here.'

'That's all right. Alex, if you had anything to do with this murder at Westbourne, if you know anything at all about it, you should tell me now.'

'I don't. I didn't kill him and I don't know who did.'

Ken Jackson tried not to show his immense relief. 'Of course you didn't. You wouldn't let yourself down like that. Not after what you've achieved in the last few years.'

'I have done something stupid, though. That's why I'm here.'

'I thought it might be. Let's have it.'

'It's over a week ago, now. I don't know what's going to happen.' For a moment, the tough little Scot looked perilously close to tears. But he pulled himself together and said, 'I went to a party in Cheltenham with two of the lads I work with. It was a last-minute invitation. I wish I'd never gone.'

'Violence?'

'Yes. I didn't start it.'

Jackson sighed. His parting advice to Fraser at their last meeting a few months ago had been to stay away from trouble, to keep his nose clean as he got on with his new life. He said automatically, 'You can't afford that, with your record.'

'I bloody know that!' For a moment, Fraser was the feral animal he'd been last week in Cheltenham, eyes ablaze and limbs triggered ready for the fight. 'I didn't ride all bloody night to have you tell it to me!'

'Easy, Alex, easy!' As he repeated the phrase, Jackson held up the palm of his hand. 'I'm on your side. I always was. You'd better tell me what happened and we'll see what we can do about it.'

Alex liked that 'we'. He had no father and a mother who'd willingly consigned him to the home at fourteen. At this moment, the man sitting opposite him was the only one in the world who might take up his cause. He now spoke in a monotone, as if he could scarcely believe the facts he was carefully announcing. 'It was a good party. We had our own room in the pub. There was plenty of drink, but no drugs that I saw. That's until I went outside for a pee and a break.'

'You don't do drugs. I hope that hasn't changed.'

Alex shook his head angrily, like a man beset by a troublesome fly. He didn't want interruptions. He just wanted the unwelcome facts out. 'I still don't do drugs. I was asked to pass on a package to one of my friends by a small-time dealer. No money changed hands.'

'Who was the friend?'

'One of the lads who works with me in the gardens at Westbourne. The ones who'd invited me to the rave.'

'And the police caught you with drugs, before you could pass them on.'

This time Alex Fraser flicked his hand in front of his face at the imaginary fly. 'No. Well, not straight away. It's worse than that. I'll tell you, if you'll let me bloody finish.'

Ken Jackson's heart sank; he felt that he knew what was coming. He waited till Fraser looked him in the eye, then said, 'I won't speak again until you've told me everything. But it needs to be everything, if I'm to be of any help.'

'Aye. We left our room at the pub together. I suppose it would be about half past eleven. There was a gang waiting for us outside. You're going to say I shouldn't have got involved, but there was no choice.'

No, not with alpha males baying for blood and you and your mates full of drink. You should have turned round and gone back into the pub, gone anywhere rather than forward into a gang fight. But that was never going to happen. Jackson nodded, but held his silence as he had promised he would.

Fraser concluded his tale in the same dull tone. 'We did some damage. We'd have won the fight, if the filth hadn't stopped it.'

Jackson waited for more, but the dull, exhausted face told him it needed his questions now. 'You say you did some damage. What sort of damage?'

'They said a broken jaw and stitches. Perhaps a couple of ribs. I haven't heard any more. Not yet.'

'But you were arrested and questioned, or you wouldn't be here.'

A quick, tortured nod; a refusal now to look into his mentor's face.

'Have you been charged?'

'Not yet.'

'Did you have the drugs on you when they took you in?'

'Yes. But they're not going to charge me with dealing. They

haven't said so, but I think they believe that I just accepted them for someone else.'

'No previous drug convictions. That must have helped you. But you're lucky.'

'That's not the worst of it. There may be a GBH charge. I'm still waiting to hear.'

'For a street fight? When the other lot were the aggressors and you defended yourselves? I'd say that was unlikely. Unless you kicked—'

'I didn't kick anyone. I had knuckledusters on. That's why they held me. That's what did the damage. That's why they'll charge me.'

'You bloody fool, Alex!' It was fierce, short, and no more than a ritual. He'd put a lot of work into this lad, almost won through, and now the cretin had thrown it away.

Except that he wasn't a cretin. He was an intelligent young man who'd had the odds stacked against him in the urban jungle that was downtown Glasgow and had come through it. Almost come through it. And now, when success and a new life had been within his grasp, he'd thrown it all away. But Fraser knew all that, or he wouldn't be here. No use screaming out your own frustration at him. Jackson said dully, 'Were you the only one with those things on?'

'I don't know. I think so. They're bloody amateurs down there, when it comes to street warfare.' A little flash of contempt, a small, warped assertion of Scottish superiority. 'There were knives, though. I'd be sure of that. Every bugger has a knife, these days.' He spoke not like a twenty-year-old in deep trouble but like a veteran warrior recalling earlier and cleaner days.

Jackson said quietly. 'Forget about the others. Were you the only one with the steel mittens?'

'Yes. I didn't see anyone else with them. Not on our side, anyway. We were attacked, Ken. They were waiting for us and they set upon us. The pigs know that.'

'They also know that anyone who goes out to a party with knuckledusters in his pocket is looking for trouble. Premeditated violence, they'll say in court. Alex, what do you want me to do? When you were in trouble up here, I knew some of the police and one or two of the magistrates. I don't know anyone down there. I can come down there and give you a character reference, if the court will allow it, but I can't do much more.'

Fraser shook his head hopelessly. He'd hoped for more, but he'd known in his heart that there was nothing to be done. 'I suppose I just wanted to feel someone was on my side. It's been pretty lonely down there, since this happened.'

'I'll bet it has! But—'

'I know I was a fool to take those things with me. I'm prepared to take whatever they do to me. But I don't want to lose my job at Westbourne. It's what I want to do and I know I can be good at it. I want to stay on permanently at the end of my apprenticeship.'

'If they bring charges, you're pretty sure to be found guilty. You might get away without a prison sentence, if they accept that the other group were the aggressors.'

'With my record? I've got previous. They'll take that into account.'

'I'll put it in writing that they shouldn't, if it comes to it. They'll have to give some weight to that. The judge at least will be aware of it, when he's passing sentence.'

'Is there any chance of a suspended sentence?'

'I don't know, Alex. I'm not a lawyer and I haven't heard all the evidence, have I? You'll need your brief to do a good job on the mitigating circumstances.' Ken Jackson mustered a grin, but he wasn't happy about even that. He didn't believe in false optimism and he always tried to be realistic with young men and women he was trying to help. He forced out the words he knew Fraser least wanted to hear. 'You need to get back there, with a murder hunt going on. This isn't the time to go AWOL.'

'No. It was a mistake to come here. I'll get straight back now.'

Jackson looked at him. The thin face looked even paler and more hunted beneath the short-cut red hair. He'd known Fraser since he was sixteen and Alex had always looked like this when in trouble. He felt a huge surge of sympathy; the strength of it took him by surprise. He felt much older – almost like a father to this boy who was but seven years younger than himself. 'You'd better sleep here. The spare bed's always made up. You can go back tomorrow. I'll ring Westbourne and tell them where you are. I don't suppose you told anyone where you were going?'

'No.' Alex wanted to protest, say he'd get straight back. But his weary body was this time stronger than his mind. 'I'll go to bed for a few hours now. I'll ride back tonight. The bike and me both like it better at night, when it's quieter. Start in daylight, be back by three or four tomorrow morning.'

Ken Jackson went into the hall. 'Eleanor? Alex is going to try to sleep for a few hours, then set off back. He'll get washed and sleep in the spare room.'

His wife appeared at the door of the kitchen, cast her eyes to heaven and mouthed the words 'Soft touch!' fiercely at him down the hall. She went back into the kitchen and firmly shut the door. She was fed up with encouraging Ken's lame ducks.

Alex Fraser now showered and laid his stained leathers carefully not on the chair beside the bed but on the floor. He wanted to cause as little trouble as possible. His brain told him that he should not have come here at all, that the rigours of the journey were absurdly out of balance with what he had achieved. But his heart was cheered by this contact with the man who he thought was his one true friend in an uncaring world.

He put his underpants back on, ignoring the clean pyjamas Ken had left on the bed for him. He savoured the bliss of cool, clean sheets for a few seconds before he fell into a deep sleep, totally undisturbed by the noises of the household.

In his study, Ken Jackson rang through to Westbourne Park, said he wanted to speak to someone who was dealing with the Cooper murder case, and was put through to a DS Hook. Jackson explained who he was, then said, 'One of the men you will want to talk to is Alex Fraser.'

'Indeed he is. He's disappeared without informing anyone where he's gone.'

'He's with me. I used to be his probation officer. He drove through the night to get to me, because of the trouble he was in last week.'

A pause. Then a voice sounding more understanding than

he'd expected said, 'Fraser's not done himself any good, disappearing like this. He's attracted attention to himself. That's not a good idea, when we're establishing murder suspects.'

'I appreciate that. But he's a lad trying to make something of himself, after a bad start. He hasn't any family to turn to. I helped him to get the apprenticeship at Westbourne. He fled to me because I'm the nearest thing he's got to a friend. He's asleep here now. He's insisting that he'll ride back through the night.'

The gruff voice sounded almost conciliatory as it said, 'That's good. The sooner he's here, the better that will be for him.'

Jackson was emboldened to say, 'I'm sure he had nothing to do with your murder, DS Hook. He came here because he's worried stiff about the gang violence he was involved in last week. He's scared that he'll lose his job at Westbourne. It means a lot to him. It's his way out of a life of crime.'

'I can't comment on that, I'm afraid. The team here is concerned solely with a murder case. We shall take note of your view that he is unlikely to be involved in that. Thank you for your call and your concern.'

Jackson understood from this sudden formality that someone else had come into the room where this DS Hook was speaking from. He felt cheered by the reception his call had received. He went upstairs and slid the door of the spare room open a couple of inches. The short hair looked startlingly red on the white pillow. The features beneath it looked as relaxed and unlined as those of a sleeping child.

He was surely right that Alex Fraser couldn't be involved in anything as vile and serious as murder?

At twilight Alex Fraser donned his leathers and his helmet and addressed the long return journey south. The lights of Glasgow blazed around him, but above the lights and over the Clyde, there was daylight still in the quiet summer sky.

At Westbourne Park, over three hundred miles to the south, darkness had all but fallen. Only a long line of purple in the western sky showed where the sun had vanished. Around the great garden, most of nature slept. There were exceptions, as always. A muntjac deer which should have settled for the night looked at the garden's walls, decided they were too high even for its greatest leap, and bounded away towards its mate and rest. A hungry vixen with cubs to feed crept towards the bank where rabbits burrowed. The first hoots of the owl announced that day was gone and his time was at hand.

Within the walls of Westbourne, the lights were on in all of the cottages and houses. Over the next three hours, they were switched off one by one, save for the security lights around the main house. Wednesday tomorrow: the busiest day for visitors, outside the weekends. In their very different ways, gardeners, catering staff, administrators must be ready for the enthusiastic hordes. A good night's sleep was a healthy preparation.

One person, however, was not asleep but active. One person had been waiting impatiently for the lights to go off and people to be in their beds for the night. One pair of eyes was still intensely alert to everything around it, one pair of feet trod securely over familiar paths. The murder room and the anteroom outside it were securely locked, as the stealthy mover had expected.

The small package in its neat white envelope slipped into the receptacle at the administrative centre near the main gates, where the morning post would arrive seven hours later. Mission accomplished.

Westbourne Park slept on.

THIRTEEN

Detective Inspector Christopher Rushton was not happy. He liked things tidy and this case was sprawling and untidy. He wanted the parameters of it defined.

Parameters was one of DI Rushton's favourite words. He liked to set limits and work within them. He was a natural bureaucrat, but a highly efficient one. As such, he was an integral member of Lambert's team. It was Rushton's presence at the centre of things, his ability to co-ordinate the huge amount of information which accumulates around a murder hunt, which allowed Lambert to be out and about among suspects rather than sitting behind a desk at headquarters.

Early on the morning of Wednesday, the sixth of July, Rushton was sitting with Lambert and Hook and trying desperately to define the parameters of this investigation. He reported rather querulously, 'Everyone resident on the site has now been interviewed. So have almost all of the people who come in daily. That's a hell of a lot of people, when you include all the part-time helpers. I've filed everything, but so far I can't see a clear pattern emerging. We usually have a list of suspects by now. That's if we haven't already got someone arrested and charged.'

Lambert nodded and said with heavy irony, 'Not every serious crime matches your exacting standards, Chris. Murder in particular can be either very straightforward or very untidy. This is one of the untidy ones. A lot of people interviewed by the team are hardly suspects at all – they're seen just because they might have important information, perhaps without even recognizing it.'

Hook said with a trace of satisfaction, 'You're not quite right about all residents having been interviewed, Chris. There's one resident we haven't seen as yet. That should be remedied today. The Scots lad who went missing. He should be back on site by now.'

'Alex Fraser.' Chris Rushton was annoyed that he'd forgotten him. 'A man with a history of violence, who was involved in a serious gang fight less than a fortnight ago. A leading suspect, I'd say. I've already got a file with the details of his past. The sooner I get your input the better.'

'You shall have it by the end of the day,' promised Lambert with a smile. 'I hope our input will help to make your parameters clearer.'

Rushton, who was thirty-two, was aware that the older men enjoyed taking the piss. Or in his terms, treating serious issues as lightweight items. He said gloomily, 'The post-mortem report doesn't tell us much. I didn't think it would.'

The three men looked down at the copies which had lately arrived in front of them. Lambert said, 'Any signs that the victim put up a struggle?'

'Nothing obvious. No skin under the nails or anything useful like that. There are indications that he made a desperate attempt to claw whatever was throttling him away from his neck.'

Lambert nodded, looking at the sheet. 'A few scratches on the front of his neck from his own nails. It looks to me as if he was taken by surprise, possibly as he turned away from whoever killed him. Still no murder weapon?'

'No. Probably something wider than a rope or a wire, because it didn't cut into the neck. Perhaps a belt from trousers or a dress. I don't suppose we'll ever see it.'

Hook pointed out, 'We now have a time of death, for what it's worth. The pathologist thinks he consumed a major meal two to three hours before death. His wife says they ate at about seven and took around forty minutes. Which means that he probably died between nine and eleven.'

Lambert concluded his perusal of the report. 'What hasn't emerged is any trace of that "exchange" we're always told is inevitable at a murder scene. The killer is supposed to leave something of himself behind; some fibres from his clothes, some hair from his head. Neither the PM or forensic have come up with anything. It rained heavily during the night after the death; that can't have helped.' Killers are always 'he' to CID men. That is no more than statistics; women murderers are simply much less common than male ones.

At this moment of collective professional dejection, there was a discreet knock at the door. A young woman DC entered uncertainly, as if she expected to be castigated for her interruption. 'Sorry to disturb you, sir, but we thought you should have this. It was left at the entrance office, where the post is delivered. But it wasn't part of the post.'

A small white envelope, with the words 'CID OFFICER IN CHARGE', in carefully printed capitals. Lambert slit it open and extracted an innocent-looking, soft-backed black notebook. Inside the cover, he read the neatly penned words. 'Strictly Private. Property of Dennis Cooper.'

She'd never rung him at work before. That was something they'd agreed as part of a policy of secrecy. But Peter was free, without a partner to deceive, as she had.

Alison Cooper realized with a profound sense of shock that she was now in the same position as Peter Nayland: she no longer needed to lie to a partner. It was surely a wonderful thing to be free to acknowledge openly her relationship with Peter. But she mustn't do that yet. She must wait until this huge fuss over Dennis's death was over and the police went away. No sense in attracting their attention, when they were searching for a killer.

Twice she picked up the phone and put it down again without dialling. She was nervous when it came to the point. Yet she felt an overwhelming need to speak to the man with whom she now planned to spend the rest of her life. That is what she wanted to do. She was sure of it now and she needed Peter to know that. She also needed to hear him declare again that he also wanted it.

She succeeded in tapping in the number at her third attempt. The phone was answered immediately and she told the strange voice firmly that she wished to speak to Mr Nayland.

The PA's voice was professionally alert, not bored as it might have been after doing this hundreds of times before. 'I'm afraid Mr Nayland is in a meeting. May I take a message?'

'No, I need to speak to him personally.'

'As I say, that isn't possible at the moment. May I tell him who called?'

'Tell him it's Alison. It's – it's a family matter.' Ally smiled nervously in the privacy of her room. Let the woman think she was a sister.

Peter Nayland rang back within five minutes. 'How'd it go?'

She pictured him at his big desk, issuing orders and receiving bulletins from the staff she had never seen and probably never would see, in that business world which both of them had found convenient to leave very vague. 'The police thing? It went all right, I think. I played the grieving widow as we agreed. They were quite sympathetic.'

'Good. They didn't know anything about me?'

'No. I'm sure they'd have raised it, if they had.'

'Good. Let's keep it that way. It's better for all concerned that we keep the police out of our affairs.'

'Yes, I suppose so.'

'No suppose about it.' He spoke sharply. 'I've found over the years that the less the police know about things, the better. They poke their noses into all kinds of things, once they find an excuse.'

She tried to make this lighter. 'But you've never been involved in a murder investigation before, have you, my darling?'

'Do you think they've finished with you now?'

She had hoped for comfort, perhaps for a little laughter together, but he was forcing her to confront the death she had been trying to put aside. 'Perhaps not. They did say they might want to speak to me again. When they'd interviewed other people and knew more about this crime, I think they said.'

'Just keep quiet, then. Keep your eyes and your ears open and your mouth shut. Pick up whatever you can, but keep a low profile.'

He spoke almost as though he knew she was guilty. Alison said, 'I need to see you, Peter.'

'Better not, for the moment.'

His answer had been immediate and firm. She said, 'I feel very lonely here.'

'I can appreciate that. But it's much better that we don't meet for a while.'

'So that you can stay out of it altogether, you mean?' It was almost an accusation. They were arguing, when she had rung him for reassurance, for a scrap of the love which would enable her to get through this.

'I thought we'd agreed on that. I thought we'd agreed that it was much better that the police knew nothing at all about us. I can't afford to become a suspect, Ally.'

She wondered for a moment why that should be. But at least he'd used her name for the first time. She said reluctantly, 'I know you're right. It makes sense. But I feel hemmed in here. I needed to hear your voice, my darling.'

There was a silence, long enough for her to think for an awful moment that the line had gone dead. Then he said, 'And it's good to hear you, Ally. And I'm longing to see you, my love. Believe me, I'm missing you and looking forward to holding you in my arms, once the time is right.'

'And when will that be?'

'I can't tell you that, Ally. It's out of our hands. Perhaps when they've arrested someone else for Dennis's murder. Perhaps when they've given up hope and gone away.'

'I need you, Peter. More than I ever thought I would.' Perhaps an independent woman shouldn't be saying that, but she didn't give a damn.

'And I need you, Ally. But once this is over, we'll have the rest of our lives together. Let's not do anything to jeopardize that.'

She made herself smile, forced herself to say, 'I expect you're right, as usual. In fact I know you are, really.'

'I am about this, my darling. It's best not to start any gossip, believe me. The police pick up on things like that. And it's best that you don't ring me here. I'll ring you, during the evening. In two or three days.'

'Promise?'

She tried to make it sound light, even girlish. It was only after she'd put the phone down that she thought Peter Nayland seemed to know an awful lot about police procedures.

He'd had a leisurely shower before putting on the clean clothes he sorely needed. He looked in the mirror before he went to meet them. Alex Fraser was shocked by the face he saw there. It looked very white and drawn beneath the familiar fiery red of his newly washed hair.

They were the two pigs he'd played golf with at Ross-on-Wye. Alex wasn't surprised, as he'd heard they were heading the murder team. He'd seen them about the place before his hasty departure from Westbourne.

Rather to his surprise, it was the burly detective sergeant rather than the chief super who began the exchanges. 'You didn't do yourself any good, lad, disappearing like that.'

'I'm sorry. I needed to talk to a friend.'

'And you haven't any friends here?'

'Not friends like Ken. Ken dragged me out of the swamp. Ken believes in me. Ken got me the job here. I trust him.'

'You were in care, weren't you, Alex?'

This must be the good-cop bad-cop act. He knew what they

were up to, didn't he? They wouldn't fool him. But the broad, tanned face seemed genuinely interested in his tale. 'I was in a council home from the age of thirteen. And in trouble. Petty thieving, bits of fighting. Ken Jackson stuck with me. Ken got me the job with the Glasgow Parks Department.'

'And from that you got your job here.'

'Yes. Ken Jackson helped me with that, too. He wrote me a reference. I think he spoke on the phone to the people who gave me the apprenticeship.'

'I see. Do you like your job here, Alex?'

He'd tried to guess what they would ask him, but he'd never thought it would be this. There surely couldn't be any trap for him here. 'I love it. I'm desperate to keep it. I want to stay on here at the end of the year, if there's a vacancy. But they usually only keep one of the apprentices, Mr Hartley says.'

'And if you're not that one, will you stay in horticulture?'

'Yes. It's what I want to do. I didn't know that. When I first went to the parks department in Glasgow, it was just a job. But then I got interested in plants and how things grow. Now I know how the different soils work and how to propagate plants. I want to go on learning. I want to make it my life's work, if I can.'

He was earnest, even slightly ridiculous, in his desire to convince them. His enthusiasm seemed inappropriate in this raw product of a great city, who spoke still with the quick, harsh accent of Glasgow. Lambert couldn't remember when he had last heard a young man so impassioned about horticulture. Another first, even at this late stage in his detective career.

He spoke for the first time. 'Golf and gardening. Two unusual ways for a young man to seek a way out of his troubles.'

Fraser was immediately cautious. This was the hard-cop bit. They'd softened him up, made him expose his weakness with this unexpected talk about his work. Now the old bugger would go for him. He'd quite liked them both in the clubhouse at Ross, where they hadn't seemed like filth at all. But golf clubhouses were odd places; real life was suspended there. They'd show their real faces here, in this room everyone on the site was now calling the murder room.

Alex said carefully, 'I've been lucky. Lucky to find a sport I'm good at and work I like. Lucky because I had Ken Jackson on my side.'

'Indeed. I agree with all of that. What I find difficult to comprehend is why you should risk all this by reverting to violence.'

For an awful moment, Alex thought they were accusing him of murder. Then he told himself that they couldn't be speaking of that, that it would be foolish of him even to show that he had thought they might be. He said woodenly, repeating the phrases he'd used to the police in Cheltenham, 'You mean that rumble last week. I didn't start that. I was drawn into it. We were attacked by another gang when we came out of the pub. We'd have gone home quietly without that.'

'Home in your case being here.'

'Yes. We had a taxi laid on. I'd only gone to the rave because two of my mates here asked me to. It was just a twenty-first birthday party. In no way were we looking for trouble.'

'Yet you went fully prepared for it. You armed yourself with illegal weaponry.'

Alex Fraser sighed. 'The knuckledusters. It always comes back to that with you lot, doesn't it?' He was suddenly transformed from the horticultural zealot of a moment ago to a whining old lag, his thin features contorted with the weight of the wrongs visited upon him by an uncaring society.

Lambert said sharply, 'Not just us lot, Mr Fraser. The rest of the world will require an answer. Premeditated violence, the lawyers and the rest of us will say. Why else arm yourself with knuckledusters for a night out?'

It was the question he'd been asking himself ever since that fateful night. There was no convincing answer to it, of course. 'It was just habit. A bad habit, I admit. When ye went out into the Gorbals or any other part of Glasgow ye went prepared to defend yourself. I did the same thing in Cheltenham.'

'And inflicted serious injuries on two men there.'

'Two buggers who attacked me. They were the ones who premeditated violence.'

'And you're the one with the history of it. Nearly killed a lad of sixteen.'

'That was in the old days. I was sixteen myself and ye were well used to violence. Ye didn't give a lot of thought to it. It was the survival of the fittest. That's what Ken Jackson said when he spoke for me in court.'

It was a tale they'd heard often enough before. A man handy with his fists who claimed he had to be. A man prepared to use any means to come out on top in a rough world, where only the quickest and most ruthless survived. Lambert looked at the now animated features steadily for a moment. 'Did you kill Dennis Cooper, Alex?'

He gasped. It was the first time the older man had used his forename, and the sudden switch to the reason why he was here took him by surprise. 'No! Why would I have done that?'

'I was hoping you would tell us that, Alex. Because he was the man who held your future in his hands, perhaps? The man who had the power to deny you this future in the gardening world which you've just told us you passionately want? Had Mr Cooper said that in view of what had happened in Cheltenham you wouldn't be offered permanent work here?'

'No. There was none of that.'

'Then why sneak away from here like a thief in the night before we could question you? Why attract attention to yourself? Wouldn't the normal action have been to keep your head down and get on with your work here?'

Fraser had kept his hands scrupulously still throughout. He was a veteran of police interrogation at the age of twenty, and one of his briefs had told him years ago that it was a good thing to control your hands. It showed them you were calm and unruffled, whatever you were really feeling on the inside. Now his control suddenly broke and he thrust both hands upwards, over the prickles of his short red hair. 'I needed someone I could talk to. Someone I could trust. There was no one like that round here. I needed Ken Jackson.'

'So you shot off from here during the night, without a word to anyone. What advice did Mr Jackson have to offer you?'

'He said the things you've been saying – that it would look bad and I shouldn't have gone up there. So I had a few hours sleep and then came straight back. Arrived here at four o'clock. The bike did well.'

With this touching but irrelevant tribute to his machine, he looked suddenly completely exhausted. Lambert nodded to Hook, who said, 'Where were you on Sunday night, Alex?'

'Sunday?' He looked totally bewildered. He had lost all sense of time with his hours of racing through the summer darkness on two wheels. 'Oh, that's when it happened, isn't it? When Cooper was killed. I was in my room. Reading, I think. I'd played golf at Ross, earlier in the day, before the rain came.'

'Is there anyone who can confirm your whereabouts on Sunday night for us?'

'You don't believe what I've told you, do you? That's because of what I've done in the past, not what I am now.'

Hook said with a professional weariness, 'We've asked everyone the same question, Alex. It's routine.'

Fraser looked at him suspiciously, then said sullenly, 'I was on my own. It was pissing with rain most of the time. I never thought of going out.'

'So who do you think killed the man in charge here?'

'I don't know. If I did, I'd have come and told you, wouldn't I?'

'Would you, though? You're not a man to give much help to the police, are you?'

'Ye don't trust the filth, where I come from.' It was automatic. And it was true enough – it was part of the city culture in which boys in care were reared. Hook leaned forward and said quietly, 'I understand that attitude, Alex. I was a Barnardo's boy myself. I know what it's like to be without a close relative you can trust and turn to in a crisis. But you should realize that this isn't a rumble between gangs. It's more serious than anything you've been involved in before. Give it some thought. If you come up with anything which might help us, it's in your own interest to let us have it immediately. You should go and get some sleep now.'

Alex Fraser looked at him hard, then decided he could take what this copper said at face value. 'No. I'm going back to work. I'll be all right once I'm in the fresh air. There'll be time to sleep tonight.'

John Lambert looked at Hook when the young man had left

them. He'd had a certain presence, despite his youth and his impetuosity in bolting to Scotland. 'He's got violence in him, that lad. Not too far beneath the surface.'

Hook nodded slowly. 'He's needed to be violent, with his background. It's dog eat dog in a lot of council homes. He's trying to make a go of it, to make something of himself. I can understand why he fled to the only man whose advice he trusted. I hope they find him a job here. I reckon he'll give them damn good value in the years to come.'

FOURTEEN

Sometimes things drop into your lap from unexpected sources. The source in this case was one of the voluntary guides at Westbourne, who came in only once or twice a week as required. When she was interviewed, she gave the facts to the most junior DC on the team. He promptly passed them on to DI Rushton and was praised for recognizing their importance.

Alison Cooper was not the grieving widow she had presented to them, or at least not only that. She had been conducting an affair with another man at the time of her husband's death. More importantly, she had concealed this from them when she had spoken to them about her relationship with Dennis Cooper.

'We'll see them simultaneously, Chris,' Lambert decided. 'You take Ruth David with you and see Nayland in his office. Let us know when you're ready to go in and Bert Hook and I will interview her at exactly the same time. It will prevent them from comparing notes.'

Two hours later, Rushton parked his car outside the modest office block in Birmingham which housed the headquarters of the businesses run by Peter Nayland. 'We're ready to go in now, sir,' he told Lambert on his phone. He tried not to look at the alert face of the woman beside him. The cloak-and-dagger phone call made him feel slightly ridiculous, rather as if he had got himself involved in one of the American TV crime series for which he professed such derision.

Nayland's PA was predictably obstructive. 'Mr Nayland has appointments throughout the morning. I might be able to fit you in later today, but you will need to tell me the nature of your business.'

Rushton flashed his warrant card. 'We're police officers pursuing a serious crime investigation. Mr Nayland will see us immediately.' He ignored her protests and was at the door of the inner office before she could intervene. Rushton was conscious not only of her opposition but of the need to display his mastery of the situation to his colleague.

Peter Nayland was sitting alone in the room behind his desk. He looked both surprised and annoyed when the pair burst into the room with his PA still protesting ineffectually behind them. Chris Rushton waved his warrant card and said, 'I'm Detective Inspector Rushton and this is Detective Sergeant David. We need to speak with you in connection with the death of Dennis Cooper.'

Nayland glared at him for a moment, then waved his PA away. 'Make sure we're not disturbed, please. This shouldn't take very long.' He waited until the door was securely closed behind her. Then he looked at Rushton with considerable distaste before transferring his gaze to DS David.

With her ash-blonde hair, green eyes and tall, willowy figure, David complemented the dark-haired Rushton, with his handsome but intense features and his determination to have what he needed from this meeting. Ruth was that object of CID suspicion, a graduate being fast-tracked through the police ranks. But she had proved herself now, and won further credit by electing to stay with John Lambert's team because she felt she was learning fast there. Peter Nayland ran his eyes over her attractive contours and afforded her a broad smile; she reacted with a neutral one of her own which was the product of much practice.

Nayland seated them in the chairs on the opposite side of his desk, sensing that it would be better for him to keep the meeting formal rather than attempt a phoney conviviality. 'I'm always anxious to help the police, but I can't think that I have anything useful to offer here. Cooper, I think that was the name you mentioned. Isn't he the chap who was murdered at the weekend at Westbourne Park?'

Rushton nodded, like a terrier anxious to get at his food. 'Cooper died on Sunday night. And you shouldn't try to distance yourself from a death which is eminently convenient for you.'

Nayland looked hard at his adversary, then down at the decorative silver desk-set in front of him, as if he needed some neutral object to control his anger. 'That phrase "eminently convenient" sounds almost like an accusation, Detective Inspector Rushton. I think you had better explain yourself.'

'Very well. We have reason to think that you have a close relationship with the wife of the murder victim, Mrs Alison Cooper. Perhaps a close enough relationship for you to wish her husband off the scene.'

Nayland leant forward and fingered the silver top of the inkwell in the desk-set, raising it and letting it drop back with a tiny click. 'You don't mince matters. But I suppose as a man with a busy day ahead of him I should welcome that. May I ask how you came by this information?'

'We don't reveal our sources. You must know enough about police procedures by now to be aware of that.'

It was a scarcely veiled insult, but Nayland didn't rise to the bait. 'My relationship with Alison is a private matter.'

'Not any more it isn't.' Rushton spoke with some relish. 'Once you become involved in a murder investigation, very few things remain private.'

'I'm not involved in this murder.'

'You are involved in its investigation, I'm afraid. And you will remain so until we are able to eliminate you from all suspicion of either committing the crime or being in any other way involved in it.'

Nayland looked hard at him, then stroked his neatly trimmed moustache. It was a gesture which had become an aid to thought for him, as well as a help in formulating the words he wished to use. He was more and more irritated by this erect, dark-haired young DI, but he knew well that he mustn't descend into anger. There was too much at stake here for that.

'I can eliminate myself from your enquiries very quickly. I believe this death took place on Sunday evening last. I was in Selly Oak on Sunday evening. Four of us enjoy a poker game once a month. I can give you the address where we met and the names of the people concerned.'

'We shall take those details in due course. They will not eliminate you from our investigation.'

Peter Nayland raised his well-groomed eyebrows and accorded his adversary a disdainful smile. 'Really? This begins to sound very like police harassment.'

'You've been a centre of interest for Birmingham CID officers for several years, as I'm sure you are well aware. You've perpetrated a series of dodgy business deals. You've been involved in drugs, prostitution and wholesale VAT evasions. You use your betting shops and gambling clubs as a means of money laundering. You are suspected of using hit men to eliminate your underworld rivals.'

'And have I been convicted even once of any of these things? In your own interest, you should be aware of the laws of slander, Detective Inspector Rushton.'

The two were bristling with hostility now, making even formal phrases into instruments of attack. Rushton said evenly, 'People who behave as if they are above the law sometimes get away with it, for a time. If they are clever, that time may extend to several years. But eventually they overreach themselves and end up with lengthy custodial sentences. Perhaps this crime will prove to be the point where that happens to you.'

'I've told you where I was on Sunday night. I'd like you to leave now.'

'And I've no doubt you can produce men to swear you were in Selly Oak at the time Dennis Cooper died. Probably people whom you employ.' The briefest flash of irritation on Nayland's face showed that he had scored a hit. 'You may even have been exactly where you say you were, ensuring your alibi for the time when you knew this killing was to take place. When you employ a contract killer to eliminate your enemies, that is a prudent thing to do.'

Peter Nayland's smile of contempt was comprehensive. It

widened to embrace the man in front of him, the woman at his side, the whole of the police service, the world of law and order beyond it. 'You're adding the employment of a contract killer to the other crimes you've thrown at me. It's building up into an impressive catalogue. I'm sure some of your superiors would be interested to read the list.'

'You employed the known hit man George French to kill not one but two men last year. We know that, but the necessary witnesses are much too frightened to come into court and speak against you. You have form, Mr Nayland. It may not yet be official form. It will become that once you overstep the mark and come to court on even one charge. We find rats desert the sinking ship very rapidly in those circumstances.'

DS Ruth David had watched these stags locking horns with interest. Chris Rushton was a quiet man, who sometimes seemed more interested in the efficient documentation of information on his computer than in feeling collars. It was fascinating to see now his real passion in the face of villainy, just as it was to see the veneer of respectable businessman cracking away from Peter Nayland as he was attacked. DS David now said, 'Mr Nayland, you'd better let me have the details of where you were on Sunday night and the people who were with you.'

'Certainly, my dear. I'm a cooperative member of the public anxious to give every help to the enforcers of our laws.'

'And I'm not your dear, but one of those enforcers, Mr Nayland.'

She recorded the names coolly, listening to the heavy breathing of the rival stags in the resulting silence. Then she said, 'As you would expect, our officers will be speaking to Mrs Cooper about her relationship with you, probably at this very moment. We should like to have your description of that relationship.'

His first impulse was to deny them, to tell them to piss off and keep out of his affairs. But he felt no shame about what he proposed for him and Ally – rather the reverse, indeed. In the shady world in which he operated, this was one of the few things unsullied, one of the brighter and better areas of his future. Even to these enemies, he wanted to declare the simple integrity of his feelings for Ally. Love can make people vulnerable, even people like Peter Nayland.

He spoke steadily, even proudly. 'I intend to marry Alison Cooper. That was our intention before the death of her husband. There will now be no need for the delays of divorce. I anticipate that we shall be united in the near future.'

There was something ridiculous but also slightly touching in this avowal from a soiled man like Nayland, thought Ruth David. Perhaps she was a romantic, but after four years of continual involvement with criminals and life's seamier side, she didn't think so.

It was only on the forty-mile drive back to the murder room at Westbourne that DI Rushton pointed out thoughtfully, 'If Nayland was being honest in what he said about Alison Cooper, that gives both of them a stronger motive than ever for this killing.'

'We'll have this out now. Whilst the kids are at school.' Jim Hartley's suntanned face was pale and set. He was determined but very unhappy.

Julie Hartley set a cup of coffee on the low table at his elbow. She had known it would come to this. Sooner or later, they had to have this out. She should have welcomed it, really, but she felt only dread. She said dully, 'You're right. We can't talk about this in front of the children.'

'There shouldn't really be anything to talk about.'

'But there is, Jim. It's a fact of life, and you're right to say that we can't just ignore it.' She was sitting opposite him and she now leaned forward and placed her hand on top of his. 'Jim, none of this is down to you. I know I've hurt you, but I never meant to do that.'

He pulled his hand roughly away from hers. 'It's time you finished with this nonsense. We've got two fine boys and we're a lovely family. Everyone says so.'

'What everyone says and sees isn't always the truth. We *seem* a lovely family from the outside, Jim. We're the only ones who know that it isn't so. And it's not your fault. In so far as it's anyone's, it's mine. The reality is that it's just an unfortunate fact of life. I discovered my real sexual orientation much too late in life. This is a mess, but a mess we can sort out.'

'We can if you come to your senses and realize your responsibilities. And if we're allotting blame, a lot of it must go down to that damned woman who's turned your head!'

'It's not Sarah's fault! You can leave her out of this!'

She had flown instantly to the defence of her lover. Jim realized that he had made a mistake in mentioning Sarah Goodwin, but her reaction had wounded him anew. He was so sick with emotion that he had no idea what to do, what were the best tactics for him in this situation. He had never imagined anything like this could happen to him.

All the arguments he'd meant to present coolly came tumbling out as he clawed at his distress. 'I'll fight you for the boys! You won't take them away from me! Maybe I'll still have you back, when you come to your senses. The lads need a mother.'

Julie felt acutely sorry for him. But she couldn't help him, could she? Not without compromising the thing which mattered most of all to her. She wanted to throw herself across the small space between them, to kneel at his feet, to put her arms round his knees, hug him and mutter consoling words, as one would do to a suffering child.

But she did none of these things. Jim would misinterpret them wouldn't he? He'd think she was 'coming to her senses'. And then she'd have to tell him that it wasn't so and hurt him all over again. She said miserably, 'I agree it's a mess. I agree none of it is your fault. But I love Sarah, and I can't alter that. I love you too, but in a different sort of way. Sarah and I will make a home together and we'll look after Sam and Oliver. They'll always be your boys. You'll be able to see them whenever you want to.'

'The boys are happy here. They love it here. They'll stay with me.'

His face set, immovable as granite. Julie said gently, 'Children are best with their mother, Jim. The courts will take that line, if it comes to it. But I hope we can agree something sensible between ourselves.'

'Between the three of us, you mean? You'll bring that woman

into it, won't you? She's good with words, so you'll throw her in against me when it comes to the arguments. She's cleverer with books and plays and music than a simple sod like me. That's what's turned your head. That's why you won't listen to reason.'

'That isn't true, Jim. And I won't bring Sarah into any of the arguments. She wouldn't want that and neither do I.' She felt wretched, felt weighed down with guilt at what she was doing, but she knew that she mustn't back off, mustn't leave him with any illusion that there might yet be room for compromise.

He had no arguments left, or none that he could think of. The reasoned approaches he had been planning for weeks had flown from him, once he was sitting opposite the face and the body he loved and hearing that Julie was determined to take them from him. He looked hopelessly into the brown eyes and white face in their frame of long black hair, then threw in the only line he could think of. 'I'll lose my job here.'

'Why should you do that?'

'You'll make a laughing stock of me if you leave me like this. They'll say I'm not up to the job.'

'Your private life has nothing to do with being a head gardener.'

'But it has, when you're the head gardener and in charge of a lot of young people. Dennis Cooper thought that. He said the National Trust was a very conservative association and would want a resident family here. He said I should sort out this situation and restore you to sanity.'

'That's ridiculous!' But as she sent him miserably back into his gardens, Julie Hartley thought that those phrases weren't Jim's. They sounded very much as if they might have come from Dennis Cooper.

'I did warn you that we would need to speak to you again when we knew more about the people involved in this crime. We are now three days into the investigation and we have reached that stage. We have studied your husband's files and also some of the private thoughts recorded in a small notebook he kept.'

Alison Cooper heard the challenge in Lambert's voice and she was acutely aware of his watching her every reaction. Her own voice seemed to come from some distance away as she said, 'I understand that. I am of course willing to give you all the help I can, but I don't anticipate that I shall be able to advance your progress.'

She had planned these words earlier, but they emerged as over-elaborate and evasive. She waited for a reaction, but the two grave-faced men gave her nothing. She said nervously, 'Are you near to making an arrest?'

Lambert smiled. 'We should be much nearer if people like you chose to be honest, Mrs Cooper.' He watched her for a couple of seconds as she struggled for a denial, then said quietly, 'Perhaps you should know that officers in the murder team are at this moment speaking to Mr Peter Nayland.'

Her head reeled. Peter had said that it might come to this and he had advised her what she should do if it did. But in her shock she could not remember his instructions. She said stupidly, 'You know about us?'

'We do. And we shall shortly know much more.'

He made that sound very ominous. Perhaps it was his words, combined with the look of challenge on the long, lined face, that brought her back to her senses. They knew that she had been conducting an extramarital affair, but nothing more than that, did they? They couldn't arrest you for something which was going on all over the country. She said carefully, 'I didn't tell you about Peter when we spoke on Monday because our relationship had nothing to do with Dennis's murder.'

'You must be aware that your concealment of it now shows you in a very bad light. You lied to us about where you were and asked your friend Carrie North to support your story. You could have landed her with very serious charges. Do you believe your affair with Mr Nayland will involve a long-term commitment?'

What a roundabout phrase for something very simple! Peter was going to be the love of her life, all the sweeter for being discovered so unexpectedly when she had reached the age of forty-nine. She wasn't going to deny what was a source of pride to her. She said quietly, 'Peter and I are serious. I don't think either of us expected that when we first slept together, so it has come as a very welcome surprise. After a decent interval, we shall get married and spend the rest of our lives together.'

Lambert nodded, then said calmly, 'Unless of course one or both of you were involved in the despatch of your husband. The mandatory sentence for murder is life imprisonment.'

Alison knew she couldn't be as dispassionate as he was, but she could try to match his steely hostility. 'We needn't fear that. Neither of us had anything to do with Dennis's death.'

Lambert did not offer her even an assenting nod. Instead, he said almost eagerly, 'Mr Cooper's death was a highly convenient occurrence for you.'

'I don't dispute that. But it has merely made things more straightforward for us. It has avoided the necessity of a messy divorce.'

'Your husband was a Catholic. He would no doubt have opposed divorce.'

She was shocked anew. It was a small fact, but one she did not think they would have known. But they'd talked to a lot of people since Monday, as they'd told her they would do, and they'd had access to Dennis's private papers. Plus that damned black notebook. She said evenly, 'Dennis was a practising Catholic. I am not. He would have opposed divorce, thrown in all sorts of arguments about his work here and the National Trust frowning upon a publicized divorce. But he wouldn't have won.'

'Things are much more straightforward with him out of the way.'

'Much more.' She spoke with a satisfaction which was almost truculent, then hastened to be more humble. 'But it wasn't a reason to kill Dennis. The idea that we would do that is preposterous.'

'And murder is a preposterous crime. People often ignore much simpler solutions. They feel frustrated and do things they wouldn't do if they were acting coolly and sensibly. How much do you know about this man you are planning to marry?'

The suddenness of the switch unnerved her. It was a new front in his attack and it was one she had not anticipated. And they had discovered a weakness. It set starkly before her what she had thrust to the back of her mind. She had been excited by this man who had declared his serious love for her, but she knew very little about him. She said grimly, 'I know quite enough for my purposes. I know that Peter Nayland loves me and that he will treat me well.'

'Perhaps.'

Lambert waited so long that she felt an overwhelming desire to fill the pause with words. But she could think of nothing sensible to say; the reality was that she knew little or nothing of Peter's background except that he was long divorced, wealthy and free to marry her. Eventually he said, 'Do you know where he was on Sunday night?'

'No. But he wasn't here, killing Dennis.'

'You're almost certainly right. Mr Nayland employs other people to do his dirty work. If you are as ignorant as you claim to be about him, we know far more than you do about that.'

'He's a successful businessman.' Alison bit her lip and twisted it between her teeth, realizing how futile that sounded, how little she could add to it.

'We would prefer to say that he is successful in some very dubious businesses. He has been under investigation by the Serious Crime Division for some time now. Did he tell you about that?'

'No. Perhaps he isn't aware of it.'

'He's well aware of it. He takes pains to cover his tracks.'

'Perhaps there aren't tracks to be covered. You seem to be finding it very difficult to bring Peter to court.'

'It will happen. People like him always overreach themselves. Maybe he has done that this time.'

'Peter has nothing to do with this crime.'

The clear grey eyes looked at her speculatively, seeming to Alison to be able to see much more than she would have wished. 'You sound very sure of that. If you could convince us, it would help all of us.'

It was tempting. She could say they had been together, give both of them an alibi. The police might not like that, but it would be difficult for them to disprove it. But at this very moment, Peter might be telling other officers a different tale.

They were deep in this already – he had warned her that the spouse of a murder victim was always a leading suspect, and these men had pointed out how convenient this death was for her and her plans. She couldn't afford to be caught out in a lie. She said as firmly as she could, 'I'm quite sure Peter didn't commit this crime, because I know the man I've agreed to marry. I don't know where he was on Sunday night, but I'd be confident he was nowhere near here.'

'You are almost certainly right. I've already indicated to you that he isn't a man who does his own dirty work. He uses other people when he thinks violence is required. It's expensive, but he can well afford it.'

Lambert did not disguise his contempt. It was a shock to her, to hear the police talk about Peter like this, an unwelcome glimpse of that business world which he had never explained and which she had always been content to leave vague. She said boldly, 'You would need to prove that. I am confident you will not be able to do so.'

She waited for a comment on this from Lambert, but it was Hook who suddenly said, 'We now know that you didn't spend the night of the murder with Carrie North, as you claimed on Monday. Where were you on Sunday night, Mrs Cooper?'

She felt her heart beating faster, though she had always known that this question must come. She looked round at the large, comfortable room, at the old-fashioned three-piece suite which Dennis had always said was too comfortable to replace, at the large black-and-white photograph of Westbourne around 1900, when there had been a house here but no real garden. The room seemed suddenly an alien place, full of danger, where once there had been only dullness. 'I was here. I read a book for a while. Then I watched a little television.'

She wondered if they would ask for an account of the programmes. But all Hook said was, 'And where was Mr Cooper?'

'He was here too.'

'But not for the whole evening, obviously.'

She stared at the Persian carpet she had never liked. She'd be rid of it when she moved out of here and in with Peter. Why was the mind always a maverick when you wanted it to concentrate hard on the questions of this seemingly sympathetic detective sergeant? 'No. We'd had a bit of a row.'

'About Peter Nayland?'

'No. About life here. He liked it and I didn't. We were very different people; it was coming here that made that more apparent to us. I suppose I was telling him that as well as not liking my life here I didn't like him.'

Hook was annoyingly slow with his note of this, so that she became conscious again of her heart thumping. Eventually the experienced but curiously innocent face looked up at her and said, 'Did he know about your feelings for Peter Nayland?'

She'd prepared an answer for this, but she hadn't expected it to come up in the context of her row with Dennis. She forced herself to speak slowly. 'I don't think he did. I can't be certain. Dennis was a man who gathered information and enjoyed it. He liked to know all about his employees, whether his information was relevant to their work here or not. A lot of the time it wasn't, but he said you never knew when knowledge might come in useful. He said you could never have too much of it.' Her contempt for the dead man came leaping out as she curled her lips over these last phrases.

Hook again irritated her by making a detailed note of this. Then he said, 'Were you aware that he kept some of this information in the notebook Superintendent Lambert mentioned earlier?'

She wanted to deny any knowledge of it. But that would hardly be convincing. She said carefully, 'A small black notebook?'

'That would be the one.'

'I saw him with it. I even saw him write something in it, on one occasion. But I never read anything he wrote. I wasn't very interested, to tell you the truth – as I've told you, we were growing apart. I think he usually kept that little book under lock and key at work.'

Hook knew that they hadn't found it there, and he didn't believe that she'd never been interested in its contents, but there was no point in pursuing that now – she would merely repeat what she'd stated. He said calmly, 'You said you argued with each other on Sunday evening. What happened after that?'

This was the key point. She felt curiously calm, glad that

they had at last arrived at it. 'I've told you what I did. Dennis went away into his study, as he often did when we'd had words. After a while, he came and said he was going out.'

'At what time?'

'It must have been somewhere around nine o'clock. Perhaps a little later. It was still daylight, but pretty gloomy after the storm.'

'Did he say where he was going?'

'No. And I didn't ask. Neither of us was inclined to say more than the minimum.' She felt a sudden stab of emotion that she should have treated him coldly during their final contact, but she tried not to show it, lest they thought her a hypocrite or a deliberate dissembler.

Hook looked her steadily in the face, his brown eyes seeming now larger and more observant. 'So Mr Cooper went out and never came back. Yet you saw fit to inform no one that he had disappeared.'

She had her answer ready. It was curious how assured she felt as she delivered it. 'That's because I didn't know he hadn't come back. He hadn't told me where he was going. I thought perhaps he'd met one of the other residents and been invited into their quarters. Or that he'd gone off to the pub in the village – anything to get away from me. I was mildly surprised when he wasn't back by eleven, but no more than that. I went to bed and went to sleep. I wasn't aware that he hadn't returned until early the next morning, when someone hammered on my door to tell me what had happened.'

Hook nodded as he wrote, then looked hard into her face again. 'Who do you think killed Mr Cooper?'

'I've no idea. I've thought hard about it, as no doubt everyone else has.' She paused. 'As I told you, my late husband was fond of gathering up information about people. Perhaps someone resented that.'

She accompanied them to the door, then said with cool challenge, 'I hope you arrest someone for this soon. That will allow Peter Nayland and me to get on with the rest of our lives together.'

FIFTEEN

Lorna Green was clearing the house of the rubbish which accumulates over the years. Rubbish was the word she had chosen to use, to make herself more ruthless. Much of this stuff had once been precious; some of it had been useful; a little of it had been merely interesting. But yesterday's pleasures were today's detritus, she told herself firmly.

Some day, perhaps much sooner than she anticipated, Barbara Green would either die or need more care than her daughter could give her. When that happened, Lorna wouldn't stay in the family home any longer. She would move into a small modern house or flat. You had to face up to these things and make your preparations for them. If it also seemed a good thing to get rid of anything which might connect her with Dennis Cooper, that of course was quite incidental.

This afternoon, she had settled her mother down for her nap and was clearing out old photographs. She would keep the three albums of pictures she had carefully mounted over the years, but get rid of all the loose snaps; if they had been of any real and lasting interest she would have put them in the albums at the time, wouldn't she? Nevertheless, Lorna found as most of us do that she lingered over the task.

There is something very evocative about visual images from our past. Half-forgotten faces and the places from which they smile conjure up whole episodes, which are part of our past and thus part of us. When we know that we are discarding them for ever, we spend longer than we planned to do before ejecting a part of ourselves. And so it was with Lorna Green.

She smiled quietly at black-and-white pictures of her father, with a full head of hair and that mischievous grin which turned up the left-hand side of his mouth – he was much younger here than she was now. It was good to see him looking so vigorous, so full of anticipation of the rest of his life. And here was another one with her mother beside him, alert and humorous in a way she would never be again. But Lorna told herself firmly that there were better ones in the albums, and resolutely flung the fading images into the bin bag she had brought to the task.

And here was Dennis Cooper, in vivid colour, smiling and masterful, with his arm round her waist and a look of proud possession upon his face. She hadn't been through these loose photographs for ages and she was surprised how many she had of Dennis. There was one of them leaning on their bikes somewhere in the country – she couldn't remember exactly where, and there was only a hedge and a stand of beech trees behind them. She wondered who had taken that. She'd never been a great cyclist and it was a long time now since she had ridden a bike – not since the days of Dennis, in fact.

'You should have married him!'

Lorna started violently at her mother's voice. She had been so immersed in her memories that she hadn't heard her come into the room. She said automatically, 'Did you have a nice rest, Mum?'

Barbara Green picked up another photograph of Dennis Cooper, taken when he was leaning back hard on the oars of a rowing boat on the river, revelling in his exertion and his expertise. He'd rowed at school and at university, and he'd enjoyed surprising Lorna with his skills. Lorna said in surprise, 'You think I should have married Dennis Cooper? You didn't say that at the time.'

'You were right for each other, you two. I thought you realized that, but you must have thought you could do better.' Barbara sniffed derisively and picked up a snapshot of her dead husband, leaning on a five-barred gate with his pipe in his hand. 'Who's that? Another of your men, is it?'

Lorna took her mother's hand and detached the picture gently from it. 'That's my Dad. That's your husband, Mum. Wally. You must remember.'

She caught the desperation in her own voice. Barbara repeated 'Husband?' as if it were an alien word. She put down the picture without another glance and picked up a dog-eared one of a young Lorna and her sister Debbie. 'They look nice children. Children used to be nicer, you know, in the old days.'

Lorna put the picture down with the others, on top of all the ones of Dennis Cooper. She slid the complete collection determinedly into the black rubbish bag. 'Yes, Mum. A lot of things used to be nicer, in the old days.'

'Come in and sit down, Mr Wilkinson. We have things to discuss.' Lambert's words sounded ominous. He waved an arm at the single upright chair in front of the desk in the murder room.

Hugo reacted with a characteristic aggression. 'You Sherlocks found who killed Cooper yet?'

'We know a lot more than when we last spoke with you.'

The chef curled his lip at this evasion. 'Observation and deduction, you know. Those were Holmes's principles.'

'And very sound they were. Conan Doyle derived them from the best detective practices of his day. But there may still be room for the gifted amateur, if you fancy the role, Mr Wilkinson. No doubt you have been busy observing. Have you brought us any useful deductions?'

'Not my place, is it? I've deduced that the police are baffled. But not a lot beyond that.'

'Not quite baffled. We are moving nearer to an arrest. We have been able to eliminate most of the people on site from suspicion. Unfortunately that number does not include you.'

Hugo was beginning to regret his aggressive stance. He'd had a hectic lunch hour in the restaurant, when two people had sent meals back into his kitchen with adverse comments; he'd had to go out among the tables and be publicly apologetic. No chef enjoys that; it is the nadir of his professional life. But he shouldn't have brought his resentment into this quiet room, where his opponents held most of the cards. He said, 'I didn't kill Cooper, so I've nothing to fear.'

'Unless we prove as inefficient as the police inspectors portrayed in the Sherlock Holmes stories.' Lambert bestowed a grim smile on the man isolated on his upright chair. 'I said we knew a lot more than when we last spoke to you. Did you ever see a small black notebook in Mr Cooper's hands?'

'No.'

'He was a secretive man. You indicated as much to us when

we last spoke. I think you said that he liked to gather information about the people who worked for him. You will not be surprised to find that you were included.'

'No. I'm not surprised that Cooper kept notes on people. Nevertheless, what you say comes as something of a shock, because you don't think of yourself as a subject for busybodies. I can only think he must have found me a very dull subject for his curiosity.'

'On the contrary, you were one of the most interesting of all to him. There are several entries about you, with dates carefully recorded. Nor do I believe that this comes as the shock you claim it is.'

Hugo had been watching Lambert's face ever since he sat down. Now he saw real challenge in the grey, unblinking eyes. 'I don't know what you're talking about. I've never seen this blasted black notebook and I can't believe he recorded anything significant about me in it.'

'Child pornography, Mr Wilkinson.'

Hugo felt the blood draining from his face. 'You must have me confused with someone else. I tell you again that I've no idea what you're talking about.'

'Oh, but you have, Mr Wilkinson.' The repetition of the surname rang like an accusing note across the desk. Lambert was not a conventional policeman, but in this respect he was typical. He had nothing but revulsion for the increasing number of men and the surprising number of women who used helpless children for their sexual gratification. He did not even pretend neutrality now. 'The group which you regularly attend is currently under investigation. There is as yet no national computer register of those engaged in this criminal practice, a deplorable situation which is now receiving attention. The details recorded in Mr Cooper's notebook have been passed to the officers investigating the indecent videos distributed to you and to others.'

Hugo thought of the material in his room. He felt the acute need of a lawyer at his elbow. He had been transformed from truculent interviewee with nothing to fear to abject offender within a few minutes. He scratched at his brain for the words the group leader had told them to use if accusations were levelled. He said dully, 'I deny all of this. I have no further comment to make.'

'Which is no doubt very wise. Fortunately for all of us, child pornography is not our business here. Except in so far as it affects the investigation of the murder of Dennis Cooper.'

'Which is not at all. Dennis was a nosy sod and I won't pretend that I'm sorry someone's got rid of him. But these outrageous allegations – and that is all they are – have nothing to do with his death.'

'You won't expect us to take your word for that, especially in view of what we now know about you. What did Mr Cooper say to you about your paedophile activities?'

'He didn't say anything. What you have told me this afternoon is the first intimation I have had that he even knew I had been to these meetings. Perfectly innocent meetings of our photographic group, incidentally.' Belatedly, he remembered the cover story they had agreed against the possibility of questioning.

'We believe Mr Cooper spoke to you about paedophilia, Mr Wilkinson. On the Wednesday before he died.'

Lambert was chancing his arm. There had been merely an asterisk against the name and the date June 29th beside it. But the detail convinced Hugo Wilkinson that the man on the other side of the desk knew everything. He nodded hopelessly, then said abjectly, 'He said he knew all about me. That he wouldn't be able to keep me on here unless I could convince him this was perfectly innocent. He reminded me again about the racialism incident in my kitchens and said there'd be no question of the Trust continuing to employ a paedophile.'

'And you assured him that these were merely the innocent meetings of men with a common interest in photography.' Lambert didn't trouble to disguise the irony. It fell into a heavy silence, which he waited in vain for Wilkinson to break. 'Did you arrange to meet Dennis Cooper on Sunday night or did you meet him by chance as you walked in the grounds?'

There was real fear now in the face which had earlier been so combative. 'Neither of those. I didn't meet him and I didn't kill him.'

Bert Hook made a note of this, then looked at their quarry

with a face which was determinedly neutral. 'Mr Wilkinson, don't leave Westbourne Park without informing us of any intended destination. You may in due course receive a visit from officers in connection with a quite different investigation. You would be most unwise to communicate with other members of your group; an attempt to warn them might well be construed as an admission of guilt. Do you understand?'

Hugo Wilkinson nodded, not trusting himself to speak, and left them without another word. The two experienced men left in the room looked at each other in silence for a moment. Then Hook said, 'What will you tell the team tomorrow morning?'

Lambert smiled grimly. 'I'll remind them of their professional duties. I'll tell them that however much we'd all like to see a paedophile arrested for murder we mustn't assume anything. We now know this man had a strong motive and the opportunity for murder. We have as yet no compelling evidence of his guilt. We must pursue our investigation of everyone else involved in this as assiduously as if Hugo Wilkinson did not exist.'

In the room where he had endured his meeting with the CID during the morning, Peter Nayland prepared himself for very different visitors in the late afternoon.

They were due to arrive at five fifteen. At five o'clock, he went into the adjoining office where his PA sat. 'You can go now, Anne. Give yourself the rest of the day off – what little of it is left.'

'I was just going to finish these letters, Mr Nayland.'

'They're not urgent. They'll keep till tomorrow. You put in plenty of extra time, when you need to. Give yourself half an hour.'

Anne's tidy mind told her that she would rather finish the day's work and begin with a clean desk on Thursday. But she knew her employer well enough to recognize that this concession was in effect a command. She wondered who might be coming in to see him and what their business might be, but she knew that the sensible thing to do was to pretend she had no knowledge of them. 'Thank you, sir. I'll give my husband a surprise, then – hopefully a pleasant one!'

Each of them smiled at her little joke, each of them waited whilst she gathered her handbag and short summer coat and made the quickest exit she could.

The two men came ten minutes after she had left. They were stocky, swarthy and strong: good Welsh mining stock, as the one who had grown up in the Rhondha Valley was prone to say. He wondered sometimes whether he might have been at the pit-face rather than the crime-face, if Thatcher and her crew hadn't seen off the mining industry in the eighties. 'Alternative employment' they'd said he should seek. Get on yer bike and find it. Well, he'd certainly found it.

Peter Nayland was different from the other men who had used him. Not many people who used muscle to further their business careers ever met the hard men whose violence they purchased. Perhaps they were able to persuade themselves they were not using such methods, so long as they did not have to set eyes upon the instruments involved. Perhaps they found it easier to deny all knowledge of illegal acts, so long as their orders had been relayed by others.

Peter Nayland had always been a businessman who boasted about his 'hands-on' methods. He liked to see the people he employed, to let them know that he was aware of what they were doing and that he expected the highest standards from them. Efficiency was demanded, even when brutality was the task. And he'd always thought it best not to put orders in writing, when directing men like this.

These men certainly looked as if they would be efficient. They sat uneasily in front of his desk, making the upright chairs look too small for the weight allotted to them. Nayland looked them up and down, gave them the briefest of smiles. 'Have you dealt with the Atwal situation?'

Atwal was a hardworking Asian retailer who had built up a chain of shops in Smethwick; he had lately seen fit to expand daringly beyond the unofficial borders of his area into Nayland territory. He had even been bold enough to open a rival betting shop. He had failed to respond to verbal warnings and thus invited something more physical.

It was the Welshman Griffith who took it upon himself to answer the boss's questions. The two men were paid the same, but he had recruited his henchman and it seemed that longer service gave him seniority. He said, 'We've done what you suggested. Knocked his stock about and emptied the till in the newest three of his shops.' He wasn't going to claim success, not yet. They could be stubborn buggers, these Pakis. Personally, he'd have gone in on the man himself, from the start; no sense in half-measures, in his view.

'Will he report it to the police?'

'No. He's got more sense. He knows we'll be round to the rest of his shops if he does that. Once things have quietened down, of course.' He added the last phrase to show the boss that they weren't just muscle men, but professionals who recognized the need for caution. Griffith wasn't stupid. Men who grew fast like Nayland always needed more violence, not less, as they expanded. You might end up in charge of his enforcement section, if you stayed with it and played your cards right.

The man behind the big desk nodded, stroking his moustache briefly as he ticked off the first item on his list. 'Did you attend to Williams?'

'Thursday night. We knocked him about a bit, as per your orders.'

Nayland looked at him hard. 'Where is he now?'

'He's in hospital. Four ribs, a broken arm, pelvic damage.' He reeled the injuries off as accurately and dispassionately as if he were announcing football scores. 'He's got the message.'

'And what's he told the police?'

'Nothing. He was half-pissed at the time. We took his wallet and made it look like a mugging. The police seem to have it down as that: they haven't given it much priority.'

'And hopefully Williams will have got the message. What about Jean Calhoun?'

Calhoun was as hard as any man. She owned a casino and was planning more. She had her own muscle, though so far they had been used only against small people who got in her way and not in direct conflict with the thugs employed by her rivals. Nayland was old-fashioned in one respect at least: he was reluctant to use direct physical violence against a woman. But he knew it might come to that, if she continued to extend the boundaries of her empire. Griffith said with a pride he could hardly conceal, 'We knifed her dog in the woods. She came round the corner and found him dying on the path. Golden retriever. Never uttered a whimper.' It was not clear whether he regarded this as evidence of cowardice in the dog or skill in its dispatcher.

'Will she get the message?'

'Should do. She was very attached to that dog. She'll know why it was killed. Good method of getting at her, we thought, since you said we weren't to touch her.' He could no longer conceal his pride in the subtlety of his thinking and the swift proficiency of its execution.

'Has she reported it?'

'She's told the police. It won't get any priority. The RSPCA will have a bleat in the local press, but that won't have any effect. There are plenty of dog haters as well as dog lovers in this country.' He delivered this view as if it were evidence of a virile nation.

'What's the latest on Mowbray?' He'd left his biggest concern until the last.

'Not much to report. His new lap-dancing club is supposed to be doing well. More upmarket, less sleazy. Word is he's been boasting about taking over some of your assets next year. It's difficult to get near Mowbray. He's got his own muscle. Perhaps it's time to take him out.'

It was a daring suggestion for Griffith. The boss made his own decisions, you implemented them. You didn't put forward your own solutions. Nayland glanced at him sharply. 'Not yet. I've told you, killing a man is the last resort. It gets the fuzz interested big-time. We monitor the situation. If and when I decide we need to liquidate Mowbray, I'll bring in a specialist. Understood?'

Griffith shrugged, glanced quickly at the man beside him. 'Understood. We'll monitor the situation.' He dwelt a little on the phrase, as if committing it to memory. 'Then we'll report to you.'

Nayland nodded, mentally ticking off the fourth and last item on his list. He gave them two other names for attention in the coming weeks, arranged to see them again in a month, and dismissed them back into the summer evening which seemed so inappropriate a cover for them. He felt a contempt for them and their violence, even though he was the man employing it. Like Macbeth's contempt for the men he hired to murder Banquo, he thought wryly. He'd been quite well educated at his private school; he was glad of that when he was with the woman he planned to make his wife.

He locked the office and left, feeling his spirits lift as he slipped into his other and more welcome role of suitor. He was a different and a better man with Ally. Perhaps in due course, when he'd made enough money, he'd give up the seamier side of his life and concentrate on legitimate business.

He kept a close eye on his rear mirror as he drove out of Birmingham at the tail end of the rush hour. He didn't think he was under police surveillance. He doubted if they had the manpower for that. In any case, he'd nothing to fear if they saw him meeting Ally. He'd told them all about his feelings for the woman he was going to marry.

He'd only been in 'their' pub in Broadway for two minutes when she arrived. That was one of the many things he liked about her: she didn't keep you waiting as a policy, as lots of women did. He rose and kissed her lightly on the lips when she arrived, then settled her comfortably into her seat beside the gin and tonic he had already ordered for her. He enjoyed squiring his lady; his careful politeness might seem a little silly in a man of fifty-six, but to him it seemed all part of this other and more admirable life he was embarking upon with Ally.

She smiled at him, ran a manicured finger round the top of her glass, glanced round the large, thinly peopled room. 'This is where we were spotted, you know.'

'Yes. I suppose it was inevitable, sooner or later.'

'It was one of the voluntary workers at Westbourne, the people who come in to give talks and act as guides. I don't even know some of them. She recognized me, but I might not recognize her.'

He put his hand on top of hers, feeling how tense she was. 'It doesn't matter, does it? The police know all about us now. We can handle it.'

'You might be able to. You're used to it.' She looked at him resentfully, feeling Dennis's death between them, dividing them like a physical barrier.

'Did the police give you a hard time?'

She found she didn't want to tell him about it. For an instant, she wanted to hug her humiliation close to herself. But she shouldn't have secrets from Peter, not if she was going to be with him for the rest of her life. 'They made it a big thing that I hadn't told them about you when they saw me on Monday. Gave me the impression that anything else I now have to say will be treated with suspicion.'

'They were bound to do that. They use anything which will give them the edge, when they're questioning you.'

'You know a lot more about their methods than I do.' It sounded like an accusation. She took a gulp of her gin and tonic, refusing to look at him.

'I know a little more, yes.'

'I don't know how you make your money, you know. I used to feel it was none of my business. I suppose it is, now.'

'It's pretty dull stuff. You'll gradually get to know more, as we go along. Meantime, we've got more interesting things to do.' He willed Ally to look at him, with her head on one side and the dark-blonde hair above the very blue eyes. That was the way he always pictured her, when she wasn't with him. When she eventually did look up, she gave him a rather bleak smile which made her seem very vulnerable. He said carefully, 'I'll introduce you to some of the better stuff when you're ready. I don't think you'll find it very interesting.'

Alison wondered about the other stuff, the stuff which wasn't for her. 'They said you had an alibi for Sunday night, for the time when Dennis was killed.'

He tried to smile it away, but she wouldn't look at him. 'I'm not sure we should be talking about "alibis", should we? But yes, I was playing poker with some of my friends. I was nowhere near the scene of the crime.'

'Whereas I have no such proof. And now they know that I lied to them on the day Dennis's body was discovered.'

'I'm sure they don't suspect you.'

'They pointed out how convenient Dennis's death is for

both of us. They implied you'd been pretty near to arrest before, but too wily to be caught.'

He found himself flattered by that word 'wily', in spite of himself. 'I expect they're prepared to blacken people, if it helps to put pressure on the person they're talking to.'

Alison sighed. A long, dismissive sigh. She said determinedly, 'I think we've talked enough about the police. Tell me about the rest of our lives.'

'That's better. Let's plan our wedding. We haven't talked about it yet. No more talk about Dennis's death.'

After all, as he'd told Griffith a couple of hours earlier, you only killed people when it was absolutely necessary.

SIXTEEN

Julie Hartley chose to see them in her own house. She hadn't enjoyed venturing into the murder room, which she had always known as the curator's office, for her meeting on Tuesday. Perhaps the CID men wouldn't make her so nervous if she met them in her own familiar sitting room.

She quickly found that the room mattered hardly at all. It was their line of questioning which discomforted her.

It was true that Lambert and Hook both looked round the room she had carefully prepared for them with interest. She had made a few changes, setting things up to give the air of a quiet, unremarkable, family room. She'd brought out the wedding photograph which had been relegated to the spare room for the last few months and put it on top of the television. Jim looked even more awkward in his morning dress than she remembered, smiling shyly but proudly at the camera with his new wife on his arm, waiting patiently for the photographer to release them.

She'd put the pictures of the children and their grandparents on the mantelpiece above the brick fireplace, alongside the picture of Jim with the Rose Bowl he had won at their first flower show, long before they had come to Westbourne. She had been aiming at a happy jumble of domesticity, to support what she had told them about her life two days earlier. The three-piece lounge suite fitted well into the low-ceilinged cottage. It was of decent quality but moderately worn, as innocent, respectable family use determined it should be. The coloured photographs of Kew Gardens in spring, summer and autumn reinforced that impression. Jim had served his apprenticeship at Kew.

She had selected a dark-blue shirt and navy trousers, combed her long dark hair, and prepared herself to play the dutiful housewife and mother, the roles she had declared to the CID on Tuesday.

Lambert's first words shattered her preparations and her calm. 'We know a lot more about you than we did, Mrs Hartley. It would have been much better for all of us if you had spoken frankly when we saw you on Tuesday.'

'I – I told you everything you needed to know.'

'You told us what you had decided to tell us. You concealed information. That was at best unwise, at worst sinister.'

She felt first fear, then an overwhelming relief that she was going to be able to speak about her new life; it was a strange sequence and it threatened to unbalance her judgement. She could not think what she should be telling them now. Eventually she managed to say, 'You know about Sarah.'

Lambert watched her closely and said in a carefully neutral voice, 'I think you had better give us your own version of this.'

'It's a mess. And I am the person responsible for the mess. But I don't see how it could have been avoided. The whole of my sheltered upbringing, the whole of my schooling and the people I knew then, told me that the thing to do was to get married and get myself a family. Oh, I know you're allowed to have a career as well nowadays, but family life is the norm. Even politicians are now trying to tell us that.'

Lambert had heard enough of this. He didn't want her to develop this well-rehearsed apologia for her situation. He said tersely, 'We're not here to take moral stances. We're interested in whatever bears upon the murder of Dennis Cooper. When you lied about your situation, it excited our attention.'

'Then I apologize. I concealed my feelings for Sarah

Goodwin from you; I didn't want her dragged into this because she has nothing to do with it.'

'Dennis Cooper knew about the relationship and was trying to disrupt it. That makes it highly relevant.'

'He wouldn't have succeeded.'

Julie was concentrating all her efforts on trying to convince Lambert, but it was the stolid DS Hook who unexpectedly said, 'Where were you on Sunday night, Mrs Hartley?'

'I told you that on Tuesday.'

'You told us then that you were at home with your husband and the boys. Do you now wish to revise that?'

This was like a card game where you were trying to make the most of a poor hand. They knew far more than she did and would take the trick if she blundered. She couldn't look the man in his annoyingly placid face as she said dully, 'I was at home with Jim and the boys for part of the evening, as I said. But I did go out. We had a row, you see, Jim and I.. A row about Sarah Goodwin. And it was her I went to see.'

Hook looked hard at her. 'Times, please.'

'I can't be certain. I think I stormed out at about nine. I didn't get back until after midnight. I wanted to be sure Jim was in bed.' She paused, watching him record the times with irritating slowness. 'That takes away my alibi, I suppose.'

'And your husband's.'

'Jim didn't kill Cooper. I'm sure of that.' She felt a surge of loyalty for the man she had hurt so much.

Lambert said crisply, 'How can you be sure? Do you know who did this?' She shook her head dumbly. 'Did you kill him yourself?'

'No.' She roused herself for a show of aggression. 'Why on earth would I do that?'

'Because he knew all about your feelings for Sarah Goodwin. Because he was putting pressure on you to abandon the affair.'

It was the word Jim had used, the word which had set them yelling at each other more fiercely than they had ever done before. She hadn't taken it from Jim, and she wasn't going to take it from this cold-eyed dissector of human passions. 'It isn't an affair! It's much more serious and permanent than an affair!'

'All right. So when it was threatened by Cooper, you were even more inflamed than you are now.'

She didn't know how they had discovered that Cooper knew about her and Sarah, but she was past rational, analytical thought, past deciding on what she could and could not conceal from these men who seemed to know so much about her. What she had thought of as her secrets were now on the table. 'Dennis said my "association" with Sarah wasn't on, that he wouldn't stand by and see Jim made a laughing stock. When I said it wasn't his business, he said that he'd make it so. He said the Trust wouldn't continue to employ Jim as its head gardener here if I left him and set up house with Sarah.'

'Could he have arranged that? Would he have even tried, if you had called his bluff?'

'I don't know. Perhaps you're right and I should have defied him. But he said it would destroy not only Jim's life but the boys' lives as well if I continued with what he called my "madcap enterprise". I certainly believed him at the time.' She looked round the quiet, low-ceilinged, cottage room. 'I came here and sobbed my heart out after I'd spoken to him. I felt quite desperate.'

'Desperate enough to kill Cooper, when the opportunity presented itself on Sunday night.'

Lambert made it sound more like a statement rather than a question. Julie's senses raced as she sought a way out. 'No. I went to Sarah's house on Sunday night. She'll confirm that for you.'

'I expect she will. Perhaps she will also confirm that you arrived in a very excited state, having dispatched the man who was threatening you.'

Julie wondered what exactly Sarah would tell them. She could picture her distress, see the too-revealing blue eyes opening wide beneath the short fair hair. Sarah wouldn't want to let her down, but there was no knowing what she might say under this sort of examination. Julie said slowly, carefully, as if trying to convince herself, 'I didn't even see Dennis Cooper on Sunday night. I ran to the garage area and got out my car. I did arrive at Sarah's in an agitated state, but that was because I'd told Jim I was leaving him, not because I'd killed Dennis Cooper.'

Lambert looked at her intently for a moment, as if waiting for her to add to this. When she said nothing, he glanced for a moment at Hook, who was recording her words, then said, 'You have now radically changed both what you said about your family relationships and about your dealings with Dennis Cooper. You have also revised your account of your movements on Sunday night. Is there anything further you wish to add to your new version of things?'

She ignored the contempt which edged his words. In a low voice she said, 'No. I didn't kill Cooper and I don't know who did.'

The sun was climbing and even the few patches of high white cloud seemed concerned to get out of its way. The temperature crept steadily upwards: twenty-six, twenty-seven, twenty-eight. It would be thirty during the afternoon; eighty-six, in Fahrenheit – most of the visitors to Westbourne Park still preferred their temperatures in what they called 'old money'.

Alex Fraser wore only underpants, shorts, socks and his digging boots. The sweat glistened on his back as he worked steadily and methodically. He was forking over a bed they had cleared for replanting. It was good to have nothing in his way; working around established plants was often necessary, but it complicated things, destroyed the healthy rhythm he liked best of all.

He completed forking the long, narrow bed surprisingly quickly. Forking an established patch was much easier than double digging a new one. He should be glad of that, in heat like this. But Alex didn't think like that. Instead, he exulted in the steady patterns of hard physical work. The outlet of regular, almost mindless labour was especially welcome after the trials he had put himself through in the last week. It seemed a long time now since he had ridden the sturdy little Honda through the night to Glasgow and back again, though it was only thirty-two hours since his return. He made that calculation wonderingly, as he paused for a moment to look down at the bed he had worked.

Then he wheeled four wheelbarrows of well-rotted horse shit and dumped them on his plot – he was feeling proprietorial about it by now. You had to remember to call it manure for the visitors, but the lads pretended to think you were gay if you called it anything but shit. He worked it swiftly into the top surface of the bed. They were planting peonies here, which would be undisturbed for years; they had spectacular flowers, but they didn't like to have their roots buggered about. You set things up right, gave them a rich foundation to get them going, and then left them to it.

He went and told Jim Hartley that the bed was ready for planting and was quietly pleased when the head gardener was surprised at the swift progress he had made. Hartley didn't question the thoroughness of his work. He knew from experience that Alex was a young man who didn't skimp things. He glanced approvingly over the turned soil, then said, 'You can collect the peonies and plant them up after your break. Keep as much soil on the rootballs as you can.' He knew that Fraser would take that as a kind of reward. Planting things in the ground you had prepared for them always gave you satisfaction. Jim wondered why things in his working life should be so much easier to arrange than those in his private life.

Alex Fraser took his mug of tea into the deepest shade he could find. He turned the foolscap envelope which had just been handed to him over and over between his fingers. He didn't get much post, but he didn't want to open this. The official address on the rear of the envelope told him whence it had come and made him abruptly afraid, as if it was a letter bomb which might go off in his hands.

It was nothing of the sort, of course. When his trembling fingers eventually extracted the smooth manila of the single sheet, it told him in officially measured terms that no further action would be taken on this occasion in relation to the incident which had occurred in Cheltenham on the night of June 24th.

Alex read it several times, fearful that there might be some sub-clause which reversed the decision and punctured his relief. This was wonderful, he told himself repeatedly. There was every chance now that the episode would be forgotten and he would be taken on permanently here. It made the whole sorry nightmare of the last week irrelevant. He must ring Ken Jackson tonight and tell him the news.

He tried but failed to wipe the smile from his face as he collected the peonies and lifted them carefully into his wheelbarrow.

Jim Hartley sat carefully on the edge of the chair allotted to him in the murder room. Unlike his wife, he had chosen to come here rather than confront the CID in his own home. He didn't want to meet anyone there at the moment. In his emotional chaos, he felt as if his own pain and shame might seep out of the furnishings and compromise him if he was interviewed in his own living room.

Lambert had no wish to put him at his ease. People who were nervous invariably revealed more of themselves and of others than people who were calm. Nevertheless, he chose to make Hartley aware of the present situation; he didn't want the preliminary session of evasions and half-truths they had endured from Julie Hartley. 'Your wife has told us what really happened in your house on Sunday night, Mr Hartley. We should now like to have your version and your comments.'

Just when as a loving couple they should have been in close touch, conferring about what they were saying to these people, they weren't speaking. Jim wondered just what Julie had said to them, whether she would have tried to harm him. Surely not? But she had been so bitter, so unlike the Julie he had known for years, that he had no confidence left. Would it be like this for the rest of his life? Would he be sure of nothing, as he felt now? His voice was barely audible as he said, 'It will be as Julie said. I can't add anything to it.'

Lambert felt very sorry for him. He was either a better actor than a head gardener should be or he was genuinely broken by the state of his marriage. But he might be the man who had killed Dennis Cooper. Lambert reminded himself as he had reminded other people that this was the single issue which concerned him and his murder team. He nodded at Hook, who said quietly, 'We need your version, Jim. Sometimes people see the same events quite differently. Sometimes they remember different details.'

Hartley had looked up sharply at the use of his forename. He studied Hook for a moment, as if conscious of his presence for the first time. 'Julie told me she was leaving me. She said she was going to live with that woman.'

'Sarah Goodwin. You've met her?'

'I've seen her twice, I think. Three times at most. I know almost nothing about her. I didn't even know she was a bloody dyke!' He released all the fury he could into the harsh consonants of the monosyllable, but it didn't give him much relief. 'And now she's got her claws into my Julie!' He plunged his face into his hands.

They waited for him to recover some composure. When he finally dropped his hands, his eyes were dry but his face was wracked with pain. Hook spoke as softly as a therapist. 'How long have you known about this situation?'

'About a week. Maybe a little longer. Bloody Dennis Cooper knew about it before I did!'

'Yes. We have the book in which he kept notes on the people here. He does seem to have been aware of the situation for rather longer than a week. But you're saying now that it wasn't you who told him of it.'

'No. Dennis had been a good friend to me. He'd helped me to make the changes in the gardens I wanted. But he was into everyone's business, I can see that now. He liked to find out things about people – he said it helped him in his job to know people as thoroughly as he could. I accepted that at the time. But now I think he was a nosy old sod who liked to have power over people's lives. Sorry! I suppose I shouldn't be talking like this about a dead man, should I?'

'Did you kill him, Jim?'

'No.'

'Even though he was threatening your job, your position here, perhaps your whole life? Much better to tell us now, if you did.'

'No. The job means nothing to me, if I'm losing Julie and the boys.'

'You'd better tell us what happened on Sunday night, hadn't you?'

Hartley nodded, apparently grateful for Hook's understanding.

He spoke in a low, swift monotone, anxious to get his version of events over without collapsing under the weight of his emotions. 'Julie waited until we had the boys in bed. They'd been swimming in the afternoon, before the storm came on, so they were tired and went off to sleep quite quickly. She told me that she was going to leave me, to set up house with Sarah Goodwin, and to take the boys with her. I said I wasn't having that, that I'd fight her for the boys if it came to it. She said the courts always sided with mothers, even – even when it was like this. I tried to show her what we had, what she was going to break up, but she's better than me when it comes to words. She said that love was what she felt for Sarah and that overrode everything else. I've never hit her, but I might have done then. She just didn't want to listen to me. She stormed out of the house without saying where she was going. To bloody Sarah Goodwin's, I suppose, but I didn't know that.'

Hook looked at Lambert to see if he wished to take over the questioning at this crucial point, but received only a slight shake of the head. 'What time did Julie leave, Jim?'

'Nine o'clock. Well, just after nine. It was going dark, but that was because the clouds were still heavy and low after the storm.'

'Did you see whether she went straight off the site?'

Hartley's eyes widened. 'This is the time when he was killed, isn't it?'

'Cooper died at around that time, yes. We aren't sure of the exact moment.'

'And you think it might have been Julie who killed him?'

'It could easily have been a woman, Jim. No great strength was required.'

'It wasn't Julie. She wouldn't do anything like that. She would never be capable of murder.'

He had sprung as instinctively to her defence as she had done to his earlier in the day. There was something touching about it, but the experienced CID pair had received such assurances on numerous previous occasions. Many of them had proved unjustified. Hook nodded but did not comment. 'What time did Julie return?'

'Twenty minutes after midnight. I saw it on my bedside

clock. She thought I was asleep and I pretended I was. I didn't trust myself to ask where she'd been.'

Hook noted the times and looked at his man in silence for a moment. 'You say that you didn't kill Dennis Cooper. You can't believe it was Julie. So who do you think tightened that ligature around Cooper's neck on Sunday night?'

'I don't know. I've thought a lot about it, as everyone round here has. I thought it might be one of my apprentice lads, perhaps – they're not above a bit of violence to settle their problems. But then I look around them and I can't see it being any of them. Hugo Wilkinson? He'd had his troubles with Dennis, but would he murder him? Or one of the voluntary workers who come in daily? I don't know much about them.' He shrugged his shoulders hopelessly.

Lambert spoke for the first time in many minutes. 'Keep your eyes and your ears open, please. You may be the likeliest person on the site to see or hear something significant. And don't leave the area without letting us know your intended address, please.'

Jim Hartley nodded dumbly, recognizing that the last words meant he remained a suspect. He had reached the door when DS Hook's voice said, 'I hope you can work things out within the family, Jim. Don't resort to violence, however desperate you feel: that invariably makes things worse.'

Bert waited a few minutes after the door had closed to say, 'I hope that poor sod didn't kill his boss. He's got quite enough trouble to deal with as it is, without a murder charge.'

Lambert smiled grimly. 'Very unprofessional, DS Hook. You know we can't pick and choose among suspects. For my own part, I hope Julie Hartley didn't do this one. I think that would cause Jim more agony than if he'd done it himself.'

SEVENTEEN

Lorna Green had known that the first talk she gave at Westbourne Park after the death of its curator would be a time of great strain for her.

For one intensely lived section of her life, she had been very close to Dennis Cooper. Even at the time of his death, she had felt her ties were closer than those of anyone, except possibly his wife. And now there were rumours that Alison Cooper was to marry someone else quite soon. Apparently she might have done that even if her husband had still been alive.

Lorna loved Westbourne Park and what it had brought to her life, but work there was certain to put pressure on her. She was surely bound to think of the man who had been in charge here as she spoke about the gardens and their history. After all, she had been suspected of his murder. But she told herself firmly that the police had been satisfied with what she'd told them on Tuesday. She'd seen them going in and out of what she still thought of as Dennis's room, but they hadn't called for her to see them again.

Lorna had been disappointed with her performance when she first began these talks. She had made the mistake of thinking that because you knew a lot about your subject you were bound to be effective, but the muted reactions to her first efforts had told her that she needed to improve. She had worked on her delivery – if you were dull yourself, people assumed your story must also be a dull one. She had learned that she must concentrate on the broad lines of the history of Westbourne and not give too much detail – that was best reserved for answers to questions. Nowadays, she got an increasing number of questions at the conclusions of her talks. That was a sure sign that people were now interested in what she told them.

Lorna found another pleasant thing was happening. As she relaxed and enjoyed her talks more, her audiences also enjoyed them more. Once you could communicate enthusiasm, you were halfway there; she remembered the best of her university tutors saying that to her many years ago.

She had revised her material for today's talk. She was now building her history of the gardens around modern features which visitors might find worth studying after the conclusion of her talk, and was pleased to see people scribbling reminders to themselves on the National Trust leaflets they had acquired as they entered. 'The gardens are planned as a series of "rooms", with different themes or different colours evident in each one. They are attractive at any stage of the year, but in early July you might particularly enjoy . . .'

She became conscious of a tall, striking woman with ash-blonde hair who had appeared on the left of her audience halfway through her talk. She seemed interested in what she heard and in the series of eager questions which followed it. She did not speak herself. When Lorna signalled the end of her performance, there was enthusiastic applause. Then the crowd melted away to enjoy the gardens.

The late arrival stayed. When she came closer, Lorna was struck by the brightness of her unusual green eyes. She gave Lorna a perfunctory smile and said, 'I enjoyed your talk. You obviously know a lot about this place. I'm Detective Sergeant Ruth David. I believe you spoke to Chief Superintendent Lambert earlier in the week. He would like to see you again today.'

Lorna stared dumbly for a moment at the warrant card which was held before her face. She said, 'I've got two more talks to give, at three o'clock and four o'clock.'

'That's fine. We're trying to disrupt the routine here as little as possible. The chief super will see you at the end of your working day. Shall we say four thirty?'

It would give her time to prepare, Lorna thought. But prepare for what? This wasn't a talk about Westbourne, where she could determine her own agenda.

Just when you had convinced yourself that things were picking up, life had a habit of hitting you with a sock full of wet sand.

Alex Fraser told himself that he had always known that. You didn't survive for years in a Glasgow council home without learning that disaster usually followed hard upon delight. And this wasn't disaster, he told himself firmly. Provided he kept his mind clear and gave them nothing, he could surely come to no harm. He should be able to do that; hadn't he spent most of his teenage years giving the filth nothing during their frequent questionings?

These reflections were prompted by an instruction to attend the murder room for further questioning at two o'clock. He had read the letter telling him that no further action was planned over the Cheltenham fracas several times during his lunch break. Indeed, he had taken it into the bog and locked the door firmly to ensure that he could spend as long as he wished relishing the formal phrases which had set his heart singing. Now he had better forget his relief and give his mind fully to the matter of Dennis Cooper's death.

Once that was out of the way, he could enjoy his work here and his leisure hours to the full. A telephone message from the secretary of the golf club had informed him at lunchtime that he had been selected to appear in the county second team in ten days' time. He'd work that news in, if he could, to try to impress the CID. Bloody bourgeois! This lot were nothing like the rough-trade coppers who'd been the enemy throughout his Glasgow years. He felt something near to affection for those hard-faced Glaswegians now.

The plain-clothes man who had come to inform him of the renewed CID interest swept his warrant card swiftly across Fraser's vision to establish that he was official police. Alex grabbed his wrist and read the rank, as most people did not. 'Detective Inspector. Top brass to send after an innocent gardening apprentice.'

Chris Rushton smiled, his gaze flitting from the sharp blue eyes to the extraordinary red hair above them. 'I saw you passing, lad: you're easily spotted. Thought I'd take the chance to examine the suspect who has the most serious record of violence.'

This pig had a handsome face, Alex conceded to himself sardonically. Dark-haired, keen-eyed, tall. Some English rose would probably find him attractive. Before he could stop himself, Alex said, 'I've no case to answer for that business in Cheltenham. Even the bloody filth have had to accept that we were set upon. We were the innocent parties.'

'Really. I'd like to say I was pleased for you, but I'm not a hypocrite. And purely for your information, I was thinking about your record of violence over the years in Glasgow, not the renewal of it in this area.'

Alex was shaken. He hadn't expected this man he'd never seen before to go immediately on to the attack. But then he was a pig, wasn't he? He also seemed to be a distressingly well-informed pig. Alex turned surly. 'Why do they want to see me? I've told them everything I know about Mr Cooper.'

DI Rushton shook his head happily. 'Ours not to reason why, Mr Fraser. Two o'clock at the murder room, please.'

Alex didn't like that 'Mr Fraser'. The filth only got formal when they were planning to charge you with something. He scrubbed every speck of soil from his nails, washed his face carefully, and presented himself at the curator's office two minutes before the appointed hour.

They left him waiting for a while, getting steadily more nervous. At three minutes past two, DS Hook ushered him into the big, stark room and sat him down opposite Lambert, who had the curator's big desk in front of him. Alex felt very exposed. Once, when he'd been in the home, he'd been 'volunteered' to be the fall guy at a church fete. People – almost all of them belligerent men and youths – had been invited to fling wooden balls at a target, whilst he had sat on a swing over a kiddies' paddling pool. When anyone had hit the bullseye, it had released the catch on his seat and dumped him into two feet of water, to roars of delighted applause. He'd had to grin and bear it; what he hadn't liked was the sign the stallholder had put over his head. Its uneven red capitals had invited the public to 'DUMP CARROT-TOP INTO THE DRINK'.

He'd almost forgotten about that day, but it came back to him now, as he sat on his chair and felt very exposed in front of a chief superintendent. Lambert looked at him keenly for a moment whilst he waited for Hook to come in from the outer office. Then he said unexpectedly, 'I hear you've been selected for the county golf team. Congratulations!'

'Thank you. It's only the second team, but it's a start.' Alex didn't question how the tall man knew. He was quite used to the police knowing all kinds of surprising things about him.

As Hook sat down with his notebook, Lambert said without any change of tone, 'Mr Fraser, have you come up with anyone who can confirm for us that you were not out and about on the site on Sunday evening?'

'Not down at the bottom of the Wilderness, you mean? Not down there killing Mr Cooper. No, I haven't.'

'I see. Pity, that. It would have enabled us to eliminate you from a murder enquiry. I'm sure that would have been even more of a relief for you than for us.'

'Yes, it would. But I can't produce witnesses out of thin air. The other apprentices go home at weekends and don't usually come back until late on Sunday nights. They live much nearer to Westbourne than I do.'

'Or much further away. From information given to DI Rushton, I gather you do not have a permanent address, apart from Westbourne Park.'

'No. I don't have family. I had a mother and a younger sister, but I haven't seen them for years. Not since I was taken into care at fourteen.'

It might have been an attempt to court sympathy in some twenty-year-olds, but it emerged only as a statement of a key fact of his life, repeated with the weary indifference of one who had delivered it many times before. Lambert nodded without comment and said, 'Matt Garton was back here quite early on Sunday. Back in the apprentice cottages by half past seven, he says.'

It sounded like a challenge, so Alex was immediately wary. 'If he says that, it's true. But I didn't see him.'

'Nor he you, according to his statement. So we can't eliminate either of you.' Lambert studied Fraser for a moment, as if inviting a comment. 'Wouldn't it have been natural for you as fellow apprentices who spend many working hours together to get in touch with each other? I know you have separate rooms, but you were in the same building. There must have been no more than a single wall between you.'

It was disconcerting to find how thoroughly they knew the layout of the cottages and where everyone lived. Alex licked his lips and conceded, 'We might have done that, a week or two earlier. But we were a wee bit cautious with each other after that rumble in Cheltenham.'

'And why would that be? You fought on the same side.' Lambert smiled grimly. 'Indeed, I suppose you could say that without you and your knuckledusters the battle might have been lost.'

Alex was uneasy. It was only this morning that he'd heard officially that the Cheltenham evening was dismissed, out of his life for ever. And here he was with the filth, being forced to live it all over again. But he couldn't see any way out of it. He explained sullenly, 'I grassed him up, didn't I? I told the rozzers in Cheltenham that he was receiving a package of illegal drugs from his supplier.'

'But you'd no alternative. You couldn't allow the interrogating officers to think the drugs had been meant for you. And especially not with charges of carrying an offensive weapon and grievous bodily harm in prospect.'

'That's how it was for me. You can't expect Matt Garton to see it like that, when he's been grassed up by his mate.'

Lambert sighed. 'Did you hear him come in on Sunday night?'

'I might have done. I might have heard him moving about. I can't remember now – and that's the honest truth, copper!' The little spurt of aggression made him feel better, as if he was in some way holding his own. 'I wasn't going to go looking for him. If he wanted to make peace, he'd have come in and seen me, wouldn't he?'

'And has he made peace since then?'

Alex really wasn't quite sure. In the arcane, often non-verbal gestures of sympathy between twenty-year-old males, it took time for wounds to heal and trust to be re-established. 'We get on all right. I expect things will be better when we've worked together on something for a day or two.'

'I expect they will, yes. And you'd other things on your mind on Sunday night, no doubt. Were you very resentful of Mr Cooper's attitude to the Cheltenham episode?'

He was shocked by this sudden change of ground. Typical bloody filth! He wondered if the whole elaborate investigation of his whereabouts on Sunday night and his relationship with Matt Garton had been a deliberate prelude to throw him off his guard for this. He tried to play for time. 'What do you mean, his attitude? We hadn't even spoken about Cheltenham. Mr Cooper was much too grand to bother himself with apprentices. He dealt with us through Mr Hartley.'

Bert Hook looked hard at him in the silence which followed. He said quietly, 'I shan't make a note of that, Alex. I'll wait until you tell us the real facts of the matter.'

'What d'ye mean? I never—'

'Mr Cooper kept notes on what he knew, Alex. He also recorded some of his opinions, on you and on others who worked here. We have now had the opportunity to study his thoughts about you in his notebook. It's one of his last entries. He speculates about your future here.'

Fraser looked from Hook's broad, earnest face to the keen grey eyes of Lambert behind the desk, then down at the floor. He said slackly, 'Wednesday of last week. That was when he saw me.'

Hook nodded. 'Four days before he died.'

Fraser glanced at him sharply. 'I didn't kill him, ye know.'

'Mr Cooper recorded what he thought about you after you'd spoken with him. Don't you think you'd better let us have your version of that conversation?'

Fraser smiled bitterly. 'It wasn't much of a conversation. More like a sermon on my sins. I've heard a few of those in my time.'

'I expect you have, yes. We used to get regular directions on being upright citizens from the governors in the home where I grew up. But you're involved in a murder case now. This is your chance to tell us exactly what happened last week.'

'He said I'd let him down and let Westbourne Park down and let myself down when I got involved in street conflict. That's the phrase he used for it. He hissed it out like an old lady chasing cats away from the birds. But I was prepared to stand there and take it and eat humble pie when he finished. I've done that often enough before.'

'I expect you have. It's the only way, sometimes.'

'Then he said the business in Cheltenham would affect my

future. He'd have to tell the National Trust administrators about it and it was only fair to warn me that he thought it would affect my prospects of permanent employment at the end of the year. They were usually only able to retain one of the apprentices and he didn't think he'd be able to recommend me.'

'And you just stood and took it?'

'No. I found my tongue when he threatened me with that. I said nothing was proved yet, that the other apprentices were involved with me and that we'd had to defend ourselves.'

Hook nodded, anxious to keep him talking. 'You weren't the aggressors. The police in Cheltenham have now recognized that. It's the major reason why you aren't facing serious charges.'

'Yes. I'd have been able to go to him today and tell him he shouldn't blacken me with the Trust, now that the police were taking no further action. That's if he hadn't been dead.'

He looked at neither of them now. Instead, he gazed at the window and the outside world and the infinite possibilities which lay there.

Lambert was silent for a few moments after Fraser had left them. Hook, who felt a bond of sympathy with the young man which derived from his own teenage years, had more sense than to voice it now.

Lambert glanced at the very blue sky which was all he could see through the window. Then he stood up, and said, 'We've a couple of hours before we see Lorna Green. Let's drag Chris Rushton away from his computer and revisit the scene of the crime.'

It was one of the paradoxes of this death that violence had been delivered not only in one of the great gardens of Britain but in the most innocent-seeming section of it. Even the more adventurous and energetic members of the public rarely moved beyond the area known as the Middle Stream Garden to the lowest and furthest portion of the estate which had been designated the Wilderness.

It was not a wilderness at all of course, but carefully designed to simulate a natural landscape. It had groups of trees deliberately planted to look informal. The bulbs which burst into flower in spring were invisible beneath the warm earth on this day of high summer. The furthest portion of the area was still cordoned off as a scene of crime, though the SOCO team had long since finished its work of gathering anything which might be significant.

Far from being reluctant to leave his computer and his records, DI Rushton was anxious to hear his chief's thoughts on the state of the investigation, and in particular on the fiery-haired young man they had most recently seen. 'What did you make of young Fraser?'

Lambert nodded at Hook, who said carefully, 'He acquitted himself well. Once he realized we had access to Cooper's notebook, he was quite frank about what they'd said to each other.'

'He was either quite frank or he contrived to give Bert the impression of being so,' corrected Lambert automatically.

'Fraser's the one with the history of violence,' said Rushton eagerly. 'He'd seriously injured a man in a street fight not long before Cooper's death. He's got a long history of violent behaviour on the streets of Glasgow before he came here.'

Hook frowned. 'I'm sure you'd find most of his male companions in that home had similar histories, if you cared to investigate them. It's a tough world when you haven't a family to fall back on. And if we're talking about serious violence, Fraser isn't in the same league as the man who now intends to marry the victim's widow.'

'Peter Nayland? I agree, but we may not be able to pin this one on him, convenient as it is for him to have his mistress now free of a husband. His poker game alibi for last Sunday evening checks out.'

Lambert grimaced. 'You'd expect that. Nayland is the sort of villain who employs a hitman to do his serious damage. We know he's done that before, though no one is prepared to go into court and declare it. So far, we've turned up no evidence that he paid anyone to kill Cooper.'

Rushton nodded. 'What about the widow herself? Alison Cooper was on the spot and lied about it. She obviously knew her husband's movements better than anyone. We've agreed a woman could have done this: whatever ligature was used to throttle Cooper, it required no great strength, especially if he was taken by surprise.'

Lambert said suddenly, 'I need to see Alison Cooper again. She may give us a little more, with luck.' He nodded gnomically, but volunteered nothing further. His two companions knew him too well to press him for what he did not volunteer. He said eventually, 'Bearing in mind the possibility of a woman, we can't forget Julie Hartley. She's very determined she's going to set up house with Sarah Goodwin. And we know that Cooper was being obstructive – threatening her with all kinds of consequences for her family if she persisted in leaving her husband.'

Rushton frowned. 'But surely he couldn't prevent her from setting up house with whoever she chose? This is the twenty-first century.'

'Apparently he thought he could do just that. He was threatening to damage her husband and her children, if she left. If Julie Hartley believed him, she might have done something desperate. People in the grip of passion aren't always logical.'

They were silent for a moment, reviewing examples of this from their own professional experience. Then Rushton said, 'That argument would apply to her husband as well as Julie. He's spent the whole of his adult life working to achieve the position he holds here. If he felt that Cooper was threatening to take away that at the same time as his family was disintegrating, he might well have turned to violence.'

Lambert, whilst listening to their thoughts, had moved a little to one side. He was staring thoughtfully at a newly planted tree which was about ten feet tall. He now said, 'You mustn't rule out Lorna Green, whom we're seeing again at four thirty today. She had what seems to have been a pretty passionate affair with Dennis Cooper many years ago. She had a successful business career with British Gas, but she never married. She'd always been interested in Westbourne Park and when she took early retirement, she chose to work here. It gave her access to Cooper, who became the curator shortly afterwards.'

Rushton had never met the lady, but he remembered the detailed information he had fed into his computer. 'She's reckoned to know as much as anyone living about this place and its history. She was maybe just following her interests when she offered her services as a guide.'

'Probably she was, because she was already working here when Cooper took up his post. But we can't ignore the fact that she increased her workload after he came, which brought her close to a man who is now a murder victim. She knows this place intimately. She's one of the few outsiders who might arrange a meeting in a remote spot at the edge of the gardens like this.'

Hook found it difficult to see the educated, respectable Ms Green as a candidate for this killing. He said reluctantly, 'She says she was at home on Sunday night, but she hasn't a reliable witness to support that. Her mother has quite advanced Alzheimer's and doesn't remember days or times. It must be a hell of a strain for Lorna looking after her.'

Rushton nodded. 'People under strain often act irrationally. Ms Green might have been looking at her life bitterly and blaming Cooper for the major disaster in it. We know from his notebook that they'd met not long before he died and had a pretty brisk exchange about the way she was correcting him in public.'

Hook grinned. 'It's a long step from a brisk exchange to murder. But I agree that there might have been evidence in that meeting that her frustration was simmering dangerously. Cooper seems to have thought so, from the notes he made about it.'

Rushton had a habit of leaving his prize suspect to the last. He now said, 'The man we can't ignore has to be the head chef, Hugo Wilkinson. He's pretty certainly going to face serious child pornography charges. We know from Cooper's notebook that he was on to him and proposed to report the matter to the National Trust. Wilkinson could not only have lost his job here but found it difficult to get another one if he'd been forced to leave in those circumstances.'

Lambert had listened to all of this with an air of abstraction. He now said quietly, 'Come and look at this.'

It was an innocent-enough looking item. He was looking hard at a sturdy flowering cherry tree, probably transplanted to here in the early spring. It had a stake beside it, but nothing to secure it to that stake. The point he was studying was five feet up both the tree and the stake, where slight wear indicated that they had once been tied together.

Rushton was no gardener, but Hook was. 'The tie's missing,' he said immediately.

Lambert nodded. 'It might have been removed merely because this tree is now sturdy enough to rely on its own roots, of course. What did forensic and the pathologist say about the murder weapon?'

Rushton had an almost photographic memory for detail. He leapt in eagerly. 'The tourniquet wasn't a cord or a wire. It was something broader, almost an inch wide – about two centimetres was the metric estimate. That's why it didn't cut deeply into the victim's neck as he was asphyxiated.'

Lambert nodded. 'I think we have our murder weapon. A simple tree-tie. Possibly the one which has been removed from here.'

EIGHTEEN

It was the first time Alison Cooper had visited Peter Nayland in his own house.

They had spent a curious but ultimately satisfactory night together. Things had been awkward at first, with the harsh fact of Dennis's death standing between them like a physical barrier. But they had stroked each other between the silk sheets of the big bed and then held each other hard. Touch was better than words. They had eventually made love in a relaxed, unhurried, affirmative way which was quite new to them.

Peter was up before her in the morning. He had appointments at work which he needed to keep. She stretched luxuriously in the bed, then used the power shower and the thick bath towel he had left ready for her in the bathroom. Everything here was the best; all the equipment was highly efficient, all the fittings and furnishings were luxurious.

Affluent but anonymous. It was obvious that someone with

plenty of money lived here, but there was not much of a personal imprint. Alison decided she liked that. She wondered if she was determined to like everything about Peter, then decided that there was more than that involved. She was pleased that there was no woman's presence evident here. That might have meant that she was one of many, just the latest in a string of women that he had brought here, but she was confident that it was not so.

There had been other women, of course, but they had meant nothing, compared with what he now felt for Ally. He had told her that, and she believed him. And he told her he had not brought those other women here, because this was his own patch and he had wanted to keep it that way. Bringing her here was another commitment, another step towards the way he planned to live the rest of his life. She believed that too.

She didn't like the things the police had told her about Peter and the way he made his money. No doubt they'd exaggerated, the way they did when it suited them. But if there was anything in it, she'd get Peter to change his ways. She was no angel, but she didn't want her man involved in serious criminal activity. She was confident that she could change him; like most women in love, she believed she could exercise a massive and beneficial influence upon the man in her life. She dismissed clichés about leopards and spots resolutely from her mind.

She'd already said she didn't want a cooked breakfast. She enjoyed a 'full English' in hotels, but she rarely had more than cereals and coffee in her normal life. She liked that phrase; her normal life was going to be with Peter from now on. He had her favourite muesli on the table and there was brown bread in the toaster. How pleasantly domestic. They made conversation a little cautiously, as was appropriate for this time in the morning. You could enjoy even the routine things, when you were with someone you loved, Alison told herself sentimentally.

There was a clatter of post through the letterbox. Peter brought in heavy envelopes. 'I asked a few agents to send us details of the properties they currently have on their books. You might like to have a look at them and pick out any you'd like to view. They're mainly in Solihull and the surrounding area: I remembered you said you didn't want to be too far out of the city. Take them with you and study them at your leisure.'

She opened one of the packages and noted from the accompanying letter that Peter had asked for details of 'properties in the two million to three million pound bracket'. She was moving into a lifestyle she had never experienced before and, far from feeling guilty, she was thoroughly looking forward to it. Dennis had always said she was shallow, but she didn't have to give a bugger about Dennis and his opinions now.

Peter encouraged her to stay behind and leave at her leisure, but she went out at the same time as him. She felt obscurely that it was too early to accept this trust, this invitation to explore his privacy. Besides, she'd already noted that the flat was luxurious but anonymous; she wouldn't find out much more about Peter and his business life by staying behind when he left.

She was to spend the morning shopping for clothes in Birmingham. She stood beside her little white Fiat whilst Peter backed the big maroon Jaguar out of the garage. 'Get yourself a super wedding dress!' he called through his open window as he drew alongside Alison.

'Not likely! I'm not going to be mutton dressed as lamb.'

'Not even with an eager old ram like me waiting for you?' He gave her a valedictory smile. 'Whatever you choose will be fine by me, Ally. And don't even consider being economical, my love. This is the last time either of us will do this!' He waved his hand and left on that appealing thought.

Alison spent a happy morning. She took the best part of three hours to buy herself a smart green dress for the wedding. It set off her dark-blonde hair and her blue eyes very well and discreetly emphasized her well-kept figure. It would be a quiet wedding but she wanted to look her best for it. Despite Peter's injunction about economy, she shuddered at the price. But she'd be able to wear it afterwards on all sorts of occasions, wouldn't she? It wasn't like the heedless and ridiculous extravagance of a wedding dress which you'd never wear again.

Morning stretched into afternoon and she bought herself a light lunch in the restaurant at the top of the multiple store. She lingered deliberately over her coffee, then descended to the ground floor, where she indulged herself by buying a cashmere sweater and a silk scarf. There'd be no Dennis waiting when she got home, wanting to criticize her purchases and asking how she'd managed to waste a whole day over them. She felt not the slightest pang of regret about that.

Indeed, all she was conscious of as she drove back towards Westbourne Park was a gathering depression. She'd never liked the place, had always resented the way Dennis had taken her away from the amenities of city life and forced her into the quiet country existence she so abhorred. She felt more and more gloomy as she neared the gates of the estate and met the stream of visitors' cars moving away from it.

A young uniformed PC was standing in the residents' garage area as she drove slowly in. She thought for a moment that he was going to spring forward like a well-drilled hotel porter to open her driver's door. Instead, he waited for her to park and then stepped forward respectfully. 'Mrs Cooper? Superintendent Lambert would like to see you for a few minutes in the Murder Room.' He gave the venue awed capital letters; it was the first time he had been involved in as big a case as this. 'It's in the main house. You turn right by the ticket office and—'

'I know where it is, thank you. It was in fact my husband's office.'

The young man shuffled back apologetically, retiring from her presence like a courtier unable to turn his back on royalty. Ally felt a little guilty; she shouldn't be peevish, after a night and a day she had enjoyed so much. Then she fell to wondering what it was the big cheese wanted to see her about, and the gloom she had felt as she approached Westbourne turned to alarm.

She slipped into her empty house, where she renewed her make-up and tidied up her hair. She was pleased to see that she looked trim and composed in the mirror. The dignified widow was the image she wished to present to the CID. Her feet were hurting after her day in the shops, so she slipped on her most comfortable shoes, with heels slightly lower than the ones she had worn in Birmingham.

Lambert gave her a cursory greeting, as if he was

preoccupied with other matters. It was Hook who settled her on the upright chair in front of the big desk where Dennis had once held court. She felt her first little stab of sorrow at the departure of her husband from this familiar place. Dennis hadn't really been a bad man, just the wrong man for her. Her regret lasted no more than an instant; it was replaced by the more familiar feeling of relief that the husband who had denied her access to lasting happiness was now permanently off the scene.

The chief superintendent looked at her for only a couple of seconds before he said, 'The extra information about Mr Cooper's relationships with the people around him has proved most helpful.'

Alison did not know how to react to this. She waited for the tall man to go on but he said nothing further; he was obviously awaiting a reaction from her. Eventually she said carefully, 'I'm glad you've been able to gather this information, if it's going to help you to find who killed Dennis.'

'Oh, it will do that. I'm certain it will.'

He made it sound like a threat. She said, 'I'm glad you think that, because I haven't really come up with anything myself. You asked me to think about Dennis's relationships with the people who worked with him, but I haven't been able to recall anything you won't already know. As I think I told you yesterday, I didn't take much interest in the work Dennis did here, so I don't know much about the people he worked with.'

'You did say that, yes. I didn't believe it was true at the time.'

It was blunt, uncompromising and all the more cutting for being delivered quietly and calmly. Alison tried again to refute it. 'I don't know why you should think that. I—'

'I'm sure you read your husband's notebook quite carefully before you delivered it to us.'

'You're still on about that notebook? Well, I'm not surprised that he kept notes, as I told you yesterday. He was a rather secretive man and he liked to know as much as he could about those around him. It gave him increased power, and he liked that.'

'He kept the book here in his office, but you removed it to see if he had written anything about you and if he knew about Peter Nayland. I believe that when you had examined its contents and found it contained nothing personal, you decided that we should have it. It would have been better if you had simply brought it here by day, instead of sliding it into the main office letterbox at dead of night.'

He seemed to know everything, this man. He would be telling her next how fiercely her heart had been beating as she had crept along the familiar path to the reception area whilst everyone slept. She said dully, 'I thought you should have the information that the notebook contained.'

'And you were right. However, the manner of delivery raises certain questions about your motivation.'

Further denials would obviously only lead her into deeper waters. Alison said dully, 'How did you know that notebook came from me?'

'It's a fairly obvious deduction, Mrs Cooper. Of those nearest to this death, you are the only one not included in those pages.'

'I see.' It was so obvious that she felt foolish. 'Dennis knew far more than I thought he did about a lot of the people here. I decided you should have that information.'

'And you were obviously right. But I have to insist that the secretive method you adopted to deliver the notebook raises questions about your own motivation.'

'I don't follow you. I merely wished to distance myself as far as possible from my husband's death. And I didn't want anyone here to think I was trying to throw suspicion on to them.'

'Really? The other interpretation of your actions seems to me much more convincing. I believe you read the notebook and found nothing within it which could damage you but a lot of things which could incriminate and embarrass the other people whose secrets are recorded within it. I believe you delivered this information into our hands to incriminate other people and to divert suspicion from you and Peter Nayland.'

'Peter had nothing to do with this.'

'That's what you'd like us to think. We have our own views

about Mr Nayland, whether or not he is innocent in this matter. I notice that you don't claim innocence for yourself.'

'I didn't kill Dennis. I accept his death is convenient for me, but you mustn't assume I killed him because of that.'

Bert Hook had so far studied the widow keenly but remained silent. Now he said quietly, 'We'd be more prepared to accept that if you hadn't tried to implicate other people by the way you slid this notebook back into our hands. You had a duty to produce it, but your melodramatic delivery of it suggests that you had things of your own to hide. A plot with Mr Nayland to remove this inconvenient obstacle to your plans, perhaps.'

She protested her innocence again and they let her go without further comment. She spent an hour sitting miserable and lonely in the house where she had lived with the murder victim. She would ring Peter tonight, despite his insistence that they should keep such contacts to the minimum.

She wondered again just what part Peter Nayland had played in this death he had found so welcome.

Another fine day. Warm, but not too warm. Ideal for visiting gardens. Superb weather, in fact, for moving through the various 'garden rooms' which made up the horticultural masterpiece which was Westbourne Park. Long lines of people did just that, waiting with cheerful patience whenever the numbers demanded it.

The restaurant was busy throughout the lunch period, with queues waiting at the door for vacant tables and a rising decibel level in the multiple conversations. Curious how the noise level always rose steadily through the three hours or so when the place was full, thought Hugo Wilkinson, as he worked swiftly but methodically in his kitchen.

He would have liked poorer weather, even a thoroughly wet day, because he wanted to get away from his kitchen as soon as possible. He had things to do, vital things. He had to get rid of the evidence. That had been the advice the leader of the group had given him last night. You've enjoyed it, now ditch it; there was no choice. Get rid of anything which could incriminate you and deny all knowledge of the group and why they met. The police probably wouldn't believe you, but without the evidence they couldn't pin anything on you. It was a pity he'd even admitted to being a member of a photographic club.

Work was normally a release for him. A kitchen working flat out is a stressful place, but this was the kind of tension he had been used to all his working life. It occupied you wholly, so that you had no time to think about the disturbing things in the rest of your life. He liked the total absorption and total concentration that he had to bring to the task. Yet today he could not cast aside the nagging fear that he should already have acted, should have cleared his flat of all the things which could land him in trouble. He should have taken it as a warning when that bugger Lambert had challenged him during the murder investigation, should have cleared the evidence ruthlessly then.

As soon as the last main courses had been served, he muttered an excuse about having to do some ordering and slipped away from the kitchen. He hurried quickly along the short path to the residences and arrived at the front door of his cottage at almost the same time as three men. 'This area is private,' Hugo said desperately. 'The main entrance to the gardens is over there.'

The leader of the trio did not immediately reply. Instead, he slipped his hand within his jacket and produced a warrant card and a larger document. He did not even trouble himself to look into Wilkinson's eyes. It seemed that it was important to him to be as impersonal as possible about this, to establish as little contact as humanly possible with the man before him. 'Mr Wilkinson? I'm DI Norman from the West Midlands Child Pornography Unit and these are my colleagues. I have here a search warrant which entitles us to enter your home and remove any materials we find which are obscene or pornographic, possession of which may constitute a breaking of the law. You are welcome to observe our search and witness that nothing is planted here and no unnecessary force is used.'

He pronounced the phrases with a cold formality, like a judge passing sentence. He still had not looked Wilkinson in the eyes. Hugo led them into the cottage, moving with the slow, steady paces of a sleepwalker.

He stood motionless and observed their movements, watching his life disintegrate before him. One of them eventually suggested that he sit down and he did so immediately, as if responding to a command.

They went through his bookcase swiftly but thoroughly, shaking each book to see if it concealed anything between its leaves. A couple of photographs fell from one, pictures of naked children he should have dispensed with long ago. The youngest of the men looked at him with a cold contempt, then slipped the photographs carefully into a polythene sleeve. Hugo wondered if the officer had children of that age himself.

In the bottom drawer of his small sideboard, they found the two videotapes he should have ditched when Dennis Cooper first revealed his suspicions. He wanted to say something jaunty and apologetic, something which might mitigate the squalor clinging about him like a shroud. But the words stuck in his dry throat. He wanted a drink, but he felt that even a move to the tap in the kitchen would somehow be a confession.

Then they moved across to the computer and the one man who had not even looked at him so far settled himself comfortably on the chair in front of it with his back to Hugo. 'You going to give us the password, Mr Wilkinson?' He didn't trouble to turn round. When there was no reply, he said in a lower voice to his colleagues, 'Shouldn't take long to get into this one.'

Hugo didn't react. Perhaps if he sat like a statue it would at least delay things. But what was the use of delay? After two minutes, he announced to the ceiling, 'The password is Henry. That was my father's name.'

'Thank you, sir. Cooperation is much the best policy,' said the man at the computer. Still he did not look round.

The first images of the children came up within sixty seconds. Hugo thought they brought a slight gasp from the man in front of the monitor, but he could not be sure of that. He had no idea whether he was shocked and revolted or whether exposure to other and worse pictures had dulled his reactions to what he found here. He wanted to offer something which would mitigate his guilt, even some light-hearted phrase to break the tension. But there was no word he could say. The steamroller was advancing steadily and inexorably to crush him.

It was over sooner than Hugo had expected. He realized dully that they would examine the full range of the material later at the station. They would no doubt question him about everything in due course, as they prepared a case for the Crown Prosecution Service. The man logged off and carefully shut the computer down.

He sat looking at the empty screen for a moment. Then at last he turned to the wretched figure who lived in this place. 'We need to take this computer away, sir. You will be given a receipt for this and everything else we remove.'

Not long afterwards, they were ready to go. DI Norman stood in front of Hugo, then took a step backwards, as if he feared that close proximity would tarnish him. 'Thank you for your cooperation, Mr Wilkinson.'

'What now?'

Norman hesitated, then said, 'We shall review the evidence. I am sure that formal charges will be made in the next few days. Do not leave the area without notifying us at this number.' He set a card down on the table beside him. 'I understand that you are at present involved in a murder investigation on this site. We do not wish to impede it by taking you into custody at this stage.'

He looked Hugo full in the face on the last sentence, for the first time in their hour's acquaintance.

Lorna Green presented herself at the murder room at precisely four thirty. Punctuality was a habit with her and she feared that any delay might make her seem nervous. How she presented herself was important to her; it might be additionally important when you were a suspect in a murder enquiry. She renewed her make-up, adjusted a few strands of her neat brown hair, and was prepared for her ordeal.

'Thank you for coming here so promptly.' Lambert studied her unhurriedly for a moment. She was a handsome woman at fifty-three, but she looked more strained than he remembered her on Tuesday. She'd given three talks today, but he fancied that it was the task of caring for her mother which was the real problem. He'd seen before how Alzheimer's carers suffered, and the situation only ever seemed to deteriorate.

This was a woman under stress, but detectives had to be aware that people under stress sometimes took strange actions.

Lorna said, 'I was here for most of today anyway. Coming in here at the end of it was no problem.' She glanced at her watch. 'I don't imagine this is going to take long.'

'You have another appointment?'

She gave him a tired smile. 'No other appointments, no. But I have a friend sitting with my mother and I'd like to relieve her as soon as I can. I don't like leaving Mother on her own nowadays. Over the last few weeks, she's become . . . rather unpredictable.' Lorna pronounced the phrase carefully; she didn't want to be brutal about her mother, but precision was important to her.

'This shouldn't take long.'

'I can't imagine it will. I'm ready to offer any help I can, but I think I told you all I could on Tuesday morning.'

'We now have material which we didn't possess then. Mr Cooper kept a secret notebook which has been passed to us. It contains his thoughts on many of his staff; there are also certain items of information which have proved valuable to us.'

Lambert and Hook were both watching her face closely to register her reaction to this. Unexpectedly, she smiled. 'Dennis hadn't changed much, then. He used to write down things like that twenty years and more ago.'

'I see.'

'He was a naturally secretive man and he enjoyed it. "Hear all, see all, say nowt!" he used to say – he was brought up in Yorkshire, you know.'

The two men opposite her nodded. Lambert thought Yorkshire origins meant nothing; Hook, who had played against a few dour Yorkshire cricketers in his time, thought it explained a lot about the man. Lambert said, 'I believe "knowledge is power" is another such saying. Mr Cooper seems to have organized his work as leader around maxims like that.'

'"*Nam et ipsa scientia potestas est*". Usually translated as "Knowledge itself is power". Francis Bacon, I believe.'

'If you believe it, Ms Green, then I have not the slightest doubt that it is so.' Lambert allowed himself the smallest of friendly smiles. 'I have to tell you, however, that Mr Cooper made notes upon you in this small black book of his.'

'I feel flattered that he considered me sufficiently important for that.'

'You are the only one of the voluntary workers here who is accorded this dubious privilege. Perhaps his interest derived from his previous history with you.'

'And again I should perhaps feel flattered that you think a long-dead affair could still be so influential.'

Lambert paused, steepled his fingers and looked quizzically at this composed woman. 'How important is your work here to you, Ms Green?'

'I know a lot about the history of Westbourne Park. It has been a labour of love for me to make myself acquainted with it. I think you were kind enough to say when we last spoke that I probably know as much as anyone alive about this place. But I am quite replaceable. There are other enthusiasts who know enough about these gardens and their history to give the guidance talks which are the main thing I do here.'

'With respect, that is not what I asked. I wanted to know how important the work here is to you personally. What sort of hole would it leave in your life if it were removed from you?'

She took her time over her reply. 'I should miss it. There's no denying that. I love this place, love seeing the gardens in the changing seasons, and I've grown even more attached to Westbourne through my work here. It fits in with the present circumstances of my life. It is part-time and I can vary my days to fit in with when I can get people to sit with Mother for me. It's highly convenient as well as highly enjoyable.'

'Thank you for being so frank. I must now be equally frank and tell you that Dennis Cooper was planning to dispense with your services.'

'Would he really have been so petty? I told you on Tuesday that I'd been a bit naughty and corrected him once or twice in public. But he needn't have seen me as a threat. He's in charge of the show and I'm an unpaid part-time worker.'

'Perhaps the very fact that you give your services voluntarily made you a greater threat to him. People who are not in paid posts can afford to be much more independent than those who work here under the curator's direction.'

'Yes. I see that. And I suppose I was a little more cavalier with him than I would have been if I'd had a full-time job to lose. But I can't believe he was planning to get rid of me.'

Hook said quietly, 'I can read you the relevant passage from his notebook if you wish me to, Ms Green.'

She waved a hand briefly and dismissively. 'That won't be necessary.'

Lambert waited until her eyes flicked back from Hook to him. 'You see now why I asked you how much the work here meant to you. Did you in fact care enough to remove the man who was threatening it? I'm not suggesting that you plotted his death carefully. I'm suggesting that tempers rose and an argument got out of hand. That you seized the nearest implement and used it against him.'

'The nearest implement?'

Lambert nodded at Hook, who said evenly, 'We now think Mr Cooper was killed by the tightening of a tree-tie upon his neck. If it was a surprise attack, possibly from behind, it would have required no great strength.'

She was silent for a moment, her head a little on one side. Then she said slowly, 'Yes. A tree-tie would have done it very well. Particularly one of the larger ones we use on the maturing saplings.'

'We think one was removed from a cherry tree a few yards from the scene of the death.'

'Then I agree that it was probably the instrument of poor Dennis's death. What I refute is that I was the person who used it.'

'You have told us that your work here means a great deal to you. We do not always behave rationally when we are threatened with the unjust removal of something we love. I'm suggesting a quarrel which got out of hand.'

He had half-expected this highly intelligent woman to fly into a rage at his renewed suggestion. Instead she treated it quite calmly.

'You're saying that I was a woman under stress and a woman with a previous heavy emotional involvement with Dennis. That I already carried a heavy resentment of the way he had treated me years ago, which was reactivated by his intention to banish me from Westbourne Park.' She paused, as if waiting for some sort of denial from him. When he said nothing, she said, 'It's feasible, I suppose. I'll admit I was much more resentful than I should have been when he took me to task for correcting him in public. I can't deny that our past history came into that. And I certainly wouldn't have welcomed a decision to axe me from the staff here. But I'm a resourceful person. I held down quite a big job for several years and I think I could easily have got other work.'

'I'm sure you could. Have you had any further thoughts on who could have killed Dennis Cooper?'

'I'm afraid not. But I haven't got the advantage of the wealth of knowledge you've been accumulating throughout the week.' There was just enough sharpness in her tone to tell them that she had enjoyed saying that.

'Clever woman, that,' said Hook after she had left them.

'Undoubtedly. But you obviously have something specific in mind, Bert.'

Bert grinned. 'I was thinking how careful she was to plant the notion that she'd no idea Cooper was planning to dismiss her.'

'Ye-es. Either that or she was genuinely unaware of it. We only know of it because of his private notes. It's quite possible he hadn't broached the idea to her at the time of his death.'

'I think you'd like Lorna Green to be innocent, because of the woman she is and because she's coping with her mother's condition so admirably. Which would of course be highly unprofessional of you.'

'Highly unprofessional. Just as it would be to hope that a young man who has needed to cope with the rigours of life in a Glasgow council home should not be our man.'

Hook nodded sagely. 'Two men as professional as we are should soon come up with a solution.'

NINETEEN

The craft of detection is not characterized by sudden blinding insights. Television has encouraged the notion that the conclusion of most cases is the sudden shaft of light into a dark world, the 'eureka' moment when the great man clutches his brow, slaps his thigh, and says, 'Why on earth didn't I see this before? It's been staring me in the face all this time and yet I've chosen to ignore it!'

Such things are not unknown in CID circles, but they are extremely rare. They occur much more in literature than in fact. In the duller world of real detection, a team accumulates facts steadily, without knowing which ones are going to be relevant to the solution. John Lambert was a Gradgrind about facts. If you gathered enough of them, every case was solvable, he often reminded his serious crime teams.

That was no more than a truism, of course. You never did gather every fact, but in your successful cases you gathered the ones that mattered and made your deductions from them. Lambert shut himself in his study at home on Thursday night and thought for a long time. On Friday morning, he made a long phone call and a few notes before he departed for the murder room at Westbourne Park.

There was no team briefing arranged for this morning. Hook was leaving his car as Lambert drove into the staff area. Lambert beckoned him over and the DS went and sat in the front passenger seat of the chief superintendent's old Vauxhall. They stared at the wall of neatly cut hedge before them and had a quiet two-minute conversation about what Lambert proposed to do. At the end of it, Hook clasped both hands briefly to his face, rubbed his eyes, and said, 'Right! Let's do it.'

'You sure about this, Bert? I could easily get Chris Rushton to do this one. Be good for him, in fact.'

Hook stared ahead. 'I'll do it. Unless you don't think I'll be sufficiently professional.'

Lambert grinned. 'I've never seen you be unprofessional in all the years we've worked together, Bert. And I'll enjoy having you beside me for this one. We can't charge the suspect until we have a confession. There'll be a good deal of bluff involved.'

'I know. I'm ready for that.'

'Good. Usual arrangement. Play it by ear and come in when you think it's appropriate. We've worked it well enough in the past. If you feel up to it, I think you might start things off – he'll open up more readily to you.'

He got out of the car stiffly and it took him a second or two to straighten. He looked ostentatiously at the gardens and not at Hook as they walked through them. It was a good time to see them, before the public were admitted, but neither man registered much of the beauty today. Lambert managed to get Jim Hartley on the phone in the head gardener's office and he agreed to send their man to the curator's office; Jim preferred that term to the murder room, which most of the workers on the site seemed happy to use; murder has its own grisly glamour, even in our violent age.

Hartley said, 'The lads are in the restroom, on their morning break. We start early, to get as much work as we can done before the visitors come. I'll send him up to you. Ten minutes?'

'Ten minutes will be fine.' Lambert despatched a constable to the exit gate, to make sure no one on a small motorbike was allowed to leave.

Hartley went to the door of the hut the apprentices used as a restroom and watched the young men down the last of their tea with his arrival. 'Top brass want to see you again, Alex. Better give yourself a wash and brush up. I said you'd be there in ten minutes.' He'd spoken as casually as he could, but the Scotsman's exit was followed by curious glances from his colleagues, as he had expected. 'Time to get on with your jobs, lads. I expect Alex will be back with you before long.'

Alex changed from his working boots into shoes, stripped to the waist, and gave himself a hasty but vigorous wash in the bathroom he shared in the apprentices' cottage. He'd washed his hair in the shower only a couple of hours earlier; he ran a comb through its wiry resistance now, wondering if this energetic cleansing was a substitute for thought, a means of thrusting away the apprehension he had felt when Jim Hartley gave him the news that the CID wanted to see him for a third time about the death of Dennis Cooper.

The pair he knew from the golf club were waiting expectantly as the uniformed copper showed him into the room. They were studying him even as he entered, before he was prepared for it. Alex realized that in Glasgow he had always waited for the police in those small, depressing interview rooms; he'd never had to make an entry under scrutiny there. He sat down carefully on the upright chair in front of the big desk, as if he felt it important to place his young limbs precisely. He felt like a boxer adopting a precise stance for a tricky opponent. To the men who had been waiting for him, his face looked very white and his hair an even fiercer red than usual.

They let him sit and sweat for what seemed a long moment. He was resisting a squirm in his legs when Hook said softly, 'Mr Cooper would never have implemented his threats, you know.'

It was a thought which had gnawed at Alex steadily through the last few nights. He cleared his throat and said, 'I don't know what you mean.'

'Wrong line, Alex.' Hook sounded genuinely concerned by the mistake. 'You told us yesterday how he'd threatened you with dismissal from here as a result of your misconduct in Cheltenham.'

'He said he might have to take it into account, that's all. If things went against me and charges were brought and I was convicted.'

'It went a little further than that, didn't it? We know from what he wrote in his notebook that he proposed to rule you out altogether from employment here. I think he rather enjoyed telling you that. Other people as well as you have told us how he relished power, and his knowledge about the people who worked here gave him power.'

'That's what got to me! I couldn't stand how the bastard actually enjoyed telling me that I'd shot my chances here.'

Both detectives recognized the key switch, the beginnings of a confession, but neither of them even glanced at the other; that would have been a wrong move in this complex and macabre game. Instead, Hook nodded and said, 'I'm sure you tried to reason with him, to tell him that he was overreacting.'

That was the word! How he wished he'd had it on Sunday night. 'I did. I tried to reason with him. I saw him wandering through the gardens after the storm had passed on down the valley. Everything was quiet and I thought this was my chance to talk to him. Everything seemed fresher and greener after the rain and it seemed the time for a fresh beginning for me too. I wanted to tell him he was going too far and too soon – that he was what you said, overreacting.' He pronounced each of the five syllables carefully, as if he were mouthing some newly discovered mantra with magical powers.

'But you followed him with a weapon, didn't you, Alex, in case it turned out that he wasn't a man prepared to listen to reason?'

Fraser looked genuinely puzzled. 'A weapon? No, I didn't have a weapon.' Then his hand flashed briefly to his mouth; they saw in that instant how tightly his fingers were clasped. 'Oh, you mean the tree-tie, I suppose. I found that in the pocket of my old anorak. It was there from months ago, when we'd been securing young trees against the spring gales. It was quite cool after the thunderstorm, so I grabbed the anorak as I went out.'

Better for him than if he'd deliberately removed it from the tree near the scene of death as they'd thought, Hook decided. A minimal difference, but one a skilful defence counsel might make something of. Just as a prosecuting counsel would imply that he'd picked up the murder instrument deliberately rather than found it by chance in his pocket. Bert prompted, 'So you put your arguments to him, Alex?'

It looked for a moment as if he would refuse to go on. His lips set into a dark, ultra-thin line. But then it seemed hopeless. The police always seemed able to collect information you didn't think they'd have, to know far more than you were prepared for them to know. Eventually Alex said dully, 'I told him that I hadn't started the rumble in Cheltenham, that I'd had no choice about fighting. He said that the police didn't think that and that I would shortly be charged with causing an affray and GBH. He said he would have no alternative but to inform the Trust and recommend that they dispensed with my services, either immediately or at the end of my apprenticeship here.'

He fell silent, his face a picture of recollected despair. Hook said, 'That seems a very premature reaction. I expect you told him that.'

Alex stared at him. If only he'd had this man or Ken Jackson at his side to argue for him. It was only when words failed him that he sprang into desperate and calamitous action. But that was a stupid idea; this man was filth. He shook his head, as if trying to clear it. 'I told him that no court had convicted me, that we didn't even know yet if the police were going to bring charges, but he laughed at that. I think it was the laughing that really got to me. It was my whole life that the bastard was laughing away.'

'Was that when you attacked him?'

'No. No, I tried to go on arguing, but I felt my words getting feebler after he'd laughed in my face. I think I told him that he should take my work here into account, that Mr Hartley would tell him I was one of the best workers. Perhaps even the best. That I was surely still innocent of anything in Cheltenham until a court of law proved otherwise. He said he'd think about it, but he really couldn't see much sense in prolonging the agony for me.' He stopped, stared gloomily at the floor for a moment and said hopelessly, 'I don't think he would have sacked me, not when he found that no charges were being brought about the Cheltenham business. I think he was just enjoying the feeling of power you talked about.'

He was silent for so long that he prompted the first words from John Lambert. 'Was that when frustration took over and you attacked him, Alex?'

He bridled for an instant at the different voice. But Lambert's long, lined face seemed as sympathetic as Hook's as he turned to confront it. Defiance turned to helplessness and Fraser said quietly, 'No, it wasn't then. Not quite. He said some stuff about the quality of my work here being now irrelevant and said we'd talked long enough. He was smiling as he turned away from me. I think that was what did it.'

Hook said quietly, 'Yes, you should tell us exactly how it happened, Alex. It might be important.'

All three men knew that he had gone too far now to fling the suggestion back into the rubicund face. Fraser looked straight ahead and spoke as if he were supplying the commentary to a video film running in his mind. 'He was grinning, like I told you. And I realized I'd been gripping the tree-tie in my pocket for five minutes at least. I used both hands to throw it round his neck as he turned his back. Then I twisted it tight. I didn't mean to kill him. I just wanted him to shut up and stop laughing and listen to what I had to say. But he wouldn't listen and eventually I felt him go limp. I put him on the ground and tried to get some air into him. But I didn't know what to do and I knew I mustn't leave prints. So I panicked and left him, hoping that he'd recover with just the fresh air. It wasn't until early on Monday that I heard how Matt Garton had found him dead.'

Hook moved the short distance forward, put his hand on the wiry shoulder, and quietly pronounced the words of arrest. Alex Fraser heard the familiar phrases about not needing to speak and not concealing evidence he might wish to rely on at a later date in court as if they were phrases in some familiar religious litany, to which he should provide the appropriate responses.

He said dully, 'What put you on to me?'

It was Lambert who said quietly, 'Once we realized that a tree-tie had been used for the killing, it was always likely to be one of the gardening staff. Only one of them had panicked and fled the scene on the day the murder was discovered. It's all circumstantial evidence, but it adds up.'

'And I'm the one with the history of violence.'

'You've tried to solve your problems with violence over the years, yes. And you were in the habit of arming yourself with some sort of weapon when you went to meetings. We couldn't simply ignore that.'

They only realized quite how perfectly erect Alex Fraser

normally held his slim frame when they saw how slumped his shoulders were as he was led from the room. Hook said, 'There are things you can do when you're locked up, Alex. You can get yourself qualifications. Horticultural ones, if you want to.'

The white young face looked at him uncomprehendingly. Then Fraser thrust his hands out to the uniformed officer in the anteroom who held the handcuffs. 'Too early, Bert,' muttered Lambert as he led him back into the murder room.

As the police Mondeo bore him away through the gates of Westbourne Park, Alex Fraser sat hunched and defeated, not even taking a last look at the gardens which were to have transformed his life.